Witch

BOYFRIEND WANTED

COLETTE RIVERA

AUTHOR NOTE

Dear reader,

This book is intended for mature audiences.
The following are content guidance and trigger warnings: anxiety, mentions of past depression, past death of a relative and mentor, career burnout and associated stress, manipulative parenteral relationship, gaslighting by side characters (often challenged), scene containing violence (minor: magical and physical), sexual content: intended for mature audiences.

Happy Reading!

LOVE & MAGIC

GIVE A WITCH A CHANCE

KEEP YOUR WITCHES CLOSE

ONE WICKED NIGHT

WITCH BOYFRIEND WANTED

Witch

BOYFRIEND WANTED

COLETTE RIVERA

1

LUCA

I was trapped on the worst blind date of my life, and that was saying something.

If there'd been no one to blame but myself, the night would have held a familiar disappointment and the solution would have been simple, but that wasn't how blind dates worked. The matchmaker had to bear some of the responsibility, and the shock of how this set up had come about left me reeling, fantasizing about drowning in my wine.

If only the waiter had left the bottle.

I wasn't good at dating, but this particular horror wasn't totally my fault. Most of the blame for tonight's situation lay at my father's feet. The fact that he was involved in my dating life at all was a serious problem. I didn't want him meddling, didn't want to be dating to begin with, but couldn't for the life of me seem to get that detail to sink into my father's mind.

I did not want to be here, stuck across the table from Herold Something-or-other, Chicago Witch and long-time friend of the family.

Herold swirled his wine, regarding me with keen interest. "Where do you see yourself in the next ten years?"

"About where I am now." I cast a glance at the door, hoping in vain for rescue.

I had under no circumstances consented to this date.

It wasn't Herold's fault. Who knows what he'd been told. Something along the lines of how eager I was to meet him, probably. What I'd *thought* I'd be doing this evening was having dinner with my father. I'd been sure to check it was only the two of us, thinking I'd learned from the last several times an eligible friend had 'happened' to be in town.

Tonight my father had lied to me outright, which was new. His deception destroyed his ability to claim he didn't realize his actions were against my wishes. It shattered the illusion that my father cared about what I wanted at all.

As a trick, he'd asked to take me out tonight to celebrate the success of my most recent case. I was exhausted from a long week—a long month—and had wanted to decline, but when he'd said it was just a quiet evening, father and son, I'd decided to keep my excuses in the bank for next time.

We weren't at the restaurant ten minutes before Herold had showed up. As soon as he'd sat down with us, my father had excused himself.

He hadn't come back.

"I know ten years isn't long." The Witch across from me smiled. I put his age at about one hundred, going by the slight graying of his hair. "But where do you see yourself going long-term? What are you aiming for? Court positions on the coasts can be tricky so it pays to have a vision well ahead of time."

"I'd rather not talk about work." I picked up my wine and took a sip.

"Oh." The man looked momentarily flustered.

Damn it. This was why I couldn't be rude and storm off. My father was fucking with Herold as much as me.

My date rallied his composure, seeming determined to press

on. "Am I being too forward? I thought you were looking for a partner with connections. I wanted to see where our goals aligned, make sure I was what you were looking for before we got to other matters."

I didn't like dates to feel like inappropriate job interviews, but saying so bordered on mean. Or at least it was the kind of mean I couldn't get away with under the guise of *'oh gosh, I didn't mean for you to take it that way.'*

Instead I drummed up a look of mock innocence. "Other matters?"

Herold's ears went red and I was officially an asshole.

Despite this not being his fault, I couldn't help hating Herold a little. I wasn't looking for some Witchy power match, or a partner chosen solely to boost my career. I didn't want to be with someone who saw our relationship as nothing but a mutually beneficial tool, devoid of feelings. I didn't want to be used or objectified any more than I wanted to do those things to anyone else.

"Um—shall we start with the more personal compatibility issues?" Herold seemed reluctant but committed to indulging me.

"I think there might have been a misunderstanding." I avoided his eyes, looking instead at the wineglass in my hand. I already regretted my mocking comment. Who was I to judge if Herold wanted to negotiate relationships this way? He could do as he pleased, I just wasn't interested in participating and that was all he needed to know. "Herold, I'm not sure what you've heard but I'm not looking for any kind of relationship."

He blinked as if he was trying to suppress his surprise. "But Marcos said you were hoping to find a husband who supported your career."

Damn my father.

This was when you felt the true age of, and disconnect in

time experienced by, older Witches. Anyone over two-hundred years old was still trying to marry off their children like it was a business transaction. My father had always accepted and supported me being gay, but he also saw no appropriate path for me other than marrying a Witch whose connections would boost my career and push me up in Witch society. It was what he'd done in marrying my mother.

My sip of wine tasted sour. "I'm sorry to have wasted your time."

"Why did you agree to meet me?" Herold appeared confused rather than annoyed, and was turning out to be less prickish than my past setups. He was significantly less arrogant than them too.

Which was a pity. If Herold was a jerk I wouldn't have to care, but he was the kind of man whose ears went red and I almost didn't know what to do with that.

"I—" couldn't think of a convincing lie and was beginning to suspect my father had found the one Witch the truth of the situation would hurt.

My unwanted date's blush spread to his cheeks, everything apparent in my silence. "Did you even want to meet me?"

"Not exactly, no. It isn't you," I assured him. "I'm sure you're great. I'm just more modern in my dating habits than my father understands."

"Oh, *god*." Herold seemed mortified, taking his turn to look around for an escape path.

Now I felt like scum for embarrassing him. I hadn't expected the guy to have feelings about my rejection. Past experience had shown me that Witches looking for this kind of marriage didn't care about me once they heard I had no interest in playing along.

"I'm sorry." I tried to sound genuine but it came out pained.

"No, Luca, I'm sorry. I should have known better than to

think a young man like you would be interested—" he trailed off, abandoning his sentence for the rest of his wine.

Fuck. This wasn't how this was supposed to go. No one my father set me up with was looking for personal connection. This whole practice was an emotionless void, an outdated business deal. Except this time I'd been set me up with someone who might actually be a good guy.

If Herold wasn't some scheming, power-hungry Witchy, why had he met with me?

This really was the worst blind date of my life. For a whole host of new reasons.

"It's not about age," I told Herold, trying to save his self-esteem. "I'm sure you're great company."

He snorted. "Yes, and that's why I'd thought meeting some who wanted me for my position in the court system sounded promising. Good company. No, I know where my appeal lies."

"Hey, don't sell yourself short." The words felt cheesy, but he was good looking in a reserved sort of way. I'm sure he had hobbies, or interests that appealed to people. His personality seemed all right.

"No, you're right. I shouldn't." Herold almost sounded convinced. "So, is there any chance you'd like to start over? Forget the setup and expectations. See where the night goes on its own?"

My body flashed hot in an unreasonable panic. The only thing worse than a nonconsensual setup was a real date where someone nice might try to get to know me. "I'm not the dating type. Is the thing."

"Ah." Herold stood and buttoned his suit jacket, his mouth a tight line. "In that case, no need for either of us to waste the evening. I do appreciate your honesty, Luca. Good night."

He left me feeling worse than usual, not something I'd have thought was possible.

2

———

LUCA

"I can't do this, Marci. I think I might curse him."

I was at Saturday night drinks with my best friend and contemplating illegal magic. Half seriously.

Marci looked at me with less alarm than I deemed appropriate. "Oh, Luca." She topped up my wine and led me up to her rooftop balcony overlooking Dolores Park and the city. "It can't be that bad."

I flopped into one of the chaise lounge chairs and swept my loose curls back out of my face. "My father's gotten devious. I thought I'd seen the worst of it when he straight up told a client's boyfriend I was a better fit for him, and that it was too bad we weren't together. It's been a year and that mortification still feels fresh. I may never go back to New York. But last night was worse."

"How?" Marci leaned against the railing and looked down at me. The wind swept her dark natural curls but didn't dislodge the circlet of crystals she wore on her head. She was the embodiment of her Witch-society nickname—Marcella Mendez, queen of modern magic—in jeans, an artfully ripped designer tee, and the iconic crown.

6

I took a fortifying sip of wine and explained yesterday's humiliation.

"Oh. Fuck that." Marci sounded vehement.

I went on, blind to the San Francisco skyline in front of me. My life had narrowed to this one nagging thorn. "He keeps saying how he and mom were together as young Witches and won't stop reminding me that's how they built their standing. But he wasn't as young as me. I don't know why he's pushing so hard. It's like my career as a lawyer isn't enough. My work doesn't mean anything on its own. He needs to see me climbing the ranks as he did, every facet of my life used as leverage. Scheming and marrying for power."

Marcy tapped the side of her wineglass with lacquered nails. "Do people even do that anymore? Surely knowing the right people is enough to take advantage of connections. I don't see why you also have to commit your lives to one another."

"Would you like to explain that to him? Stars above know I've tried. I don't see why he's so hellbent. Besides, all his scheming is irrelevant. I honestly think I've reached the peak of my ambition, Marci. I'm tired. And just don't give a shit. I don't want to make laws or join a Judicial Committee. I'm good where I am." Though this was partially untrue. I wasn't good. I was indifferent to my career and current job title.

"Maybe that's why he wants you to marry well, to cure your lack of ambition." Marci's eyes flashed in amusement as she belatedly hid a wicked grin behind her glass.

I couldn't see the humor. My ambition wasn't lacking, it was spent. I'd focused my whole life on one thing: working to land a prestigious job at a top Witch-law firm. I was a successful lawyer working in magical law, the youngest Witch in the region to get the kind of promotions I'd achieved. Why couldn't I be done now I was finally here?

I set my glass down on a nearby table. "I can't take another date like last night."

Marci shrugged. "Stop meeting your dad for dinner." Her parents were the opposite of mine, low-key and respectfully hands off.

I crossed my arms like a petulant child. "Easier said than done. I'm not convinced my father wouldn't start sending Witches around my house to court me."

Marci giggled.

I found the idea horrifying.

"It's not fair Aria got away with dating a Mortal," I complained, not for the first time. I wasn't about regressive values or saying our parents should be on my twin's marriage prospects because she was a woman, but suffering alone felt deeply unfair.

Marci blinked in a way that suggested she was expending effort to not roll her eyes. "There's no rule to say you can't follow Aria's example. Isn't there anyone you're interested in dating, Mortal or otherwise?" She was very good at pretending we hadn't had this conversation before.

I frowned. "That's the whole thing, I don't *want* a boyfriend. Even if I did, I doubt I could get away with a 'disadvantageous' match like Aria." I loved my twin but she'd embraced our parents' disapproval in a way I never could have, and was oblivious to the way they'd transferred all their expectations onto me.

"Are you sure you don't want a boyfriend?" Marci took out her phone and tossed it to me. "There's this new dating app. I hear all the Witches are using it."

I snorted. It was her app, utilizing a magically enhanced algorithm to determine compatibility as people matched with each other. It was only open to Witches for ethical and legal reasons—you know, the secret existence of magic and consent being required to enchant Mortals—but still, the limited launch had gone well, and working on the ethics case with Marci had been a good experience for me.

Another stand out line on my resume.

I set her phone aside. "I don't want to date."

"So what's your solution? Just lie? Tell your parent's you're in love, so they stop throwing every gay Witch they know at you?"

"Oh god, I'm drowning in a deluge of gay Witches. My problems are ridiculous."

Marci made me smile without fail at our weekly drinks night. I used to only see her monthly, but she'd worn my antisocial ass down and I wasn't sorry about it. I needed the weekly stress relief with my sixty-plus hour a week schedule.

"I'd rather your problems than mine," Marci said, her tone turning more serious.

I sat up. "Why, what's up?"

She huffed. "Nothing terrible, I've just had a strange day. This one developer whose contract we didn't extend has been causing problems. He showed up at the offices unannounced today, demanding to see me. My poor reception staff had to threaten to call security."

"Security? Was he dangerous?"

"No." Marci shook her head. "He just wouldn't leave."

"We can totally swap problems if you want," I offered. "Seriously, if you need anything, let me know."

Marci made a shooing gesture. "No, I'm hoping that'll be the last I'll hear from him. It's not like I'm going to be providing a reference now anymore than before. He should know trying to bully one out of me was doomed to fail. Your father on the other hand might prove harder to shake off. That's the problem with relatives."

I picked up my wine and took a contemplative sip. "Yeah, I don't think a lie will work." I frowned, wishing it weren't true. "My father's been a lawyer for over two hundred years, he's almost as good at spotting lies as a psychic. They'll ask for proof-of-boyfriend in the flesh and I'll be right back where I started."

Marci waved her wineglass, exasperation with me apparently returning. "So go on a date with someone you're actually interested in. See where it goes. Then you won't have to lie."

"Now you're just telling me to get a real boyfriend. That's what I'm trying to avoid."

"Is it?" Marci looked at me pointedly, seeming to lose patience with me. "I don't see why. You're smart, technically not bad looking—"

"Hey, are you complimenting me, or what?"

"All I'm saying is, I know a bunch of guys you'd hit it off with. If you tried. Let me set you up. It won't be so bad."

I arched a brow. "A bunch of guys?"

"Okay," she huffed. "One guy. But he's great. And one is all you need. You two would be the loveliest couple. The others I alluded to would probably find you annoying, but Theo—"

"Wow. Annoying. Thanks, Marci. You're really helping sell dating as an appealing option."

"*But Theo*," she said at an increased volume.

"Will ultimately find me disappointing, if not annoying. Working too much is the most generous feedback I've received from my exes."

I didn't need to tell Marci I'd given up on relationships. She'd known me since we were kids, and we'd roomed together in our twenties. These days she knew me better than Aria did.

I'd started off strong on the casual sex game, too wrapped up in myself in college to want to put in the effort for a steady boyfriend. Then I'd met someone who'd changed everything. I'd wanted that one person by my side forever. Of course it hadn't lasted long. Once the honeymoon had been over and the real getting-to-know-you stuff had begun, he'd left.

My desires had changed but that hadn't stopped all my

subsequent boyfriends from leaving me. When the end of every relationship I'd ever had was a breakup I hadn't seen coming, I couldn't pretend I wasn't the problem. Marci thought I needed to try, but I had the feeling I tried too hard, yet when I was less than perfect I got dumped.

The only way to get something right was to try, but somehow my dating efforts always led to failure. It stung and I didn't know how to fix it. I didn't know how to be the kind of boyfriend someone wanted, so I'd told myself I didn't need a relationship. With too much pressure in my life already, it was best not to have to add another set of expectations.

"What I need is an actor who I can hire to pose as my boyfriend." I stretched out on the lounge chair as I thought. "That way my lie can be accompanied by manufactured proof."

Marci looked caught between a laugh and a groan. "Don't be absurd."

I tipped back the last of my wine. "I'm not. Fake Witch boyfriend wanted. Do you know anyone who'd respond to that ad?"

Marci knew way more people than me, and people who weren't connected to my career in magical law. I wouldn't 'date' anyone I worked with, fake or not. She humored me with a real answer. "Can't say that I do. The only Witch actors I know are too high profile to fuck with this sort of thing."

"Damn."

Marci looked at me like I was cause for concern. "Luca, you either need to stand up to your dad. For real. Or get your own damn boyfriend. Make a decision because I'm getting bored with this conversation."

I glowered. "Do you think Theo would be down to be my fake boyfriend?"

"No." She looked offended I'd asked. "He has dignity."

"Good for him."

"I actually think you two would be good together, Luca. Please, let me set you up?" Marci joined me on the chaise lounge and put her hands together, under her chin, deploying her best Bambi-eyes.

I tried to scooch away. "If he's after a relationship it sounds doomed, Marci. That's just not what I want right now."

Her innocent look turned shrewd. "You want a relationship, Luca. Stop lying to me as well as yourself. Do you know how much I hear about Aria and Owen? A lot. I hear about them *constantly*, and not from Aria herself. Instead of living vicariously through your twin's happily ever after, try and find your own."

I felt exposed. "Why do you have to see right through me, Marci?"

She gave me an evil grin. "Because I know you, and I'm almost always right. You're dying to fall in love."

It wasn't that I was jealous of Aria and Owen, but I couldn't deny wanting something like what they had. I just didn't know how to make it work. I figured I'd put off the real love stuff until later on. Eventually I'd figure out how to achieve romantic success. It wasn't like being a Witch left me with any lack of time, we lived for centuries.

I needed to balance out my stress before I let anyone in. I couldn't take any more failures. Going after what I actually wanted scared me when I didn't know how to succeed. Which was ironic because being successful was the thing that defined me. I had a plan for everything except this.

I'd told myself I wouldn't try again until I'd figured out how to not overdo it, how to be the perfect partner and make it seem effortless and natural. But I was lonely. I could tell myself I didn't want a relationship, but that didn't make it true.

"If I go on one date with Theo, will you stop trying to push me into getting an actual boyfriend from here on out?" I didn't mind Marci's meddling like I did my father's. She was coming from a place of actually caring about me and my happiness. And I trusted her assessment of compatibility. She'd created the app after all.

Marci brightened. "Yes. Maybe. It won't matter because you two are going to be great together and I won't ever need to set you up again."

I stood, heading back inside to refill my drink. "Fine. I'll meet him."

Marci squealed and picked up her phone, fingers flying.

If Theo rejected me, I'd just see if he was game to do me a favor and fake it for my family. How I'd make that appealing I wasn't sure. I was desperate and unable to deal with my father in any other way.

Still, I wasted the next half hour wondering if Theo might actually like me. It was a fantasy I could get lost in.

3

THEO

I was going to cancel. My phone was right there waiting to be picked up, an out of place piece of modern technology burning a hole in my well-worn vintage countertop. Marci would understand. I just wasn't ready.

The brass bell above the shop door jangled.

My hand hovered over the phone but my eyes snapped up. Mr. Finnigan entered my apothecary shop, tipping his hat at me before disappearing down a narrow aisle of dried herbs.

I pushed my glasses up the bridge of my nose. Such a stereotypical gesture, I couldn't help thinking every time I did it, but necessary. Not that it mattered, no one was even looking at me.

I should text Marci now, while my customer was out of sight. My hesitation didn't make any sense. I didn't want to go on this blind date. I had no idea what I'd been thinking when I'd agreed to it last weekend. After spending the week worrying about it, canceling was the only good option.

Mr. Finnigan brought a bundle of sage and a vial of dried mushrooms up to the cash register, an original nineteenth century model from when the shop first opened. "Business been good today?" He offered me a soft smile.

"The usual. Can't complain." I took his items and wrapped them carefully in tissue paper.

"Can I trouble you for a tea this late in the day?" Mr. Finnigan eyed my ornate tea set.

It was five thirty, time to close the shop and realistically too late to cancel drinks without being rude. "I can always make you a tea, Mr. Finnigan."

"Perfect, Theodore. You're a gem."

The shop—Graywoods Apothecary—had been doing business in San Francisco for two hundred and fifteen years. It had started as a street vendor and moved into this particular building in Noe Valley back in 1918. I'd taken over proprietorship from my uncle six years ago, and was here to continue serving the local Witchy community with quality ingredients and expert advice.

The work suited me perfectly, as it had my Uncle Theodore, whom I was named after. Some customers joked we were the same man, or twins defying age. But he had just been my uncle, and a friend. He'd been the kind of guy who had a cushy armchair tucked behind the curtain to the back room so he—or now I—could curl up with a book when no one was around.

I rang up Mr. Finnigan for a tea and his purchases before going to make the brew.

Graywoods magically refilling teapot hadn't been empty since the shop opened. I pressed my hands to the cold metal and felt my crystal rings heat as I coaxed the water to temperature. Then I handed my customer the ceramic cup. He held it reverently with both hands, the dark red and deep earth tones of the glaze shifting at his touch. The tea set was enchanted to produce a perfect brew, unique to the cup's holder.

I had tea bags and regular shop branded mugs under the counter for when Mortals tried to request the legendary tea.

They took Graywoods to be an overpriced novelty shop when they occasionally wandered in.

As I poured the steaming water into the enchanted cup, murmuring the accompanying spell, the bell sounded. Tea took my full attention so I let the customer come in unacknowledged.

The water glittered in the ceramic cup, swirling of its own accord and slowly turning from crystal clear to the color of a lightly steeped brew. I put the magic teapot back on its pedestal. It let out a satisfied hiss as sweet steam wafted around me and my customer.

Mr. Finnigan thanked me for his perfect tea, which smelled of ginger and tarragon. He drank it almost meditatively before wishing me a goodnight and departing.

I waved a hand over the cup to clean it with a poof of smoke, before stowing it next to the teapot.

Making tea was my favorite part of the job. People often had visceral reactions to their first cup. I'd had more than one person cry. The experience could be cathartic if you'd never had Graywoods tea before. For Witches like Finnigan, it was a regular part of their self-care and helped them maintain their connection to earth magic.

Rituals like this were what being a Witch was all about, for me anyway. Giving people what they almost didn't know they needed, a cup of comfort and understanding. Unique magic was in the details. It's what made it special. The experience never failed to leave a positive impression on a Witch. It was a way to improve their day. And mine.

Maybe I'd bring my date back here for tea later tonight.

That was, if the date went well. Which I had serious doubts about.

The remaining customer was out of sight. I hated to be pushy, but they needed to be prompt. It would figure someone would come in at the last second after I'd spent most of the afternoon on my own, with nothing to do but measure out common ingredient kits and finish my reading—a murder mystery with more than a few scares at the end.

I came out from behind the shop's counter and made my way down the narrow central aisle. I had a direct line of sight from the register to the entrance, and used the short walk to peer down the aisles branching off on either side. I didn't spot my customer before reaching the front door. I flipped the sign to *closed* and made my way back, checking again.

I settled behind the register.

It wasn't unusual for someone to be out of sight in the shop. The rows of packed shelves were by no means straight. I didn't need to watch people to prevent theft when there were enchantments in place. Still, I was on edge, like my uncertainty about the date had infected the rest of my thoughts, or maybe the creepy book I'd been reading had me more freaked out than I'd first thought.

"Closing in ten," I called out.

For a moment there was such a pure silence that I wondered if I'd imagined the bell, too wrapped up in the tea service. Then a man stepped out from behind the specialty candles, making my heart jump.

"Good evening, Mr. Landon." The Witch had a much less friendly tone than Finnigan, and wasn't holding any purchases, or looking interested in the nearest displays. He stared at me with focused gray eyes.

"Hi." I returned his greeting with my usual friendliness. "Can I help you find anything, sir?"

He wasn't someone I recognized. Witch communities were tight knit, even in large cities. I didn't know all my customers by any means, but most had been shopping here for decades, if not centuries. Completely unknown Witches were in the minority as far as my customer base went, but it wasn't uncommon for them to know my name, the shops reputation being what it was.

The Witch continued to assess me, so I returned the favor. He was unremarkable in scuffed jeans and sturdy boots, his skin pale and face plain. His attention held no hint of attraction or romantic interest in me, but it didn't feel casual. Like he was looking for something.

After a strained few seconds, he seemed to make up his mind. "I'm hoping you can help me, but I'm not here for a purchase."

I stifled a sigh. Wasn't Friday night too late in the week for strange enquiries? I pushed my glasses up my nose again and waited for him to go on.

The man pulled something small out of his coat pocket. "I've heard you're an expert at detecting the specific magical properties of objects."

"Not all objects," I corrected. "Only the earth magic of naturally occurring materials." I found myself hoping he'd brought a spelled locket, or something similar with no inherent power of its own, so I could send him away.

The man set a crystal on the counter. It was barely two inches long, cut and polished. I'd never seen anything quite like it. The shape was usual; the color, however, was not. It was a deep wine red, almost black, making it appear fake or man-made.

My curiosity snagged.

"May I?" I reached out, hand hovering, waiting for the man to agree.

"Be my guest, Mr. Landon." He looked at the small item with narrowed eyes.

I picked it up and turned it over in my hand. It was cold, slightly cooler than you'd expect in the current ambient temperature, or after coming out of a pocket. The crystal was real, a quartz and not synthetic as it had first looked. The strange coloring seemed to come from the additional magic it was imbued with, rather than manufacturing.

"Examining this will take time," I told the man. "My expertise is in natural magical properties, but I can try to figure out how the crystal's inherent magic is interacting with the enchantment it holds."

The man nodded and took his eyes off the crystal to check his watch. "I don't know what it does."

"If you leave it with me I can try to have an idea of how best to use it, in say, two weeks?" I took a scrap of paper out from under the counter and passed it to him along with a pen. "Your name and number, please. I'll call if I have any information sooner, but I don't know how long this will take."

Enchanting objects like crystals, that already held their own power, was complex earth magic and while not outside my area of interest, I didn't get a lot of requests like this.

The man glanced toward the front door like he was anxious to get going, before picking up the pen. If he was in such a hurry he shouldn't have waited until the last moment to come into the shop. He considered before scribbling on the paper, then folded it in half and set the pen squarely on top.

I slid the pen and paper back toward me. "Is there anything you can tell me about the crystal to get me started? Anything specific you're wondering? And if you know its place of origin, that would be helpful."

People generally had more to say when seeking my input. Crystals were conduits, so I'd have expected him to ask if this one's unique properties might be best suited to one brand of spell or another, if it enhanced magical flow better or worse than crystals of other, unaltered varieties, that sort of thing.

The man shoved his hands in his pockets. "It's just a family heirloom. Found it in my father's attic. Wondered if it was worth much, or did anything interesting. I'm sorting through his estate."

None of that was useful information. I'd meant the geographic origin of the thing, not where he'd gotten it from. Crystals didn't *do* anything in themselves, as he put it, interesting or not. They were elemental tools, like herbs, fire, or water. Maybe he wasn't an experienced spell caster. Magical ability ranged, as did individual Witch interest in using their powers.

Each of the four elements had magic of their own. Earth elements had the greatest variety of magical properties when you considered everything from herbs and other plants to crystals, and the variations seen within any one natural indigent. Sage grown here and sage grown on the East Coast weren't exactly the same, magically speaking. These were things apothecaries had been studying forever, but that the average Witch might not spend too much time thinking about.

I only nodded, like the man's answer was expected. "Okay. Thank you, sir. I'll take payment for the evaluation upfront. Be aware, if the item is left here with no contact from you for more than six months, I reserve the right to sell it."

The man only shrugged, so I rang him up. He didn't thank me before leaving the shop.

It was way too late to cancel my blind date now.

I frowned at the crystal; something about it made me wrinkle my nose, and not just because I blamed it for being stuck going on this date. I held it up to the light. The surface was too opaque to create any light refraction; instead it shimmered like an oil slick. The closer I looked the more it seemed to darken the air around it, like a shadow that didn't fit traditional physics. The evaluation might actually prove interesting.

I opened a lockable drawer under the register and set the crystal inside, before scooping up the piece of paper with the man's details. He hadn't even introduced himself. A little common courtesy never hurt. I wasn't the legend my uncle had been in life, but people usually had manners and respected Graywoods regardless of it being in younger hands.

I unfolded the paper to see who the guy was, but he hadn't written his name. There was no contact number, only three words: *Tell no one.*

I re-opened the drawer and stared at the crystal. It was odd, rare without a doubt, maybe even one of a kind given it was magically altered, but not dangerous. No strong power emanated from it. Was it really worth a warning?

Perhaps it was stolen. Theft would explain the man's cagey manner. Or maybe I was wrong in my brief assessment, and there was something sinister about it. If the crystal was dangerous, I didn't want it in my shop. Except, I couldn't give it back to the guy now he was gone, or even call him and ask him what the deal was.

I took a breath. I couldn't worry about this now. Not when I had a date to agonize over. How much danger could it really be?

Dropping the useless note on top of the crystal, I closed and locked the drawer. Whatever it was, it wasn't my problem tonight.

I closed up the shop, dawdling and taking the opportunity to reorganize the central potion display.

Graywoods was deceptive, small but laid out in a way that created nooks and extra crevices, the layout mostly unchanged from its opening days. I checked each of the winding aisles. Not because I was uneasy. I needed to make notes in my little book about replenishing certain stock, but while I did so I couldn't help checking no one lingered in the corners.

Looking for loiterers wasn't a typical part of my nightly routine and I didn't know why it felt necessary tonight. Was it just the uncertainty the note had left me with? It shouldn't have been, unless I thought the warning to tell no one meant people might try and sneak into the shop to steal the crystal, like it was some valuable prize. But if that was the case, why would the man say he wondered what the crystal was worth?

Thieves were unlikely, so it wasn't surprising that I found no evidence of any. Not even outside when I glanced out the window. For some reason, after confirming no one was here, the quiet became oppressive. I didn't know if I was unsettled by the nameless man or just lonely.

I checked everything twice, for good measure.

At last I stood in the back room looking down at the change of clothes I'd previously laid out on Uncle Theodore's chair. Thoughts of the bothersome man and his crystal were replaced with more pressing worries.

Was I putting in too much effort for a blind date? It wasn't like I was dressing up, only swapping a rumpled shirt for a pressed one. Yes, I'd laid out three to choose from, along with a nicer waistcoat, but these limited choices were better than standing in front of my whole wardrobe and being paralyzed by indecision.

A strange shiver coursed through me and I almost abandoned the clothes to go up to my apartment, just to get out of there. Maybe I should have been reading a romance novel instead of a murder mystery to get me in the right mood. I'd been in a serious rut since my last relationship ended and needed to be doing everything I could for tonight to go well, not freaking myself out with creepy books and paranoid thoughts about robbers.

My ex, Jason, had done more than break up with me. He'd said some very unkind things, judged me unfairly, and had hurt me in a way I'd found hard to get over. It had been too many years and all my dates still seemed to turn into disasters. My inability to get back out there had gone from embarrassing to, I don't know, something worse and more permanent.

Marci had the suspicion I was self-sabotaging and not even realizing it. I wanted to disagree, but maybe she had a point. I should try tonight. Hope for the best. So, I changed and cleaned my glasses.

As I waited outside for the rideshare I'd booked to take me across the city, an unexpected thrill of anticipation filled me. Spending most of my time inside Graywoods was comforting, but leaving the familiar walls was like a cup of strong coffee tonight. It was a fresh autumn evening, chill and clear. Alive. I was ready to have a good time, stop thinking so much. See this guy Marci said was going to make my day.

If it went well I'd bring him back to the shop for tea. Then ask him upstairs to my apartment. I blushed at the thought, but *god*, I needed it.

4

THEO

My confidence had waned by the time I reached the bar. The place was so obviously a Marci pick. Too trendy and modern down to the molding.

I was officially nervous and cursing myself for thinking about taking someone home with me. Sex did not need to be on my mind. I was more often a slow and steady kind of guy than a jump into bed sort. But what I'd been doing up until now hadn't been working. Maybe I needed to change my game. I just didn't know, and overthinking everything from my shirt to my hair, to my damn horny thoughts, wasn't helping.

Marci had gone full matchmaker queen for this date, and had refused to tell either of us the other's full name so we couldn't look each other up. If we weren't using her app, we were going old school, apparently. Marci had insisted on a token as a form of recognizing each other. My date was supposed to have a red rose on his table and I was wearing a red pocket square in my tweed coat pocket.

I scanned the mood-lit room for a Witch with a rose.

Most of the bar was set up to cater to large groups with long high tables. A DJ spun slow tunes in the corner. I tentatively made my way into the growing crowd. Voices and laughter volleyed amongst the sound of cocktail shakers. Everyone was occupied with themselves, a sea of smiles and flashing eyes. My presence went unnoticed.

Being stuck on a date in the middle of all the bustle would be disappointing. Distraction wasn't going to help this go well. I adjusted my pocket square nervously.

Not seeing any roses around, I looked to the perimeter of the room where cozy two-seater booths were full of couples. I relaxed a fraction. Surely we could sit over there, out of the way of all the people.

Yes. A dried red rose was placed on the table nearest the door to the bar's terrace. A waiter stood in the way, blocking my view of my date, almost melding into the surrounding black booth upholstery in his all black serving attire.

I took a shaking breath, gave up on quelling my nerves, and began to make my way over.

As I extricated myself from the crowd, the waiter moved on, freeing up the view. Surprised jolted through me. The Witch at the table was gorgeous, but of course he was. Luca Belmonte had always been hot.

He sat there, casual as ever in what looked like an expensively tailored suit, jacket nowhere in sight. He'd probably hung it in the coat check, something I should have thought to do. I was suddenly sweating, my pulse pounding.

Luca was all relaxed and comfortable looking in his pristine white shirt, sleeves rolled up to his elbows, top buttons undone to reveal a hit of dark chest hair on brown skin. He was facing outside, his stubble-lined jaw in perfect profile. Luca had the same long hair I remembered, falling down to his shoulders in untamed brown curls. He brushed it back, tucking a few strands behind his ear, exposing a long row of crystal earrings. They glittered in the low light.

But he couldn't be my date. How could Marci think I'd ever like Luca? Not that she knew. But still. She'd said the man I was meeting was her oldest friend. Marci would never be friends with a jerk like him.

I scanned the table again. The rose was still there, mocking me.

I was standing dumbstruck, not thinking fast enough to duck behind someone and hide, when Luca looked my way. He almost glanced over me, his serious expression lined with curiosity and expectation, but his eyes caught on the ridiculous red silk in my pocket.

He smiled in a slow, sensual curving of lips.

I walked up to the table.

Luca gave me a quick, appreciative but not intrusive, once over and held out his hand. "Luca Belmonte, pleasure to meet you."

No.

This. Was. Not. Happening.

The jerk didn't even recognize me. What the actual fuck? Seriously? Had his mind been altered? Was he already drunk?

I didn't know what to do. I kind of wanted to die of embarrassment.

Luca's cool, supermodel smile slipped as I failed to shake his hand. "Not what you expected?" He gave me self-deprecating chuckle.

That laugh. It made my blood boil.

"Sorry—um—" I reached out and clasped his hand, belatedly realizing he'd notice how sweaty mine was. With all my internal rage, I was still stumbling and shy on the outside. "Th–Theo Landon." I fixed my gaze on the dried rose.

"Lovely. Theo, here, take a seat." Luca gestured to the space beside him in the booth.

Oh, hell. The setup was way too romantic. We didn't even

have separate chairs, just one half circle shaped seat curling around the small table.

I slipped into the booth, careful not to get close enough to touch Luca. What was I supposed to do? Ask him what he was playing at? If this was a joke? Or if I was just that forgettable?

Marci was a dead Witch—or realistically, she was banned from tea service. Something.

"I already ordered a drink." Luca half turned so he could look at me, putting him way too close. His brown eyes were deep and flecked with hints of gold that almost glittered. "Sorry if that was rude of me. The waiter was being persistent and I got here early."

"Th–that's okay." I turned my attention to the cocktail menu.

I almost choked on the prices. I did well at the shop—it was a San Francisco Witchery institution—but I wasn't into splashing my money out on stuff like this. Damn Marci times a thousand.

"My treat." Luca gave me a conspiratorial smile, like he'd noticed my reaction.

Great. I was acting like an incompetent mess, as usual. Not that this was a real date. Not anymore.

I refused to be disappointed the night was already ruined.

Luca's attention remained fixed on me. "What kind of drinks do you like, Theo?"

Was he being attentive? What was this? Was he a good date now? I supposed he'd had ten years of practice since the last time we'd sat down for a drink together.

"I like—um—aromatics." Good lord, why I was blushing?

Luca seemed to notice, his gaze on my flaming cheeks. "So a classic. I went with one of the specialty drinks, but I respect a man with taste." His attention turned to my clothes, eyes sweeping over me again.

I wasn't sure if he was making fun of me or not. "I'll get an old fashioned, I think."

Luca flagged down a waiter and ordered my drink. He turned back to me and tapped my pocket square. "This was a cute idea. Figures Marci would be dramatic, huh?"

I felt his touch like a shock. Those good kind of chills wound through my traitorous body. I may even have shivered, given Luca seemed to pick up on my reaction to the brief brush of affection.

His hand was back on my chest, tracing an outline of the silk with a single tattoo-lined finger. The symbols inked on the backs of his hands radiated power and looked cool as hell. His touch set my pulse racing.

Oh my god, what was happening? Was I seriously being seduced by Luca Belmonte? This easily? Did I have no dignity left at all?

"Looks stupid with my outfit." I took the cloth out of my pocket and balled it up in my lap.

"Not at all. I won't try to tell you it matches. I doubt you usually pair formal accessories with tweed. Just as I almost never tote around flowers." Luca sounded like he was trying to make me smile. With anyone else I would have, but looking at him was starting to hurt.

His flirting was effortless, full of confidence and probably honed by way more practice than I'd ever had. I could fall for it easily. If he'd realized who I was when he'd first seen me, who knows, maybe I'd have said to hell with the past and seized this fluttering feeling and seen where it went.

But Luca still hadn't remembered. Even after I'd said my name and looked so deeply into his eyes.

Luca had seamlessly shifted closer to me as he'd fondled my pocket decor. With one arm stretched out on the back of the booth, I was already half in his embrace. For some reason I wanted to lean right into him. I wondered what he'd do if I moved closer. If I returned his touch.

Ugh, this was ridiculous. I clearly needed to get laid. Just not with him.

Again, Luca was too perceptive. He seemed to pick up on my lusty thoughts like they were inscribed on my forehead. "You have beautiful eyes, Theo." He reached out and pushed a curl of hair off my brow and back into place. "I'm glad we're doing this. I think we'll have fun getting to know each other better."

"You don't remember me?" I asked at last.

Luca's smile twitched like he was trying to catch up on a joke. I scooted back from him and wiped my sweaty hands on my pants.

Our drinks arrived. Luca didn't even acknowledge his glass as he stared at me. I thanked the waiter and took a generous sip.

"What do you mean, Theo?"

I barked a nervous laugh and took another long sip of my drink. It was already half gone. "This isn't our first date, Luca."

"Come on." He gave me another mischievous grin, but it fell quickly.

My face mustn't have looked friendly. There, I'd finally gotten over my stupor and found my self-respect. Fuck this guy.

Luca ran a tattooed hand roughly through his hair. "Shit. Really?"

I managed to roll my eyes and turned back to my drink. I downed it and flagged down a passing waiter to order another.

Luca turned to his own flamboyantly garnished, and admittedly fun looking, cocktail. He seemed to be thinking hard. Wracking his brain. Still I was nothing to him. A blank. A ghost.

"I'd have remembered sleeping with you," Luca said like he was sorry to have forgotten. His eyes ran over me again, maybe trying to picture what was underneath my clothes.

I stiffened. "I never said we slept together."

His reaction was almost comical. "What? Wait—when did we go on a date?"

"It–it was—um—" Now I didn't know if I wanted to remind him. No way was I spelling it all out. I was embarrassed by the memory, bringing back my stuttering uncertainty. "Um—"

"In college!" Luca snapped his fingers like he was excited to have solved the puzzle.

I tried to hold onto my confident rage and failed. "R–remember now?"

"Yeah, Theo, or should I say Theodore? You didn't use the nickname back then." He looked genuinely pleased to be uncovering our last encounter. "We had a class together—"

Which I'd dropped.

"I took you out to that student bar. You weren't even twenty-one."

"Nineteen," I reminded him.

"Yeah. I got us cokes, and worried you'd only come out with me because you were hoping for a sneaky beer."

What? I hadn't known that. Luca had been twenty-one then, but hoping to drink booze wasn't why I'd gone out with him. He'd always been nice to me in class. He'd been older than the rest of us because it was an elective he'd skipped. Past Luca had been smart and hot, driven and serious, but always smiley when he'd talked to me.

"You turned me down." Luca didn't appear fazed in the least by the old rejection. "Maybe this is our second chance."

"S–second chance?" I was stunned. Were we remembering the same date, or did he have me confused with some other guy? "You laughed at me."

That brought him up short, smile disappearing. "What? No."

"Yes, you did." My face burned in a painful blush.

The date hadn't been long after I'd come out as bi, and was the first time someone had asked me out. I'd been so excited, nervous and bumbling as I always was, but I'd been having fun. Luca had been into me. Our conversation had flowed easily. Then he'd leaned in close and whispered in my ear that he wanted to take me home with him, get on his knees for me. I'd nearly choked on my soda, and said I wanted to go on a few more dates before all that. It was too fast. Too overwhelming.

Luca had been straight with me and let me know he was only interested in hooking up, he wasn't looking for a boyfriend or anything like that. I'd blurted out that I'd never been with anyone, and wanted to do that stuff with someone special. I should have just walked away once I'd figured out we didn't want the same things. Instead I'd overshared and he'd laughed at me.

Now, all these years later, that first date reminded me of Jason in the worst way. Luca was just another person who'd judged me and thought my genuine desires were stupid and something to make fun of.

And the asshole didn't even remember it.

5

LUCA

*T*heo's second drink arrived and he took a sip immediately. The man was doing an impressive job of avoiding my gaze in such close quarters.

Damn it, I felt terrible.

I'd genuinely been into him when he sat down. He seemed sweet, and there was no denying how fucking pretty he was. Of course I went straight to seduction mode in order to stave off panic at having to impress him with my personality, but it had seemed like the right move. The way Theo had reacted to my soft touches spoke to some serious chemistry between us. I'd thought I'd had a chance.

Now I wondered if it had been nothing more than simmering anger on his part.

I let Theo nurse his drink for a moment while I tried to figure out what to do. I couldn't seem to keep my eyes off him. He had a distinct hipster vibe, from his tweed coat to his waistcoat and button down, all in earthy browns and faded greens, clothes which showed off his slender frame and poised mannerisms expertly.

Theo had short sandy brown hair that curled artfully, and a

soft-featured face complimented by thick-framed glasses. His white skin gave away his blushes beautifully, and the rest of his emotion I could read in his vivid green eyes.

He'd changed quite a lot since college. He seemed to have grown into himself and embraced his own style.

"What I remember," I began slowly, drawing Theo's attention back to me. "Was taking you out and getting shot down."

"Well that's not what I remember," he muttered, but didn't elaborate.

Was he embarrassed that he'd told me he'd never had sex all those years ago? We'd been young, it hadn't been uncommon, and I wouldn't have judged him for it even if he'd said the same was true today.

Back then, I'd been worried I'd scandalized him with my blunt proposition, but surely he wouldn't be upset about my forward manner all this time later. And I hadn't laughed at him. I'd been delighted he was so open about what he wanted. It had been like a breath of fresh air. No games or guessing. He'd had the guts to say what he was after. Hell, he'd had the confidence to openly want things I'd always been afraid of.

"I'm sorry, Theo." I hoped he could hear my sincerity. "I didn't mean to laugh, or didn't mean it in an at-you kind of way. I think, from what I remember, I was surprised."

"Sure. Whatever." He didn't appear to believe me. "I'm ordering another drink."

"We should get some food." I flipped the menu over to reveal the tapas on offer.

"This isn't a date, Luca. Don't bother."

My gut twisted. I didn't know how to help him understand I'd never meant to make fun of him. I hadn't seen it that way at all. And I didn't know how to make up for not recognizing him. I'd always tried to forget the guys who didn't want me, erase my failures and pretend they hadn't happened.

"Theo—" I abandoned the menu. "I'm truly sorry. For being an insensitive idiot back then, and for not remembering. I didn't mean to hurt you. Please, I don't want to completely ruin your Friday night on top of everything else."

Theo looked uncertain, like he thought I might be lying to him.

The waiter reappeared and stole his attention. I managed to order a few small dishes at random so Theo could eat and balance out his drinks.

"Look." I had to try one last time. "I'm not about shaming people for sex, whether for having a lot of it, or not having it at all. I wasn't laughing at your inexperience, or desires for something meaningful. I promise. I only—um—found it refreshingly funny how different we were. And was too young and dumb to think how my reaction looked from anyone else's perspective. That's all it was."

Theo considered, hints of hopefulness reflected in his eyes. "Really?"

"Yes, really." I gave him an imploring look.

"I guess I can accept that. But if you're apologizing hoping this"—he gestured between us—"is going anywhere, you're out of luck. We are *so* not happening."

"It wasn't an apology with an ulterior motive, Theo." That he assumed it was let me know what he thought of me. It wasn't a picture I liked.

Theo huffed. "What are you doing going on a date anyway? Is all that 'not looking for a boyfriend' stuff in the past? You all grown up now?"

"What?"

"Done with hookups and ready to settle down?" Theo sounded like he was mocking me, more confident than he'd seemed before.

I frowned. "There's nothing immature about preferring casual sex."

His amusement disappeared. "Right. Sorry—I didn't mean—"

I waved a hand flippantly. "It's fine. And no, I don't particularly want to settle into a relationship." This wasn't true but I'd already been rejected. Failed before I'd even been able to try, so it was better to pretend I'd never intended to.

"Then why are you on a blind date?" Theo gave me a newly offended look. "Marci must have thought you were the relationship type or she'd never have set you up with me."

"Yeah, I don't know. I was considering it for a moment there." I picked up my drink. "The truth is, my family is pressuring me to find someone and Marci suggested I try and head them off by finding a guy I actually like." Too bad finding someone who liked me back was going about as well as I'd expected.

"I don't know what she was thinking," my not-date muttered.

I felt a twinge of embarrassment. "You deserve better, Theo."

He cringed at my words. "Oh—um—no. You're not—um—I just don't think I can get over how badly this started off."

"I get it. No need to cushion the blow." I gave him a quick flash of a smile. "Hope we can still enjoy our drinks, but if you want to go, I understand."

His third drink and the first of our tapas arrived. Theo smiled sheepishly at the sight of his cocktail. "You're right, I should eat." He reached for a side plate.

I was surprised he wasn't bolting. Maybe I could salvage some shred of his respect. It wasn't likely, but I should try. I helped myself to some tapenade, trying to figure out how I'd possibly achieve such a thing.

Theo turned away from the food to assess me, as if he'd just thought of something. His face was flushed, probably from going through his first two drinks so quickly. "Just so we're clear,

I'm not interested in being someone's convenient boyfriend. And I'm not looking for someone who's only following their family's orders to settle down."

"Of course not. To be honest, tonight part of me was only looking for a body to fill a seat so I could get my father off my back, but another part of me—" What? Hoped Marci had my perfect match tucked away, waiting to come out and find me, give me all the things I wanted most in life?

Well yes, exactly that. But I didn't like admitting that to myself and certainly wasn't telling Theo.

"Never mind. I shouldn't have gone on a date if I was only looking for a convenient boyfriend, as you put it."

"Thanks for being honest. I guess you've always had that going for you. It makes me believe our first date could actually have been a misunderstanding." Theo seemed satisfied with the new perspective on our past. He picked up a piece of bread. "I've been hopeless at dating lately and wanted this night to go well. I want to meet someone I can be me with. Someone who wants what I want, you know?"

"Sorry to disappoint."

He looked up from the hummus he was spreading with wide eyes. "Oh. I didn't mean—"

"It's okay. I'm over here desperate enough to consider a fake boyfriend and you're looking for like, love and companionship. We aren't in the same dating hemisphere."

"A fake boyfriend? Really?" Theo laughed in surprise, looking at me like he'd just discovered something significant.

I grinned. "Yes, I know. It was a silly thing to even consider. Marci's already made me aware only one of us had any dignity—"

"Theodore!" a blond haired white guy—Witch—shouted from halfway across the bar.

"You've got to be fucking kidding me." Theo dropped his

remaining bit of bread back onto his plate. He looked around as if he was considering bolting, all traces of laughter gone from his face.

I set down my knife. "Who's that?"

"No one—oh *god*—he's coming over." Theo's voice pitched like he was starting to panic.

The Witch reached our table, smile wide across his face but giving the impression it was devoid of genuine pleasure. He sat down uninvited next to Theo, who scooted reflexively away, almost into my lap.

"Theodore, sweetie, so good to see you." The man leaned in to hug him.

"Hi, Jason." Theo patted the guy stiffly on the back before freeing himself.

Jason leaned around Theo to peer at me. "You must be the elusive boyfriend."

"Uh—" I stalled, confused and ready to deny it since Theo looked horrified, but Jason spoke over me.

"You aren't what I imagined." He seemed to find me lacking and didn't attempt to keep his skeptical dislike hidden. "Are you going to introduce us, Theodore?"

Theo responded to the rude demand as if it were perfectly reasonable. "Yeah, this is Luca. Luca, this is Jason, the ex I mentioned."

"Hey, man." I extended my hand.

Jason shook it briefly, already turning back to Theo. "It's so good to see you out, sweetie. Being cooped up isn't good for you."

"I'm fine." Theo's voice was tight with suppressed emotion.

"Because you're getting out there. Actually having fun. This bar is great, right? Honestly, it's the last place I'd expect to run into you." Jason paused as if he expected Theo to make a comment. When he didn't, the guy barreled on. "Stella was just telling me she was *still* waiting for an introduction to your boyfriend. Can't believe I beat her to it. You guys have been together a while, yeah?"

"Uh-huh, yep." Theo picked up his drink and hid himself behind a sip.

Wait. Had Theo been telling people he was seeing someone? Had he been lying about having a fake boyfriend? Is that why he'd laughed at the idea when I'd brought it up?

If so, I might as well play along. I owed him that much. Theo seemed even more frazzled by the appearance of his ex than he'd been upon discovering I was his blind date. Surely I could help ease whatever he was feeling. Besides, I didn't like how Jason was talking to Theo, and didn't think he'd come over here intending to make Theo's night better.

I put my arm around my fake-date and gave Jason a smug look. Theo melted into my side and my heart rate spiked at his closeness. "You're not joining us, I hope? Sorry, Jason, but it's kind of a special night."

"Oh." Jason looked disappointed. "Just wanted to say hi. Theodore's kept you hidden, almost like you didn't exist. No one knows anything about you. He said you were too busy to accompany him to my engagement party. Was that true?"

The smug jerk. There was no good reason to say any of that.

Theo balled a fist in his lap, looking away from Jason.

"Oh, yeah. I forgot about that, sorry." My tone made it clear I wasn't sorry at all. "I'm a senior associate at Ellicott & Pearson. My free time is at a premium." Name dropping was obnoxious and not my usual style, but my words had the desired effect in quelling Jason's arrogance. "Engagements of people I don't know aren't my first choice of activity, and you haven't come up a lot in our conversations."

Theo turned, his back to Jason, and mouthed *thank you* out of his ex's line of sight. I squeezed Theo's shoulder.

"No big deal." Jason frowned at us. "I should leave you to it. I'm meeting my fiancé and some workmates." He scooted out of the booth.

Theo's alarm made a reappearance, his body stiffening against mine. "Is Stella joining you?"

"Ha. Of course. I'm surprised she isn't here already. See you two around. Maybe at the wedding." With a smirk, Jason left for the bar terrace.

"Thanks, Luca." Theo stared after his ex, sounding thoroughly disheartened.

"Hey, no problem. Happy to help." My arm was still draped over Theo's shoulders. Should I move away? Holding him suddenly felt overly intimate and way too presumptuous, even as part of an act.

Theo turned back to me, looking sheepish. "I may have—um —told a few lies about my relationship status."

"You don't have to explain."

Theo smiled shyly, seeming full of genuine gratitude, his eyes like dark emeralds in the low light. "We do need to hide, though."

I was very aware of everywhere we were touching and the fact that neither of us had moved away. "Hide?"

"Before Stella gets here. She works with Jason, that's how I met him." Theo looked away from me. "Oh, thank you."

The waiter had returned to deposit the rest of our tapas and when he walked away, it became apparent it was too late to avoid Stella.

Theo let out a small whimper but didn't pull away from me.

"Baby brother." A green-eyed, brown-haired Witch approached the table excitedly. "And the mysterious boyfriend. No fucking way!"

"Am I mysterious?" I asked in a purposely dull tone of voice.

She laughed and sat down, this time next to me. "Six months and no one's set eyes on you, I'd say you're mysterious all right."

"Stella, please," Theo whined.

"I just don't think I've ever met someone so busy." Stella eyed me as if she'd never liked Theo's boyfriend, despite never having met him. "I'm not sure my brother should be with a guy who barely has time for him."

"I'm sorry. I'm a lawyer, it comes with the territory." I grimaced in a way I hoped looked regretful.

"A Witch-lawyer. Interesting." She turned her assessing gaze on her brother. "You kept that quiet too."

Theo squirmed. "Yes. Well. His name is Luca, by the way. Can you leave us alone now, Stella? We're on a date."

"I know, I know. I have eyes. I'll be gone in a second. Can I take a picture to send to Sadie? I've been telling her your boyfriend was real but she's had her doubts."

Theo glared at her. "Oh my *god*. No. Stop it."

Stella took our picture anyway. "So are you coming to the party?" She glanced up briefly from her phone, eyes narrowing at me.

"No, he isn't," Theo cut in fiercely. "I told you he has work next weekend."

"It's true." I nodded, maybe playing it up too much. "Big case, long hours. You understand."

Stella pointed her phone at me accusatorily. "But what you don't understand, Luca, is missing our mother's two hundred and fiftieth birthday is an unforgivable offense. You've been together too long to keep avoiding the family. We're going to start taking it personally."

I had to resist laughing, covering the stifled sound by clearing my throat. I wasn't the only one in dire need of a fake boyfriend. "I see, but I really can't make any promises. Ultimately my time is at the whim of the firm's partners."

Theo's sister pursed her lips. "Fine. I'm only trying to save you two future trouble." She got up from the booth and departed for the terrace.

Theo dropped his head onto the table with a *thunk*, narrowly missing the bread. I pulled my arm away and scooted to give him as much space as the cozy set up would allow.

"This is the worst night of my life," he said into the table.

"Hey, it's not so bad."

He picked himself up and gave me an exasperated look. "I've been lying to my family for months. It's been three years since my relationship with Jason, and yes he's my most recent ex. I was sick of them feeling sorry for me, trying to give me pep-talks and advice every five minutes. So I pretended. But my lies were starting to get out of hand. I was going to tell them there'd been a 'breakup' before I got caught out, but now—*fuck*."

"We could still break up," I assured him. "You could be sick of my long hours or something. Say anything you want about me. No one will know you lied now they've seen me with you. It'll be okay."

"Maybe." Theo selected a few of the tapas and put them on his plate.

I followed suit, finishing my drink in the process.

Theo cut into a wheel of brie, looking glum. "I'll be back where I started if I tell everyone we broke up."

That was true, however I could already see a few holes in Theo's fake boyfriend logic. "Maybe, but what were you planning on doing if your date had gone well tonight?"

Theo looked at me with wide eyes. "What—what do you mean?"

"If you started dating someone after tonight's blind date, what would you have told your family about the 'new' person?" What had he thought I'd meant?

Theo's nervous laugh and pink cheeks made me wonder if

he'd interpreted my question to be about what he did on successful dates. Which had me disappointed I'd never find out the answer.

"I don't know what I'd have said." Theo ate his brie with a little too much focus. "Didn't get that far. As you can see, nothing about this is well planned."

I chuckled, prompting Theo to smile along with me. "So, do you need help making the breakup convincing?"

"I doubt it." Theo sipped his drink thoughtfully. "Or you could, you know, come to the birthday party with me? That way I can keep my lie alive a little longer." He shrugged in a half hopeful, half resigned way.

"You'd take me as your date to the party?" There was no need to get excited as Theo nodded in answer to my question; he didn't actually want me there. I was literally one step above breaking up with a boyfriend made of lies. "I do have to check my schedule before I commit. Long hours wasn't a lie on my part."

"Oh." Theo's disappointment set my stomach swirling.

"But I'm sure I can swing it. If this is what you want. I haven't taken time off in at least ten months. I'm due."

Theo examined the ice in his glass. "You really don't have to. It was a silly idea. I shouldn't have even suggested it."

I nudged his shoulder with mine and he looked at me. "Fake boyfriends was my silly idea too. And I want to make up for that awful date in college. I owe you a favor at the very least."

Theo bit his lip. "You don't owe me. Besides, it's not really a favor if you get a fake boyfriend out of it too."

"Wait, you'd agree to be my fake boyfriend as well? Like help me convince my dad?" I hadn't expected that.

Theo looked at me as if him helping me in return was an obvious part of this. "Isn't that how it works? It's a team effort."

"Yeah, but you don't have to meet my dad and sell this for my benefit. I'll help you out with the party either way."

Theo gave me a funny look. "It's only fair if we both get to benefit from the lie. I can't ask you to come to the party and leave you hanging."

He could have, but the fact he wasn't the kind of person that would gave me rush of affection for him. "Sounds like we have a deal, then."

6

THEO

My day was in disarray.

Closing Graywoods early to drive to Lake Tahoe for my mom's birthday party should have been a breeze. I only had the last of the inventory to do, maybe a few orders to put through, and a book to finish. But no, Witches decided today was the day to seek me out unexpectedly. From people in need of detailed advice on herb combinations for their bespoke spells, to new vendors trying to convince me to stock their potions.

I was run off my feet.

On top of all this, I was inexplicably jumpy and uneasy. A nagging feeling pulled at my consciousness every time I passed the locked drawer under the counter. I'd only half started analyzing the crystal, intending to look at it more in depth today. Then I hadn't had time, which left me feeling somewhat guilty about my lack of progress.

I'd be away all weekend and then only have a few days to sort it out before the man was due back. I'd half expected him to come in today precisely because I wasn't ready, but there was no sign of him.

His warning note seemed even strange now than before, but less worrying. The crystal wasn't dangerous, I'd looked at it enough to know that, and no one seemed to be looking for it. I hadn't had any more mysterious customers.

Luca had confirmed he'd come to the party with me promptly after our blind date, his work having agreed to give him half a day off today. I couldn't decide how I felt about his apparent desire to help me. He'd saved my ass on Friday night, but getting set up with a guy who was unfazed by fake relationships didn't feel like a win.

The fact that I had my own fake relationship going on was irrelevant. Marci didn't know about that. I still had no idea why she'd set me up with Luca, partly because I'd completely avoided talking to her since the disastrous date.

The bright idea to continue bolstering my lies with an in-real-life fake boyfriend had one hundred percent been the result of sucking down old fashions like I'd been in a drinking competition. Sober me was smarter than that, but not bold enough to take it all back.

Now I was stuck with Luca for a weekend. Not mere hours at a party, but days. I couldn't believe he'd still agreed to come when I'd told him we'd be gone for two nights.

I'd checked multiple times, over text, if he was sure he was okay doing this. I didn't want him to feel like he had to. But Luca had told me not to worry about the weekend away, saying he needed a fake boyfriend as much as me and that my idea was a great way to solve both of our problems.

After such a major time commitment on his part I was apprehensive of what he'd ask me to do in returning the fake boyfriend favor. All I knew was he wanted to convince his dad he wasn't single. But when? And for how long? I couldn't bring myself to ask. This plan wasn't much more thought out than my last one and, even with Luca's reassurances, I was already regretting the whole scheme.

The point of telling my family I had a boyfriend had been to get a little space, a break from their judgment and well-meaning but persistent comments. I'd hoped the ease in pressure would help my confidence, and therefore my ability to get out there and date like I wanted to.

Instead I'd got Luca Belmonte for my trouble.

I hadn't heard from Mr. Sexy-Lawyer since our texts on Monday when he'd agreed to make the trip with me. I had no idea how he was feeling about the upcoming charade. Not that I should care beyond knowing he was comfortable with the plan. And I didn't expect us to be in constant contact, so it shouldn't matter that we hadn't talked much. I didn't even want to talk to him.

In fact, I'd tried my best not to think about Luca at all, but he was like the crystal: always half on my mind but not so intrusive that I could be bothered confronting my half-formed concerns head-on.

I shot the closed drawer under the counter a narrow eyed look. I wasn't sure why I hadn't found anything in my first analysis of the crystal. I hadn't been able to detect its natural properties as I normally could with earth elements.

Maybe the spell it was imbued with was some sort of concealment, but I hadn't checked that yet. It wasn't my usual sort of analysis. Now that I'd had half a look, the crystal didn't seem like it had been enchanted to enhance any of its natural properties, and really, it might not be the kind of thing an apothecary would normally look into.

I was much better at discerning if particular mushrooms would add more or less animation to your spell than others. Or if you should use quartz from a particular region over another to better ground your enchantments. That kind of thing.

If I came up with nothing useful I might have to give the guy a refund, but there was no point worrying about it now. I was busy balancing out the cash register, my last task for the short day. The iPad I'd set up for credit card payment was, as always, hidden in the drawer under the counter next to the blasted crystal, so as not to disrupt the vintage vibe of the shop. I balanced those takings separately, and had already done so for today.

The bell at the front door rang.

Curse it. I'd meant to lock the door already but distraction had made me sloppy.

"You're going to have to be quick," I called out as I closed the envelope containing my cash takings. "Closing early today. Sorry." I looked up to see not a customer, but Luca.

My brain took a moment to absorb the sight of him in my shop. He fit in, almost too well. Luca had a classic Witchy style from his celestial tattoos to his pristine formal clothes. He looked damn good in my doorway, all modern and gorgeous framed by the contrasting timelessness of the old building.

Luca closed the door. "You didn't tell me you worked at Graywoods."

My back stiffened at the hint of amazement in his voice. "I don't work at Graywoods. This is *my* shop."

"Wow, really?" Luca scanned the place as he came further inside, lingering over shelves of bundled dry ingredients and pausing to run a finger along a display of potion bottles.

I couldn't help taking Luca's surprise personally. "What, you didn't expect me to have a good job?" I locked the register then turned on my heel to put the takings in the safe out back.

"I didn't mean it like that," Luca called after me.

When I returned he was standing at the counter, black suit bag slung over his arm. "I've heard of this place. I mean, everyone in the Bay Area has. It's legendary. I wasn't expecting someone so young to be in charge. That's all."

I walked past him to the front door where I flipped the *closed* sign and locked the door. Beneath the sign I hung a little chalkboard displaying a message that the proprietor was away until Monday.

Graywoods wasn't a hire-someone-to-open-while-you-were-away sort of place. Witches would rather come back when I was here. I prided myself on the selection of ingredients in stock, but the shopkeeper's knowledge base was the main appeal of Graywoods. Well, that and the tea.

After drawing the front curtains I was left with nothing to do but look back at Luca. "I took over from my uncle. He was the original owner. I—um—guess you'd know that if you were my real boyfriend."

"We do need to agree on a story. Cover some basic facts." Luca was eyeing the famous teapot, his bag abandoned on the counter. He leaned forward, hands behind his back, squinting in the gloom of the closed up shop. He didn't touch the teapot or ask for me to fix him a cup.

Should I offer?

The idea of brewing Luca his perfect tea felt more intimate than it did with other customers. I wanted to share my favorite piece of magic with him—which was a desire I wasn't sure I should trust. We weren't actually dating or trying to get to know each other. That wasn't even something I wanted, and I didn't know if Luca would care about the tea. If he was genuinely interested, surely he'd ask about it.

"We should get going. I want to be there by dinner." I made my way back to the counter. "We'll get our stories straight in the car. Come on. There's another exit down the hall." I pulled back the curtain intending to lead Luca out the door that opened directly from the apartment stairs to the street.

Luca looked around. "Aren't you bringing a bag?"

"Oh—right, *shit*." I'd meant to close an hour ago and go

upstairs to pack. Worry that I'd be found out for lying crashed over me anew. I'd never live it down if my family found out I'd been lying about dating someone. I let the curtain fall back into place, running my hands through my hair. "I'm just all over the place today. I don't know if I can do this. How will I keep myself together enough to convince people I haven't been lying for months if I can't even remember to bring a change of clothes?"

Luca came up to me and put a hand on my shoulder. "Breathe, Theo. It's only a weekend and you'll have my help. I'm very convincing." His eyes flashed mischievously. "It's a lawyer thing. What we're paid for. That and interpreting the law I suppose, but keeping facts straight and conveying believability is second nature. I'm good with details and—despite what you may think—have an excellent memory. I'll help you convince your family of whatever you want. There'll be no hint it's fake, I promise."

He still had his hand on my shoulder. I fidgeted, more out of self-consciousness than anything. I liked the way his touch calmed me a little too much, and wished I was still as mad at Luca as I'd been upon first seeing him at the bar. Anger was easier to deal with than amorphous shifting feelings.

Only, I couldn't be angry when seeing him again after so many years, and hearing his side of the story, had allowed me to let go of an old humiliation. Finding out Luca had never meant to laugh *at* me, and hadn't judged me for my inexperience or romantic notions about first times, was precisely what I needed right now.

These days it was beginning to feel like so many people around me harbored hidden thoughts about how I was silly and a bit of a loser. Jason had. After what he'd revealed during our break up, I'd started second guessing so many things. I needed reminders that not everyone saw me so negatively and that some of the things I feared might not be as they seemed.

That old memory of Luca could be that reminder. He'd given me so much more than he knew by explaining.

However, this left me unsure where I wanted Luca to stand in my life now that he wasn't in the awful jerk box. He seemed like a good guy. He was frank, never seemed to hesitate to be honest, and appeared to care about helping me out, all of which boosted his attractiveness to a new level.

It was too bad Luca had never been after a real boyfriend. Would he have been interested in me if he had? I wondered if I would ever find out what he thought of me now, or if it would all be confused by fake relationship lies. Not that it mattered. What I really needed was to focus.

The silence between us had gone on for too long as I'd gotten lost in my thoughts. Luca dropped his hand from my shoulder, calling attention to the awkwardness.

I took a breath. "If you're that confident we can pull this off, I won't argue. Maybe you should come up while I pack, so you see what my place looks like. For—um—details or whatever."

Luca grabbed his bag off the counter. "Perfect. Lead the way."

I ushered him behind the curtain. Instead of continuing past the chair to the storeroom, I unlocked the door to the stairwell. As we ascended, I tried to remember how clean my apartment was. I didn't attend to it quite as meticulously as I did the shop since no one saw it but me.

The living room turned out to be respectable. My books were always in order, and my study was only just visible through the open door to the right. There were no dirty dishes around, not even in the small adjoining kitchen, just a mess of crumpled papers and haphazard candles around the couches and dining table.

After a brief look around Luca followed me up to the third floor. We bypassed the first smaller room—it had been where I'd slept when my uncle was still alive and we'd shared the apartment—and entered the master bedroom.

I should have told Luca to wait down on the couch. There were piles of clothes all over the floor, definitely underwear in sight, and more than a few used tea mugs around. All that was fine, sure, but as I glanced at my bed—sheets all over the place —I wasn't able to keep my blush at bay.

Trying not to think about Luca all week had led to one rather notable exception. Yes, it had been a dream, but not one I needed to relive while the man was in the room with me.

"Did you draw this?" Luca was standing over by my dresser, distracted enough to probably not notice my heated face as he looked at a colored pencil sketch of a redwood forest.

I'd drawn it last year. Hanging up my own art seemed conceited, but I'd really liked this one and how it matched the colors in my room. "Yeah. I—um—like drawing."

Luca was actually the first person to see that particular sketch. *God*, I needed to get him out of my room. There were too many personal things in here, and now I'd seen him in my space, it would be way too easy to imagine him here with me on lonely nights.

Luca turned away from the sketch, his brows knitting together in concern. "You all right, Theo?"

I tried to smile, then abandoned the effort, quickly ducking down to grab my bag from under my bed. "Just spacey, sorry."

And way too pent up. Luca had gone from never-in-my-life to I-could-do-a-lot-worse disturbingly fast, but I needed to think less about being attracted to him and more about how to convince people he was a normal part of my life. I wouldn't be this hopeless around Luca if we'd really been together for six months.

An inconvenient crush on my fake boyfriend wasn't going to be the thing to blow this.

7

THEO

By the time we pulled up to my childhood home I was feeling marginally more confident the weekend wouldn't be a total disaster.

During the drive Luca had interviewed me about my life. He'd even brought a small notebook in which he'd written potential how-we-got-together scenarios. He'd scribbled notes, offering complementary details about his own life as we'd talked.

Luca's organization was medicine to my overwhelming doubt. I wanted to be touched he'd put so much time into this fake dating thing, but I suspected he was fastidious about everything. It reminded me of the Luca I'd known in college. Besides, he had a vested interest in us being believable to help his own family situation. All this work wasn't just for me.

"Did you like growing up here?" Luca asked as we got out of the car.

"Yep. I've swum in this lake every summer of my life. If it wasn't for my uncle and the shop, I don't know if I'd ever have considered moving to a city."

Luca scanned the surrounding trees. "I couldn't wait to move to San Francisco."

I imagined he liked the nightlife and all the excitement.

"It has its perks," I offered, in my case meaning Graywoods and every conceivable type of food delivered.

My parents resided in a three-story lake house located on a large plot of land. Warm light spilled out of the many windows into the twilight, beckoning us in. The forest came right up to the house, providing a protected atmosphere. It made our property ideal for Witches who might want to do a little magic outside.

Luca grabbed our bags out of the car and offered me his other hand. "I'm looking forward to meeting your family, sweetie." He gave me a mischievous grin.

"Don't call me that," I snapped.

"Sorry." Luca's face fell, along with his empty hand. "No pet names then? I just thought it would be a good way to signal intimacy."

Something about him saying that—so calculated—made me sad. He was only doing a good job at his fake boyfriending, but it made me acutely aware of how badly I wanted someone to say tender things to me out of genuine endearment.

"Pet names aren't a bad idea." I took my duffle bag from him so I didn't have to think about my hand not being held by his. "Just pick another one, all right?" Sweetie reminded me too much of Jason.

"Okay—*babe?*" Luca raised his brows in question.

I sighed. "Fine. Let's go with that."

I walked off toward the house. Luca followed. I opened the front door and gestured for him to go ahead.

Inside we were enveloped by the warm smells of candle smoke, herbs, and magic. The ingredients of my childhood memories. I clicked the door shut behind me.

"Theodore brought a man with him!" my brother Tobias yelled from the stairs like an old-timey town crier.

"Fuck off. No he didn't," came a yell that sounded like my sister Sadie.

Luca's gorgeous brown eyes went wide, his thick brows traveling up his forehead.

I tried to smile. "Having regrets?"

I'd avoided telling my family Luca was coming as my plus-one, saying he couldn't confirm until the last minute. It was a lie born out of defensive panic and deployed in an effort to avoid their prying questions earlier in the week.

Everyone was used to me acting cagey about my boyfriend by now, so there'd been little resistance. I wanted to be offended how many of them were surprised Luca was real—Stella's photo had made the rounds—but I *had* actually been lying, so I couldn't be mad they'd assumed it more likely my boyfriend didn't exist than someone actually wanted to date me.

Tobias reached the bottom of the stairs, ignoring Luca in favor of scooping me off my feet and into a bear hug. "Baby bro, so good to see you."

"Put me down, please."

I was, as everyone constantly reminded me, the baby of the family. Stella was only five years older than me at thirty-four, Tobias was fifty-one, and Sadie—who'd made it from the depths of the house to the bottom of the stairs—was almost sixty. Being Witches, we all looked relatively the same age but they lorded their advanced years over me constantly.

Tobias, who was also a giant and a full head taller than me, put me down at last. He and Sadie stood side by side forming a human wall of pale freckled skin and narrowed green eyes.

"Hard to believe he came," Sadie muttered to Tobias.

"Looks tolerable, though," Tobias muttered back like Luca wasn't standing right here.

"So nice to finally meet you both. Tobias and Sadie, I presume." Luca didn't miss a beat, putting his considerable charm on display.

Sadie eyed me. "Not bad, Little Theodore. I'd almost say he seems worth the *long* anticipation of his arrival."

I cleared my throat. "Yeah, okay. Thanks guys. Meet my boyfriend, Luca Belmonte. Luca, meet these overgrown children." I stared my siblings down, adjusting my glasses unnecessarily to better convey my judgment. "Your welcome only confirms that keeping Luca away was the right choice. Can we please be released from the entryway?"

Tobias ruffled my hair like a menace, before taking our bags to stow in the hall closet. "Theo, relax. We missed you. And it's not our fault you built up your boyfriend with all your mysterious mentions of him. Take Luca through to meet everyone. You guys can settle in after dinner." He seemed to think I'd been about to go off and hide in my room.

And maybe I'd entertain the idea, but so what?

My siblings led the way through a wood-paneled hallway lined with a hodgepodge of family photographs. It always comforted me to be home, but like my last several trips, all my warm feelings were muted.

"Sorry," I muttered to Luca.

He took my hand. "No worries, babe. They seem great."

My heart fluttered like I was actually welcoming Luca into my family. Like his approval mattered. I couldn't even tell if he was being truthful about liking my siblings or not. Luca could be hating every second of this and I'd never know.

We found the rest of the Landons in the living room. The large space overlooked the lakeshore and our little dock. With high ceilings and a wall made almost completely of glass, it was almost like being outside.

What looked like a game of competitive potion brewing was

abandoned all over the coffee table. Cases of ingredients, small iron pots and glass vials were everywhere. From the smell, they'd been brewing wellness elixirs and at least one person had gone overboard with the mental wellbeing.

This was what apothecaries did for fun, at least in my family. The person with the best brew won. Playing without me was the only way any of them could challenge my title of All Time Champion.

Maybe I should have brought the crystal and made a game out of analyzing it, changed up our typical Friday night, and saved myself the brunt of the work.

Stella had driven up from the city earlier in the week and was busy chatting with Katherine, Tobias' girlfriend, while Mom and Dad were sitting on the dark leather couch playing cards.

"Look who's here with Theo," Tobias announced to everyone.

Mom and Dad both looked up and hastened over. I braced myself for a barrage of cheek kisses.

Luca received the exact same welcome. He looked a little overwhelmed and blushed more at my parents' attention than I'd seen him do in my presence thus far. Maybe it was embarrassing to have such a loud touchy-feely family, but I loved them. Even if they hassled me.

"I hope you'll forgive me for not making myself available sooner," Luca said as my mom hugged me a second time.

"Nothing to forgive. It's good to have you here now." My dad, a tall, pale and gray-haired man dressed in a worn knit sweater and jeans, smiled genuinely at Luca.

"Yes. We understand, dear. I'm just happy you're both here." Mom placed a hand on Luca's shoulder, turning serious. "Now tell me, how's your potion making?"

Dad chuckled and turned away, returning to the couch.

"Um—" Luca looked at me nervously. Apothecary games

hadn't come up in the car. "Brewing my own isn't something I do often, but I did well in school."

"Hm." Mom considered him. The fine lines around her dark eyes making an appearance. "I don't think I'll take you onto my team, in that case. But don't worry. I'm sure you have many other talents, Luca."

"Uh—" My fake boyfriend only seemed more confused.

I almost laughed. "He'll be on my team."

"Of course he will, dear." Mom cupped my cheek with ring clad fingers, gazing at me with affection.

I had to look away. Seeing how happy she was to see me happy made my stomach hurt.

Mom fussed with my hair. "How's the shop, Theo?"

"Good. Same as ever." I briefly wondered about mentioning my strange customer, but there wasn't really anything to say other than I'd procrastinated at the work he'd paid me for.

She nodded, taking her hand away. "Did you bring me any sketches?"

"No. I—maybe I'll do one while I'm here."

"I'd like that. But only if you feel up for it. Does Luca ever draw with you?" She looked at him in question.

"I'm not much of an artist, I'm afraid." Luca seemed worried she'd find this disappointing, his frown serious. "Even if I had the skill, my career takes up the majority of my time."

"Remind me what you do again?" Mom folded her hands in front of her.

Luca shifted nervously. "I'm a lawyer."

I hadn't expected him to be nervous. On our date Luca had been flawless and confident in front of Jason, even before I'd explained why people thought I was dating him.

Mom nodded politely. "Do you enjoy being a lawyer?"

"Sure." Luca looked at me and I couldn't tell if he was only acting, but he seemed off balance. "It's rewarding. I've worked on some pivotal cases with my firm, Ellicott & Pearson."

"Lovely." Mom gave him a warm smile but was clearly not interested in asking more about his job. "Come sit, boys. Friday night is for relaxing, especially after your long drive."

Luca looked confused but recovered quickly. "That sounds great, and thank you for having me here."

"Any time. I hope we'll be seeing more of you around." Mom gave me another hug and left us to rejoin Dad on the couch.

Tobias was in the kitchen—attached to the living room in an open plan set up—making drinks, while the others dealt playing cards. The novelty of our arrival seemed to have officially worn off.

Luca shifted closer to my side so he could whisper, "What teams was she talking about?"

His breath tickled. I moved away, leading him over to a couch across from Mom and Dad, while explaining the apothecary games.

Luca blinked at me like he didn't quite understand the concept. "But what do you win?"

"Nothing really. Just bragging rights."

"Huh." Luca settled close to me even though the couch was spacious, his thigh rubbing against mine.

I glanced around uneasily, avoiding looking at the man next to me. Just as I was about to take out my phone to combat the growing feeling of awkwardness, Luca took my hand. I couldn't keep from sucking in a breath of surprise at his touch. Luca laced his fingers between mine, resting our hands on his leg. His palm was cool against mine, like I was burning up. Even if our relationship was fake, the physical contact was very real. There was no way to act desensitized when all my body seemed to want was more.

I eyed the lines of celestial tattoos on his fingers and the back of his hand, trying to focus on them rather than how our hands looked together. I recognized the symbols as magical links to his birth signs, but had never known anyone who'd gotten into that kind of magic before.

"Is this all right?" Luca asked in my ear, squeezing my hand. "Not making you uncomfortable?"

"It's good," I breathed. "You can—um—hold my hand whenever."

A soft chuckle rumble through Luca. He could probably tell my enjoyment of the affectionate gesture wasn't an act. I tried not to be embarrassed about it.

"Perfect," he said, voice still low. "And just so you know, that was a delighted laugh, nothing more."

Delighted? But was he really, or was that only what a real boyfriend would say? No one was listening to us, or even looking at us, so he had no reason to lie. I wanted to believe Luca didn't find my inability to be cool about snuggling up to a hot guy amusing, and had to remind myself he hadn't been laughing at me all those years ago. He hadn't been judging me. That whole first date was a misunderstanding.

But then what was this?

8

LUCA

e ate a pizza dinner in the living room, everyone sitting around on couches and the floor. It was like something Marci and I would have done in college rather than a typical family dinner, at least compared to the ones at my parents' house.

After the intense greeting I'd expected an interrogation, but everyone left us pretty well alone. Theo's family wasn't what I'd expected. Maybe I'd assumed his mom and dad would be similar to my parents, given he'd been lying about his relationship status, but sitting here I had to figure Theo and I had vastly different reasons for needing fake boyfriends.

"My room's in the attic," Theo said as everyone dispersed for the night.

I followed him up the stairs. "It's a big house, I'm surprised you're all the way up here."

Theo paused on the stairs to look back at me. I didn't quite know what to make of his expression. "I've had my room up here since I was little. I've always liked the extra space."

He led me into a large room, the edges of which were too close to the downward slope of the A-frame roof for you to stand

60

under. The space ran the length of the house with what looked like a door to a bathroom on the opposite end. There were three little square windows set low along each sloping wall, close to the wood floor. The ceiling itself had been painted to look like a forest canopy.

"Wow." I did a full turnabout, taking in the reading nook by the door, an easel and stacks of canvases, and a large desk piled with sketchbooks. Tucked down the far end was a cozy looking bed with a dark green duvet, lots of pillows, and a teddy bear propped carefully in the center.

"Yeah, it's the best room in the house for sure." Theo went straight to the closet by the bathroom to hang up our suits for the party.

I stooped to peer out one of the windows into the dark forest outside. "And I thought the attic at my parent's house was top notch."

"You slept in the attic too?"

I straightened to find Theo looking at me, a wad of poorly folded pajamas clutched in his hands. "No, my room wasn't in the attic, but my twin Aria and I had a playroom up there. It was the only part of the house that was just ours. Even our bedrooms were decorated by our mother and were more elegant than cozy. The attic was where we hung out."

Theo gave me a funny look. "I can't imagine not decorating my own room."

I shrugged. "I'm not artistic like you, so I can't complain about leaving it in someone else's hands."

We stared at each other for a long moment.

"So—" Theo glanced over his shoulder. "I'm going to go change and brush my teeth." He disappeared into the bathroom.

I took off my shoes and plugged in my phone near the night-stand. As the screen lit up I caught sight of a bunch of email notifications. I sat down on the edge of the bed and swiped to the app, quickly getting lost in catching up on the afternoon's correspondence.

A small twinge of anxiety pinched my chest as more emails came in, the phone vibrating faintly in my hand. It wasn't like taking half a day off meant I had any less work to do, and the thought of putting it off all the way till Monday didn't sit well.

I was in the middle of typing a long reply when Theo returned. It sounded like he was moving around by his dresser, probably putting his clothes away. The room was quiet except for my tapping fingers and his rustling.

At last I looked up to find him hovering, still over by the dresser, wearing green flannel pants and a loose T-shirt.

"Work?" Theo gesture to my phone.

I put it down. "Yeah, sorry."

Theo came over to the bed and sat on the other side, snatching the teddy bear and tucking it behind a pillow. "It's still kind of early. If you need to get some stuff done we can leave the lights on. I'll read."

I watched him fuss with the pillows. "I left my laptop at home to avoid work, so I should probably try and ignore the emails too."

Theo nodded, not looking directly at me.

The awkwardness between us seemed to be escalating. Not quite sure where the shift in mood had come from, I got up to go brush my teeth.

In the bathroom it clicked. We'd be sleeping together in the same bed.

My instinct was to say it was no big deal. There was no confusion about us not actually being together like that. But I couldn't pretend I hadn't noticed Theo's small reactions to me. He seemed to find me attractive and liked it when I was physically affectionate, even if he didn't actually like me in a way that translated into wanting to date me.

I wasn't the kind of guy Theo wanted for a boyfriend—he'd made that very clear on our date—but he might be interested in other things.

I returned from the bathroom feeling uncharacteristically flustered. I didn't think it would be a good idea for Theo and me to fool around.

Surely I was being ridiculous. No way Theo wanted me like that. He'd hated me on our blind date, and probably wasn't interested in hooking up outside a relationship given everything I knew about him. But part of me knew I'd won Theo over, just a little. If he'd still hated me he wouldn't have brought me here, and assuming he wasn't into casual sex was just that, an assumption. One based on decade-old information no less.

Even though I wasn't the no-strings-attached guy I'd been in college, casual was all I'd let myself have since deciding dating wasn't worth the rejection. I shouldn't have been bothered by the possibility of our arrangement shifting to include a bit of fun. Why was I? Was it because I still wanted a real chance with Theo, despite that not being an option?

I made my way over to the closet and began unbuttoned my shirt.

"What are you doing?"

I twisted to look over my shoulder. "Getting ready for bed."

Theo was under the covers, a book on his lap. I slid my shirt off and he looked away.

I turned around abruptly. We were both blushing, but it wasn't like I was stripping off in a showy way. I just wasn't going to sleep in a work shirt and slacks.

Maybe I'd read Theo totally wrong and the awkwardness came from him not wanting to be too near to me in bed, *not* him wanting something to happen tonight. Man, I was being an idiot, projecting my hopes onto him. I suddenly wished I'd brought pajamas. Not that I actually owned any.

Theo seemed very focused on his book as I slid into bed wearing just my boxer briefs.

I adjusted the blankets over my lap. "Look. I didn't give much thought to the sleeping arrangements on this trip. I'm not a pajama guy, but if you'd prefer, maybe I could borrow something to sleep in?"

"My clothes wouldn't fit you." Theo didn't look at me. He turned a page of his book.

He was right. I was a little taller and more thickly built. We'd have to look up an alteration spell to stretch anything of his to fit me comfortably, but he undoubtably knew that was an option. "It's not bothering you that I'm in your bed like this?"

"Nope." Theo turned another page.

I ran a hand through my hair, not sure what to do.

Theo looked at me then, his eyes sweeping over my chest. Predictably, he blushed and my insides fluttered at the sight. Seeing Theo cozy in bed, dressed down rather than in his usual impeccable clothes, had its own appeal. He'd looked stunning earlier in a wine-red sweater, but now he looked pretty in a more personal way.

Theo had freckles on his arms that I wanted to trace with my fingers.

I lay down and scooted under the duvet, covering myself better, and turned on my side to try and sleep. Theo went back to the book I suspected he wasn't really reading.

I STARTLED awake in the middle of the night.

Theo was kicking my shin. I grunted in annoyance, but as I came all the way to consciousness I realized he was whimpering. Not in a pleasurable way. It was a sound of pure helpless fear.

I sat up. "Theo?"

He thrashed under the covers, his breathing short and sharp.

"Theo?" This time I was louder, not sure what to do. He must have been having a nightmare but I didn't know if touching him to try and wake him would make it worse.

With a sharp intake of breath, Theo's eyes flew open. He looked around and jolted at the sight of me looming over him, his hand going to his chest. I leaned away.

"What—Luca?" Theo blinked and squinted at me.

I had no idea how well he could see without his glasses. "Yeah, it's me. I think you were having a dream."

"Was I?" He was still griping the front of his shirt, breathing quickly.

I sank back down onto my pillow, leaning on my elbow to look at him. "Are you all right?"

Theo frowned. "Yeah, why wouldn't I be?"

"It didn't seem like a good dream."

He ran a hand over his face and turned his head toward me. It seemed like he was glaring but I didn't know if that was just him straining to see. "Was I talking in my sleep?"

"No. Just making sounds."

Theo rolled to his stomach and buried his face into his pillow with a groan. "Sorry." The word was muffled.

"No problem. I was worried it was a nightmare or something." I wanted to ask if he had dreams like this often, or if he was used to talking in his sleep, but that felt intrusive. I rolled to my back, looking at the celling, figuring it would give Theo a little more privacy than staring at him.

There were stars on the roof, interspersed amongst the forest canopy mural. They glowed faintly, giving a good impression of the night sky. They seemed to have been magically done, and weren't at all like the plastic glow stars Mortals bought at the store, but little specks that seemed to twinkle.

"I like your stars." A smile stretched my lips.

"Thanks." Theo's reply was still muffled by the pillow he had his face planted in.

He seemed to get embarrassed easily and I caught myself hoping he'd become more comfortable around me over time. I wanted Theo to know that it was safe to share things with me without fear of judgment. But that hope felt misplaced. It was the kind of thing I could expect if we were actually together, not pretending. There was no expectation of growing trust in what we were doing.

The covers rustled. "I can't actually see the stars without my glasses anymore. My dad and I made them when I was little and my vision wasn't as bad. Tobias helped me paint the trees back then too." Theo's voice sounded clearer, as if he'd freed himself from the pillow.

I kept my eyes on the ceiling. "That sounds like it would have been lots of fun."

"Yeah." Theo shifted again. "It was magical. And like, I know we can do magic, but when I was really young it all felt so special. Doing stuff like creating stars and burying crystals in the garden with my mom to help the plants grow. I thought I lived in a fairytale." Theo huffed a laugh like he thought that was silly now.

"Magic was never like that for me. At least not that I remember. It wasn't much different than other school work." I'd never seen it as something whimsical. Learning spells had been serious from the start. My earliest magical memories were of grimoires, private lessons and practicing for hours. Our parents had my sister and me linking our power from an early age to see how far our abilities went, but Aria and I hadn't done a lot of creative things with our magic.

"Really?" Theo sounded surprised. "That's hard to imagine."

I shifted to look at him. "I mean, magic was still pretty cool." I'd just never believed in fairytales.

"Magic is cool, isn't it?" Theo sounded dreamy. He closed his eyes and drifted back to sleep.

I woke the next morning to pounding on the bedroom door.

"Everybody better be decent in there." Tobias didn't wait for a response before barging in.

The door swung open and I sat up in alarm. Theo groaned beside me and threw the covers over his head. I stared at Tobias.

"I see that Luca isn't decent." Tobias was in pajamas so I felt the comment was a bit unfair. It wasn't like he was dressed. "You two need to get downstairs for breakfast, everyone's waiting."

I frowned. "Can you give us a minute to get ready?"

Tobias shrugged. "Someone has to pull Theo out of bed."

I glanced at the rumpled blankets hiding the man beside me. "Why don't you leave that to me?"

"Fine, but if you're not down in ten minutes I'm coming back." He gave me a pointed look, then turned and left.

I ran a hand through my hair. "That was fucking weird."

"Sorry." Theo's voice came from under the covers. "He's serious though. He'll be back in ten minutes."

I got up and went to retrieve some clothes from the where I'd hung them in the closet. "I'm guessing you like to sleep in?"

A huffing sound came from the bed. "Not as much as I used to. And it's like, I get up on my own every day, but as soon as I'm back here it's as if nothing's changed."

"So are you getting up?" I pulled a polo over my head.

"Yes." Theo made no move to unearth himself from the duvet.

I pulled on a pair of chinos, smiling to myself. "I can't help thinking Tobias may have had a point after all."

Theo threw back the covers, quickly sitting up to glare at me. His hair was mussed, half of it standing on end. "He does not. How dare you."

I laughed and Theo cracked a brilliant smile. He reached for his glasses on the bedside table and slid them on. A yawn stretched his grin and he blinked before poking his fingers behind his glasses to rub sleep from his eyes.

I shook myself, realizing I was staring, and went back to my side of the bed to retrieve my phone. There were half a dozen new emails waiting. I clicked into the app, feeling resigned.

Theo got up and hovered by the foot of the bed. "We really should head down."

"Oh." I put the phone back on the nightstand. "I thought I had a moment while you got dressed."

"It's pajama breakfast." Theo shrugged and grabbed a robe off his desk chair. "Come on. No one will care that you're in your clothes."

"Um." I followed him out of the room, snatching up my sweater on the way.

I had no idea why a group of adults would be having a pajama breakfast, but sure enough, all the Landons were in the kitchen wearing various flannel items and slippers.

Sadie's eyes swept over me as she passed, carrying a plate of pancakes and a coffee. "I'm surprised you and Theo aren't matching. He usually can't pass up cutesy couple coordination."

"Oh, well—" Theo looked strained as he scrambled for an excuse.

"I don't think Luca wears pajamas, Sadie," Tobias called from across the room.

I felt hot and weirdly exposed by his teasing, considering I was the only one dressed, but despite the man's loud voice everyone seemed to ignore Tobias as they fixed their plates from the food set out on the counters.

People slowly filed out of the kitchen, going past the living room and out the back door to the lakeshore beyond, where picnic blankets had been laid out around a small bonfire. Soon only Theo's mom was left behind with the two of us.

My fake boyfriend was steeping himself some tea, so I claimed the rest of the coffee in the pot.

"Here Luca, I've made you a special pancake." Mrs. Landon handed me a plate. "I always make one for Theo and since you're his special someone, you get one too." She kissed me on the cheek, turned to hug her son, then took her own food outside.

I looked down at the plate as a weird mix of emotions washed over me. I felt acutely guilty for lying to her and accepting her affection under false pretenses. I didn't know if anyone had ever shown me such unconditional acceptance immediately upon meeting me. Her kiss burned on my cheek and I found myself longing for something, I just wasn't sure what.

The plate held one large pancake in the shape of a teddy bear. The batter had been poured with such minute detail that it had to have been created by magic.

Theo was eyeing me from behind his teacup. "My nickname used to be Teddy."

"That's so sweet." I looked down at my plate again as my chest constricted.

"I guess." Theo turned away, picking up his own plate and piling fruit on top of his teddy bear pancake. "I grew out of the nickname, but couldn't bring myself to tell my mom to stop with the pancakes."

"I don't know why you'd want to." I brought mine over to the counter next to Theo and dished out some fruit, careful to put it to the side of my pancake.

Theo watched me, biting his lip like he was thinking. I had the sudden urge to lean over and kiss him.

"You don't think this is weird?" Theo gestured to our plates. "No one else gets a personalized breakfast."

"It's not weird for people to show they care about you."

"Oh." Theo seemed startled. "I mean, I know that. I just thought it would seem silly to you."

"Why? I'm not judging you. Or your family. I'm overwhelmed by them, but I like them. And feel kinda bad that I'm lying—"

"*Shh*—" Theo hissed, glancing over his shoulder like he was afraid I'd blown his cover. "It's fine, they're all outside." He looked back at me. "I just didn't think you'd like this kind of sappy stuff. You don't have to pretend you do when no one's around."

"I'm not pretending." I picked up my coffee and plate to avoid looking at him. "And it's not like you know me that well, so I'm not sure why you thought I'd have a problem with sappiness or affection, or anything like that."

"Um, yeah. You're right, sorry." Theo seemed startled again, like he'd really thought I'd been secretly judging him this whole time.

"I'd have loved magical teddy bear pancakes growing up." There was more longing in my voice than I'd intended, but I pushed thoughts of my own family aside.

Silence filled the space between Theo and me for a long moment. I didn't really want to think about why this was making me emotional.

Then, Theo smiled softly. "Well, I'm glad to share this one with you." He placed an arm over my shoulders and gave me a quick half-hug. "Come on. We should go join everyone before Tobias comes looking for us."

9

LUCA

"**W**hat do you mean you haven't taken Luca foraging?" Tobias asked Theo in what appeared to be genuine bafflement.

Theo squirmed on the picnic blanket where we were sitting. "We live in a city."

"Has that ever stopped you before?" Tobias frowned at his brother before reconsidering and fixating on me, like I was the problem here. "How will you know if he's *the one?* Maybe he'll hate it."

"I won't hate it," I said out of solidarity.

Tobias ignored my comment, nudging Theo in the shoulder. "I thought traipsing through the woods was a key part of your game, little brother."

My fake boyfriend bristled, turning away from Tobias toward the bonfire and extending his hands toward the warmth. He hadn't shaved this morning. Light brown stubble lined his jaw in a way I found appealing. "Maybe I'm changing up my game."

"Ha. Yeah right. You're very predictable, Theo. Something's up." As Tobias continued to scrutinize us, I caught a flash of worry on Theo's face.

I doubted Tobias was about to make the leap to Luca-is-your-fake-boyfriend but Theo didn't seem to share my confidence. It was as if he feared our lies might crash down around us at any moment, and while I doubted that would happen, the Landons knew a lot more about each other than my family knew about me. It made lying trickier, leaving the deceit feeling more personal.

"I'm not predictable," Theo muttered.

"You are, but it's not a bad thing." Tobias nudged Theo's shoulder again, trying to get his younger brother's full attention. "I'm just surprised I haven't heard any stories about the rare mushroom the two of you spotted together, or how Luca found you the perfect flowers to press. It's like you've been subdued ever since Jason."

Theo focused resolutely on the bonfire. "That's not true."

I shifted closer to him, ignoring Tobias, who was starting to get on my nerves. "Could we go foraging today, before the party?"

Theo's eyes raked over my face like he was trying to read into my request.

I raised my brows. "I'm intrigued."

He hesitated a bit longer before giving me a tiny smile. "Okay. It will be fun, I promise."

"See, you're perking up already." Tobias got up and stretched. He flicked his fingers, cleaning all our empty plates with puffs of smoke. "The rest of us will probably come on the trail with you. I think Katherine and the others wanted to go on a run." He collected the dishes with a wave of his hand, summoning them into his arms, and departed back to the house.

Theo tracked his brother's progress across the lawn. "You're really intrigued? It's okay if you're not."

"I'm intrigued. And it's only partially due to envy of all your past dates." I hadn't planned on admitting I was envious of Jason, or whoever else Theo had taken on romantic outings in the woods, but I couldn't remember the last time I'd experienced anything truly romantic.

Theo's attention snapped back to me, a vulnerable look on his face. "Are you teasing me?" His tone made it clear he didn't think it was a friendly type of teasing.

I hadn't considered the possibility he'd take the comment as me poking fun at him. It threw me off balance. "No, I'm not teasing. It sounds like a unique way to get to know someone."

Theo mulled this over, cocking his head slightly.

Did he second guess everything I said? It was as if Theo still took me for the guy who'd laughed at him unkindly, even though he'd said he believed my side of that story. I didn't know what to do to help Theo realize I wasn't making fun of him now, any more than I had been back then. He'd accepted my apology, so where was this coming from?

"I'd never have thought you'd be envious of anything *I've* done. It's like you actually want to go on a date with me." Theo sounded cautious, as if he was considering believing I was being genuine.

"Maybe I do." I shrugged, feeling a bit hot in the face. Perhaps if I kept being honest with him, he'd trust me at my word. "I'd like a date, going foraging with you."

A slow smile spread across Theo's face, as if he'd accepted what I was saying at last. "It really is my signature move." He displayed a hint of smugness, confidence that had been nowhere in sight a moment ago straightening his posture and lighting his eyes.

I didn't hold back my flirty response. "So you're a pro at seducing people in the woods?"

"I mean, no. It's not like that." Theo tossed a crumpled

napkin at me, trying to suppress an even wider grin by biting his lip as his cheeks heated.

"I guess I'm about to find out. You can give me the classic Theo Landon date experience." I stood and offered a hand to pull him up.

"You'd be lucky to get it." Theo's slender hand slipped into mine, his many crystal rings shimmering. "What's a classic Luca Belmonte date? Maybe we can do a swap."

I pulled him in a little closer than getting him to his feet required. "Drinks and a private place to get to know each other."

Theo blinked in a flutter of lashes, dropping my hand. "I suppose I could have guessed that."

I suddenly worried my comment was too close to the proposition I'd made that first disastrous time we had drinks together. "Sorry, I didn't mean—I was just messing around, and that is—um—my honest answer."

I'd gotten too caught up in the moment, not sure exactly where the line between us was drawn. It felt like we were genuinely flirting. Maybe Theo disagreed. Was I the only one who wanted this woodsy date to be real, even though Theo had seemed pleased to discover my sincerity?

"No need to apologize." Theo waved my concern away with a renewed smile. "I'm clearly the creative one of the two of us."

"Now *you're* definitely teasing *me*," I laughed, relaxing again.

Theo huffed. "Come on, Luca. I thought you wanted to see my woodsy charm."

I waited for Theo in the living room while he got dressed, replying to another work email.

The other Landon children and Katherine filtered into the

room, all dressed in activewear. They didn't disturb me from my work but I had a feeling I was being rude by not attempting to join their chatter.

It was odd—the urge to make a good impression was as strong as it would've been if I were visiting a real boyfriend's family, but it didn't actually matter what these people thought of me. Theo and I would 'break up' before too long, the confusing discussion about foraging dates notwithstanding. No one here had to like me. I'd probably never see any of Theo's family again after this weekend.

Regardless, work was frustrating me enough that I half ignored these thoughts, along with the question of exactly how long Theo and I were going to keep up this ruse.

Another email came in.

I should have been able to switch off given I'd taken some paid leave—and it was a Saturday—but my job never really stopped. I'd have been in the office this morning if I wasn't out of town. Something major had come up, and while I wasn't the primary council on the case, I was part of the team assigned.

"Ready?" Theo stood in front of me wearing a soft brown sweater and carrying a canvas shoulder bag.

I shoved my phone away. "So ready, babe."

Theo made an exasperated face and huffed a soft laugh. He didn't seem to like the pet name *babe*. I wanted to find one that he liked, but maybe it was better not to confuse things more than I already had by telling him I wanted to go on a date.

Theo grabbed a well-worn walking stick from the back porch as we exited the house. "It's for poking around in the leaves."

"Of course." I followed him away from the house and past the lakeshore, the rest of the Landon's were a ways ahead of us. "Do I need one?"

"No, we'll be okay with one. You won't really know what you're looking for yet anyway."

Theo's combination of the nice clothes and walking stick made him seem like he was out for a stroll in an entirely different century. It was adorable. I wanted to compliment him but wasn't quite sure how to put it. Would he appreciate a compliment from me, or would it only be met with doubt?

Stella turned to us as we reached the tree line where the group was waiting. "We'll run up to the first lookout and back. See you soon."

Theo waved in acknowledgment, already turning his attention to the ground. The others jogged off and were soon out of sight.

I peered down to where Theo was poking around with his stick. "What are we looking for?"

"On this trail, mainly moss and mushrooms." Theo adjusted his bag. "The soil here enhances the natural magical properties of certain plants better than others. I've found that the difference in particular mosses and fungi are worth the effort of foraging from this region rather than sourcing from elsewhere."

He paused to brush away some leaves at the base of a tree, but didn't see anything interesting and moved on to a spot further up the trail.

I followed. "I didn't realize the location a plant was grown in could affect its magic."

Theo glanced up at me, fixing his glasses as they slipped down his nose. "Location always makes a difference, but it's very precise earth magic. Not something most Witches bother with."

"How does it work?" I came closer so I could inspect the ground with Theo, his attention shifting back downward.

He swiped the stick through the leaves. "It's—well—you know how soil essentially gets incorporated into a plant via transfer of nutrients? Same with magic. The magical essence of the place the plant came from can be found in the plant itself."

I looked at the trees around us. "Can magical essence vary enough to affect a spell the plant is used in?"

"To an extent. If you think of magic like an art, essence is like adding small details to a painting to give it depth and richness, or changing details to change the tone. It won't make a difference to the spell's strength to use—say—sage from the Mediterranean, but it will give most spells a more wholistic tone."

I was fascinated. "I had no idea. I don't remember this from school."

Theo chuckled. "They don't bother with essence in school. It's like astrological magic, on a much smaller scale. Instead of your stars influencing your magic through their positioning at your birth, the earth influences natural elements as they form. But like I said, it's not about power or core spell function, so lots of Witches don't bother with it."

I rubbed the knuckles on my right hand. Aria and I could link our power to each other as twins, but had also linked ourselves to our birth stars more permanently. It took the general astrological magic that influenced everyone, as Theo had mentioned, to another level.

Linking to your stars was a move that was all about power, a kind of magic that let me call on something outside myself when casting spells. It wasn't the kind of magic many Witches did. Channeling celestial objects was physically taxing, but if you had a twin to help bear the burden it was somewhat easier.

Our parents had been thrilled to have twins for this very reason. Aria and I had the potential to be more powerful than our peers, and in our parents' circles, power mattered. Even in my job where most of my work didn't require magic, just interpreting Witch law, power was valued. My celestial link was what made me a desirable potential partner, both to my law firm and to romantic interests. My ability to harness celestial magic was what my father used to tempt Witches with higher social standing into considering me worthy of their favor.

A flare of resentment surged through me. I tried to push it down.

Theo explaining things in relation to astrological magic made it easy for me to understand what he'd meant about essences. It also highlighted how different he was from the rest of my life. Theo had seen my tattoos but never asked about the extra power they signified. Instead, he'd focused on the other side of astrological magic—the way birth signs influenced everyone—and used that as a way to relate our two vastly different magical experiences.

Fresh affection for him replaced my bitter feelings, loosening the twinge in my chest.

I smiled, watching Theo still poking around in the leaves. "Did you learn about all this when you were training to be an apothecary?"

Theo bent down to brush more leaves away with his hand. "Sort of. I have a strong earth affinity that allows me to sense the magical differences between plants grown in different regions; same goes for crystals or any of the earth elements."

I squatted down next to him. "And you experimented with the different mosses and stuff out here to see which were best for certain kinds of spells?"

"Yeah." He shifted to a kneeling position and plucked a mushroom from the ground. "I sell lots of this particular one in the shop."

Theo opened his bag and took out a glass jar to place the mushroom in. He then grabbed a small notebook, flipped to the last half-used page, and recorded what looked like the scientific name of the mushroom and today's date.

He glanced up from the book. "What?"

I'd been staring, a wide smile on my face. "You're amazing, Theo. You know that, right?"

He bit his lip. "It's just an earth affinity. My uncle had it as strong as I do. All the stuff I sell at Graywoods comes with location details, and a lot of customers ask about adding extra sparks to their magic. Even if they can't detect the difference in the ingredients themselves, they can feel the extra essence once the potion or spell is complete."

It wasn't just his earth affinity I was talking about. My sister had the psychic air affinity, while I was more average, but extra magical ability wasn't what had impressed me with Theo.

"I love that you think of magic like art." I took the jar from him. "I'd never think to see it that way, but hearing you talk about it, no other way seems to fit so perfectly."

"Oh." Theo closed his notebook and busied himself stowing it in the bag. "I'm glad you're enjoying all my rambling."

"I am." I handed him back the jar to put in his bag. "I'm enjoying being outside and digging in the leaves with a ridiculously clever man. I don't think I've felt this—refreshed in a long time." I'd been about to say happy but held myself back.

"It is relaxing, isn't it?" Theo let out a contented breath, then handed me another empty jar. "See that other mushroom by that log? You can put it in here."

My fingers brushed his as I took the jar.

We shared a smile that felt soft and brittle, like something new was forming between us. The dappled light filtered in through the trees, falling on Theo's face. The green of his eyes made it seem like he was born to be out in the woods, like this place was part of him, his to tend to and coax small wonders out of.

Theo reached out and tucked a stray one of my curls behind my ear, his fingers sending tingles over my scalp.

He cleared his throat and then delved back into his bag for

the notebook, needing to record the second type of mushroom. I plucked it from the ground and placed it in the jar.

We walked in silence until we came to a large patch of moss.

Theo grabbed my hand and pulled me off the path. "I've been harvesting from this patch for years." He pulled a pocket knife out of his bag and knelt down.

I'd been teasing him earlier about seducing people in the woods, but Theo had my heart in a chokehold. It seemed like he'd let go of all the hesitance and embarrassment that had tinged the rest of our time together. Theo seemed so fully himself right now, and I never wanted him to close off again. I wanted more of Theo, more of the way he saw the magical world, and more of how he made me feel.

We were carefully wrapping bits of thick furry moss in wax paper when the rest of the Landons came jogging back down the path.

"You two didn't get far." Tobias stopped, slightly winded, and bent down, putting his hands on his hips.

Theo didn't look up from his notebook. "We didn't need to go far to find some quality specimens."

"Here, give me your camera." Stella walked up to us, her hand out. "I'll take a picture for your scrapbook."

"Scrapbook?" I looked curiously between her and Theo.

"Oh come on, there's no way you don't know about the scrapbook." Stella waved her hand impatiently for the camera.

Theo had gone pink. "There is no scrapbook, Stella."

His sister looked shocked.

"Liar." Tobias joined Stella, the two of them looking down at us where we knelt on the ground. "You're telling me you have a partner and there's no scrapbook? It's like you're not even dating."

"That's not—that's ridiculous," Theo sputtered.

I couldn't help my annoyance at the others, thinking they'd

ruined our moment. I didn't want a reminder this was fake—I may have said I wanted a date, but Theo hadn't said this woodsy outing was anything more than the rest of the lie-filled weekend, neither of us had been clear—and I didn't like seeing Theo so stressed about being found out.

"You're not doing any of your usual couple stuff with him." Tobias pointed at me.

I stood up. "People are allowed to change."

"Yeah, but are you changing him?" Tobias narrowed his eyes. "Are you making him feel like he can't do the things he wants with you?"

"That's not it at all." Theo stood as well, closing his bag with an air of deep frustration. "I've told you guys to butt out so many times before. I don't need the constant commentary. Maybe I just don't want to share all this stuff with you."

"What, why? We didn't mean it like *that*, Theo." Stella made an impatient gesture. "You've just been acting different and we want you to know you can talk to us."

I wasn't sure that was the message they were sending but Theo didn't argue.

Tobias didn't seem like he wanted to let it go. "You two are different together."

"And maybe that's a good thing," muttered Theo.

"You know what? You're right, little brother. I've always said trying new things was what you needed." Stella looped her arm through Tobias'. "Come on. We'll walk with you guys a bit before we do our next run. And if you change your mind about the picture, I won't say anything."

We followed them back to the path and the conversation lightened. Everyone seemed to forget the odd argument except Theo, who was back to acting subdued.

I slipped my hand into his, not knowing if it was because I wanted to ease his worry, help show the others there was nothing odd about our relationship, or if I wanted to show Theo something much more personal. Maybe it was a bit of both.

After a while Theo held me back under the guise of poking around in the leaves, turning his back to his siblings.

"Do they always bother you like this?" I asked.

"*Eh—*" Theo let go of my hand, eyeing the others warily to make sure they weren't within earshot. "I just don't want to deal with how annoying they'll be if they find out I've been lying. They've suspected it from the start."

I wondered if annoyance was all it was. Something deeper would have prompted him to start lying. His family didn't come across as unkind, but his siblings seemed oblivious when their well-meaning comments bothered Theo. At least that was the impression I was starting to get.

"I don't know how well this whole thing is going. I just wish they'd accept that you were my boyfriend and stop pushing." Theo paused, chewing his lip. "I think we need to kiss."

He caught me completely by surprise. "Need to?"

Theo nodded rather seriously. "They know something is up. I'm acting different around you than I would normally. It would help sell our story. I'm usually—um—more affectionate with my partners. Not like heated PDA but, you know. I'm acting like I just met you, not like we're together-together."

"Okay. But I doubt your family will assume you're lying just because they haven't seen us kiss."

Theo's face fell a fraction. "Do you not want to?"

"I didn't say that." My heart rate picked up. I'd much rather have kissed him when we were kneeling by the mushrooms, but I didn't *not* want to kiss him now. Only, nothing about my desire had anything to do with proving things to his family. It was all about Theo, wanting to feel him close to me, show him how much I was beginning to like him. I wanted to strip away all the pretending. "If you want to kiss me, just tell me."

Theo didn't say anything. Maybe he didn't want to kiss me for any deeper reason than the one he'd stated.

My fake boyfriend glanced over his shoulder to where the others were stretching, preparing for the next section of their run. He faced me, then pulled me close, his hands at my waist. "Kiss me, Luca."

My stomach flipped. "Okay."

As I leaned in, Theo closed his eyes. Was any part of this something he wanted? Would he have welcomed my kiss when it was just the two of us? I might never know and tried to push away my disappointment.

I tilted his chin just a bit and pressed my lips to his. Theo's arms snaked around my waist as he kissed me back. I let my hand caress his cheek and the underside of his jaw as we shared soft careful kisses. To me it felt tender, like something delicate I could get lost in. Something new that might grow.

After a moment Theo pulled back and glanced across the path again. I couldn't bring myself to look, preferring to forget any of this was for show.

Theo turned back to me quickly, tucking his head into the crook of my neck. "They saw."

I made an acknowledging sound, feeling nervous and weird about the whole thing.

The sound of footfalls caught my attention, then faded away, hopefully meaning the others had all left. Theo untucked himself from me, but didn't pull away as I'd suspected he would. He wrapped a firm hand around the back of my neck and pulled my mouth back to his as he shifted back to lean against a nearby tree, taking me with him.

I pressed into Theo, one of my hands coming to rest tangled in his lovely hair. As I touched him, Theo's kisses became more forceful, almost greedy. A deep feeling of affection sparked in my chest. We felt so good together.

Did Theo realize the others had probably left? He must have. Our first kiss had been proof-of-boyfriend; this was something else, too raw for an audience.

Theo made a small humming sound, then released me. "You're good at kissing."

"Thank you." I sounded pretty pleased with myself. It was impossible to resist pressing one more kiss to the corner of Theo's mouth, catching the feel of his stubble on my lips. "So are you."

A quick glance around from both of us made it clear the others had indeed left us behind.

Theo still held me close, his back up against the tree. "I think I do have a thing for seducing people in the woods after all."

"Yeah?" I ran a hand through his hair.

He tilted his neck in invitation, lips slightly parted and just a bit rosy from being pressed against mine. His green eyes seemed bright with longing.

Still, I searched his expression, not sure what we were doing now that there was no audience. Did this mean he shared some of the same feeling I was starting to have? Then why even pretend the kiss was for someone else to begin with?

"Please?" Theo whispered, his hold on my waist tightening, naked desire on his face as he pulled me closer.

I stopped trying to figure everything out and I leaned into him, kissing more deeply than before. He groaned and opened his mouth to mine. I let my tongue find his and Theo's fingers dug into me, his arousal becoming firm against my leg.

I slid a hand to the small of his back and his hips twitched. A deep noise emanated from the back of my throat and Theo swallowed it in a gasp. I let my hand move lower, until I was cupping his ass. Theo rolled his hips more deliberately this time and I encouraged the motion with my hand.

I released his mouth, kissing along his jaw to his neck.

"God, yes," Theo moaned as he moved against me, sounding completely unrestrained.

I wanted to whisper in his ear, ask him what he wanted. I wanted to say that I'd never experienced a kiss quite like this. Being wanted had never felt this good before.

I pulled back.

Theo had his eyes closed, his head tilted back to better enjoy my lips on his neck. He looked stunning, totally absorbed in his pleasure, loose limbed and flushed. After a second his eyes fluttered open and found mine.

I shifted so we weren't pressed so tightly to one another, sliding my hand up to Theo's hip.

He'd caught me completely off guard. I didn't know what it would mean if we hooked up, and needed a better idea before I went there. Was this just lust to him, a convenient opportunity for release, or could it be something more?

Theo's grip on my waist slackened. Reality seemed to hang between us, quickly turning things awkward. We both shifted out of the embrace in unison. Theo ran both hands through his hair, tugging on it a little.

"I guess we should keep going. That spot up ahead looks good for mushrooms." He pointed up the path.

I grabbed his walking stick and bag off the ground. "Cool, yeah. Let's check it out."

10

THEO

I made it through the rest of the day without touching Luca.

He seemed to be subtly avoiding touching me too, but other than this silent agreement, things hadn't gotten as weird between us as I'd feared.

I didn't know why Luca had pulled back from our kiss—more than a kiss—and I tried to convince myself I was glad he had. If we'd been somewhere more private I'd have been ready to take things much further. Even out in the woods it wouldn't have taken much to get me on board with hooking up against a tree, but I didn't need to be making any rash decisions. Right?

Despite our jokes, I'd never gotten that heated with someone while out on a trail. I'd never felt reckless enough, caught up enough in a partner to forget my inhibitions. I'd never needed someone more than I worried what might be happening around me. Or maybe I had just never been pent up and horny enough to disregard the rest of the world, but that explanation had the ring of unwarranted dismissal.

I'd been attracted to Luca in a physical sense from the start, even when I hadn't wanted to see anything good in him. Now I was starting to wonder if I had any reason to hold myself back. He wasn't a bad guy, unkind or uncaring. He kept showing me that my fears of his judgment were as misplaced today as they had been back in college.

But at the same time, maybe it only felt safe to want Luca knowing things wouldn't get complicated. He couldn't hurt me, break my heart and shatter my hopes on the floor around me. We weren't together. There wasn't any risk when our relationship wasn't real. Nothing to lose.

I was getting out of the shower, Luca having had one before me. It was time to get ready for my mom's birthday party, which I felt excited for in a way I hadn't expected to. Maybe that was down to Luca too.

Things with my family still felt off, but that had always been more my siblings than my mom. Their behavior this weekend had only confirmed that I was always under their scrutiny and subject to their critiques.

Luca had been right; them not seeing us kiss shouldn't have made me worry I'd be found out, but I didn't know where the line was for them. No one should be grilling me about why I didn't have a relationship scrapbook this time around. It was none of their business, regardless of whether the thing with Luca was real or not, and it's not like my siblings hadn't teased me about the damn scrapbooks when I'd made them.

I could never get away. I knew they loved me and probably saw keeping tabs on all the little things I did as a way to look out for me, but the constant assessment and questioning was stifling.

Contemplating all this as I shaved was killing my good mood. I told myself to ignore it as I exited the bathroom, rubbing the towel against my hair. The party was going to be fun. They'd be too distracted with the celebration to hassle me. Everything would be fine.

Luca was sitting at my desk typing on his phone. I stopped a moment to look at him. He'd dressed already in a dark navy blue suit and white shirt, top buttons undone just as they had been on our blind date.

His mouth was set in a serious line of concentration that made me want to kiss him, mold those lips to mine.

I turned toward the closet before he could catch me looking. I'd come out of the bathroom in my underwear and quickly grabbed my pants. Not that I'd mind if Luca looked up and saw me like this. The thought even made me smile, which surprised me given how I'd hidden in the bathroom to change the night before.

I slid on the pants and selected a shirt. If I wanted Luca to look at me undressed I should probably ask him if he wanted to see me first, rather than be all *oops you caught me* about it.

He'd pulled back from our kiss, I reminded myself, and I needed to know why before anything more could happen between us. If we kissed again it wouldn't be with the excuse of being for show, and if we went further it wouldn't be a rash decision made in the woods.

I did up the buttons on my shirt. It was formal dress for the party and I'd gone—unsurprisingly—with shades of dark green. Over my white shirt I shrugged on a forest green waistcoat, a shade lighter than my pants. I didn't like suit jackets and hadn't brought one with me, but I'd planned to roll my sleeves up anyway.

"Green looks good on you."

I whirled around. "It's the eyes."

Luca's gaze traveled up my body. "It's more than that."

"Well, thank you." I smoothed the front of my waistcoat, feeling pleased.

Luca seemed happy I'd taken the compliment. Then he frowned at his phone.

"Is everything all right?"

He set the device down on my desk and rubbed his temple. "Yeah, fine. I missed some calls while we were in the woods and the emails haven't stopped."

A wave of guilt swept over my good feelings. "If you need to return the calls I can head to the party without you."

"No." Luca straightened, brushing back his long hair. "I told them I was unavailable this weekend." He sounded stern, giving me a good picture of what he must be like at work.

I took off my glasses to give them a quick clean. "I appreciate it. And—um—I'm really glad you came on this trip with me."

Maybe I'd also removed the glasses so I couldn't see Luca's reaction to my words. Sometimes being in my blurry world felt like hiding—an impervious shield from scrutiny—even though other people could still see me.

"So am I, Theo. I'm having a good time."

I rubbed the lenses with a cloth, my heart fluttering. "Me too."

"Can I ask—I mean, I've been wondering since we got here; why did you lie about having a boyfriend to begin with?"

I looked up even though it was largely useless. Luca was a blur. "I told you. Everyone kept trying to give me life and dating advice, butting in. I needed space." I'd needed people to stop judging me and acting like the way I was handling my personal life needed fixing.

My siblings were always pushing me to do things I didn't want to do, and having a 'boyfriend' gave me an excuse to avoid their meddling. They couldn't judge me for not being busy when I had a 'relationship' to occupy me.

With my glasses back on, Luca looked thoughtful. "I get why you lied to your ex, the way he was acting that night he ran into us. He seemed like a total jerk, so I'd wondered if your family was like that too, since you'd been lying to them all for so long."

I had no idea what to say.

Luca grimaced. "Sorry, I probably shouldn't shit on your ex."

All of the sudden I felt tired. "No, it's an accurate assessment of Jason. He hasn't been great since we split, and he wasn't great before. But I couldn't lie to him about seeing someone and not give the same story to everyone else when he works with Stella."

Luca opened his mouth then seemed to reconsider what he was about to say. "So is that how it started, lying to Jason?"

"No." I turned away and grabbed my phone from the dresser, pretending to check something.

"Well, I'm glad I was wrong about your family." Luca stood up and crossed the room, coming toward me. "When Stella said your mom wouldn't forgive me for missing her birthday I assumed she would be—honestly—like my mother."

I wasn't quite sure what he meant since I'd never met his mom and Luca hadn't said much about his parents. "She'd never be mad someone missed her birthday or hold it against them, just sad we all didn't have our special someones with us. Mom would worry I was feeling lonely. Wonder if you were good to me if you were never around—which was maybe a flaw in my whole fake boyfriend scheme."

Luca stood beside me at the dresser. It didn't seem like he was judging me for concocting a fake boyfriend when it didn't really make sense, at least not the way I'd explained it. This whole thing had never been about lying to Mom or Dad. My siblings were the ones that would hold it against my 'boyfriend' for never showing his face. It had become another thing for them to hassle me about, almost canceling out the whole point of the fake boyfriend in the first place.

Luca's phone buzzed and we both looked over at the desk.

"I'm going to leave it here tonight." Luca sounded like he was telling himself more than me.

"Okay," I agreed anyway. "We should probably head out."

The party was in the woods. I led Luca to another path, this one following along the lake before cutting into the trees. Lights danced in the leaves and among the tree branches, illuminating the way in the twilight.

Luca draped his arm over my shoulders as we walked and I slipped mine around his waist. It felt natural, an easy comfort, no longer the shocking thrill it had been yesterday, and not strange after avoiding contact for most of the day. It was a transformation almost like earth magic, a small shift in the elements of the spell giving it a whole new feel even when the result—an arm on a shoulder, a hand on a waist—was the same.

The path led us to a clearing in the trees. Hedges pruned into swirling shapes marked the north, south, east and west points of the clearing, each with sizable crystals constricted within the tangled lower branches. Tables of drinks and food were set around the periphery with a section of chairs and couches to relax on clustered on the far side. Most of the space had been left clear for dancing and mingling, and plenty of Witches were already here.

Everything glittered with magical light. The trees shimmered. Even the fallen leaves on the ground sparkled.

"How beautiful." Luca sounded almost reverent.

I tightened my arm around his waist, feeling a rush of affection for him. He seemed to appreciate magic's softer charms like I did.

My mom appeared at Luca's side. "Thank you, dear. Dressing up this space is one of my favorite things to do."

Luca and I wished her a happy birthday and received cheek kisses in return. "Do you have events out here often?" Luca continued to look around, admiring the colorful lanterns strung overhead.

"Yes. We do something every solstice, and on any other occasion the family wants to celebrate. Theo did some really nice drawings of Stella's thirtieth birthday here. You should share them." She looked at me with warm encouragement.

"We have photos too." I caught Luca's eye and gave him an awkward smile.

"Sketching captures your unique interpretation. It's more personal than a photograph. Besides, I feel like this space was always meant to be drawn."

I stared at my mom, at a loss for what to say.

"I'd love to see." Luca gave me a look of genuine interest. I didn't second guess him. All day I'd been trying not to.

Yes, some of this weekend was pretend, but Luca wasn't secretly judging me or only acting interested in me as a person because he had to. Picking mushrooms together had seemed to make him happy. He'd said he wasn't pretending to have a good time, so I should believe him.

Luca might not be looking for anything serious but he seemed to be interested in me on some level. He'd said he enjoyed my company. Both of those things made me feel lighter inside. Happier. More comfortable with this odd thing we had going on between us, and more confident in following my instincts when it came to liking Luca. Liking his kiss and his touch, and accepting his returned interest.

"I can show you later tonight," I found myself telling him. "I've got piles of drawings in my room here. And more back in the city."

Luca beamed at me. He seemed to be doing that a lot today.

"If you like the clearing tonight, you should join us for Winter Solstice. This place will be even more spectacular with magic flowing through it, and we'd love to have you." My mom rested a hand gently on Luca's arm.

"Thank you." Luca faltered, eyes darting to me then back to my mom. "But I might—um—"

"Luca's family does a big thing for solstice too," I finished for him.

"Of course." Mom seemed understanding. "But we'd love to have you one of these years. Maybe summer will work better for you. Your family can come too, if they like."

Luca muttered more thanks, curling his hair behind his ear in a nervous gesture. The crystal earrings he wore sparkled in the magical light bouncing around the clearing. I'd never seen anyone who wore their crystals as earrings rather than rings, but I supposed Luca had all those magical tattoos on his hand to contend with.

Mom was called over toward the northern shrubbery by a friend who'd just arrived, and Luca's shoulders sagged in relief. We looked at each other. The question of how long this ruse was going to continue seemed to hang between us.

Winter Solstice was three months away. There was no way our lies would continue until then.

"Should we get drinks?" I eyed what looked like a small champagne fountain off to our left.

Luca gave me a relieved smile. "God, yes."

I laughed and led the way.

The champagne fountain was set up next to a bar complete with a bartender in a white tux. I ordered an old fashioned as Luca filled a champagne glass.

"The only problem with your family not being jerks is I feel terrible for lying to them," Luca said in a low voice. "And the feeling gets worse when your mom does stuff like that, not better."

I eyed the bartender who was expertly crafting my drink. It wasn't like he was going to tell anyone what we were saying. "I'm sorry, but you really don't have to worry, Luca. This is all on me if it goes bad anyway."

"I just—" Luca stared off into the growing crowd. "I don't know." He seemed almost wistful.

"Let's have fun, okay?" I took my drink, thanking the bartender, and looped my arm through Luca's. "We'll figure out what to do about this mess on the drive home tomorrow. And I promise I won't ask you to do anything that makes you feel guilty again."

Luca frowned slightly. "I didn't mean to imply I wouldn't keep helping you out with this, it's just feeling complicated."

"No, you're right. It is complicated with so many people to lie to." I felt the first twinge of my own guilt. "It'll be easier when we get back to the city."

"True. And regrouping on the drive home sounds like a good plan." Luca held out his glass and I clinked it with mine.

After sipping our drinks in comfortable silence, we milled around. I found myself introducing Luca to everyone. He kept himself reserved but charming. Even if he wasn't beaming with genuine happiness, as he had been when we were alone, he still easily won everyone over.

Knowing he was feeling guilty was rubbing off on me. I didn't like that Luca felt he was doing anything wrong, and the more people we chatted to, the more I had to admit that bringing Luca here was only making things messier for me. Now instead of just dealing with my siblings prying into my love life, I'd have to deal with almost all the people I knew asking after Luca. I'd have to tell them all we'd broken up, deal with all their sympathy and wonder if they were being genuine, or if they secretly thought someone like Luca would never stay with someone like me.

At least I lived in San Francisco, away from everyone. My life there was quiet other than my friends Marci and Jacob, who was my neighbor and as reserved as I was. I didn't see many people outside Graywoods. The shop was safe and comforting. No one coming in was asking me personal questions or judging my life choices. I was respected. Seen as an asset. Someone knowledge-able who helped people with their potions and spells, maintaining an important part of the Witch community, serving tea and happiness.

As with all my recent visits home I began to long to be back at Graywoods where it was easier to remember all these good things about me were true.

"What's he doing here?" Luca's unfriendly tone caught me by surprise.

I looked around the clearing, now full of people. Jason was over by the drinks laughing with his fiancé. My stomach twisted.

"I don't know." I continued to search until I spotted my sister. "Let's find out."

Stella, Tobias and Katherine were lounging on one of the couches.

"What's Jason doing here?" I peered down at Stella, letting my frustration fly free.

Her brows rose. "He's here?"

"Yes, and I didn't invite him."

"I let a few people from work know about the party. The Witches only. You know how Mom always wants everyone to come." Sadie sounded casual, like this wasn't a big deal.

I couldn't believe she'd invited Jason. She knew things had ended badly with him. I crossed my arms, unable to not get defensive. "You could have warned me."

Sadie frowned. "And risk you not showing up. Hiding away in your shop. No way. Besides, I had no idea Jason would actually come all the way out for it."

"Yeah, Theo. You know Witch circles are small. You're going to see him around." Tobias made it seem like I was the one being unreasonable, which wasn't fair.

"You're right. I will see him around. But I shouldn't have to at Mom's birthday." I turned and walked away.

Luca followed, a silent calming presence. I didn't stop until I was outside the clearing.

The magic lights didn't do much to brighten beyond the area they'd been cast to illuminate. The shadows were deep, the surrounding woods almost pitch dark. Even the sound of the party was muffled due to a spell cast to keep noise of the celebration from reaching the ears of our far-off Mortal neighbors.

My eyes stung.

I was probably being ridiculous, but I was so mad. It didn't matter how long ago Jason and I had broken up. He shouldn't be here.

"Do you want to talk about it?" Luca asked softly.

"Not really." I cleared my throat and blinked until my tears disappeared. I wasn't crying over that man anymore.

"What would you like to do?"

I turned away from the darkness beyond. Luca had gone serious but somehow managed to make it feel tender. Maybe it was the bad lighting or my wishful thinking. Either way, the sight of him comforted me.

A tightness in my shoulders relaxed.

"Jason said some really nasty things to me when we broke up." I folded my arms around myself and glared down at our feet.

"Do your siblings know that?"

"Yeah." I kicked at some leaves. "But they don't get it. Sometimes I wonder if they just think I'm being dramatic." My words came out pinched with emotion and my eyes burned again.

One of Luca's hands came to rest on my shoulder. The touch was light, as if he wasn't sure if he should have reached out. I moved forward and leaned into him, letting my face tuck into the crook of his neck. He folded both of his arms around me.

"Knowing he hurt you should be enough for them to understand," Luca whispered.

I cleared my throat. "They think I should be over it by now. It's been three years."

Luca wrapped me up tighter. "Don't think that's up to them."

I huffed a bitter laugh. "True. But I'm afraid the reason they don't get it is because, on some level, they secretly agree with Jason."

I'd never told anyone this, not that I had anyone to tell other than Marci or Jacob. But I'd also tried not to tell myself, and avoided thinking about it.

Did everyone think I was pathetic and boring? Did people only act like they cared because they felt sorry for me? Were my interests silly and something to laugh at?

Jason had judged every little thing I'd done while we were together, done it all behind my back, and then sneered openly at me the second he was sick of me. As soon as he realized I wasn't some project he could fix, some loser he could break out of his sorry little shell and improve, he'd told me all the ways I wasn't good enough.

And I didn't really think my family thought the same, at least not with as much malice. I knew they accepted me, but it felt like their acceptance only went up to a point. My siblings kept pushing me, trying to change me like they too only liked me when they thought I was on my way to morphing into something different. A Theo who was a bit more outgoing and confident, like growing up automatically meant I'd turn into them rather than my own person.

Luca ran careful fingers through my hair. "Your family should know better than to agree with a smug prick like that."

"I'm not going to argue, but you don't actually know him, or my family."

Luca made a *humph* sound. "I know enough."

His loyalty made me feel better. I trusted Luca wasn't secretly judging me right now in a way I hadn't with anyone in more than three years. I felt safe talking to him like this, being held in his arms.

A twig snapped behind me, off in the dark woods. Luca's head snapped up from where he'd been resting it against mine as I spun around.

Something was moving off in the trees.

11

THEO

s a figure approached, Luca conjured a small ball of light. Tattooed fingers twitched in the corner of my vision, his muttered words loud in the darkness. The light hovered in the air above our heads. Luca coaxed it forward with a flick of his wrist.

"Mr. Landon?" The voice was low and unfamiliar.

"Guests don't usually leave the clearing," I called as the light illumined the approaching man.

My startled curiosity turned to unease. It was the man who'd left the strange crystal at Graywoods. He was more put together than the last time I'd seen him but not quite dressed for a formal party.

"I didn't realize you were a friend of the family." I stood rigid, glad Luca was beside me. There was no reason to be afraid of the guy, but his presence here didn't feel right.

"It's a wonderful party." The man gestured toward the revelry with a ring-clad hand. He wore an untucked button-down shirt and slacks that looked like they'd seen a few days of wear in a row. He'd have stood out from the other guests, making me think he hadn't actually been among them before wandering into the woods.

"How do you know my mother? I'm sorry, but I never got your name the other day." All my Jason-related insecurities had disappeared. I sounded confident, almost authoritative. I was the Graywoods proprietor, and while customers always got my respect, that didn't mean I wouldn't challenge them.

The man didn't react to my tone. "I'm not a friend of your mother's, just the plus one of a mutual acquaintance. I'm actually here to see you."

"How'd you know I'd be here?" I narrowed my eyes, not that it was likely he could see my expression in the low light. Luca and I were further out of the sphere's illumination than the man was.

He took a step forward. "Everyone knows the Landons."

Maybe. But why come all this way to seek me out? Even if he'd heard of the party, we were way too far from the city for him stopping by on an off chance to make sense.

"You're a friend of Theo's?" Luca was stern and commanding in his own way, making it clear he knew this man wasn't my friend.

"A customer." The guy shoved his hands in his pockets. "I was hoping you could tell me more about my crystal."

I frowned, annoyance overshadowing my unease. "I said I'd get back to you in two weeks. I'm afraid I don't have any news for you yet. As you can see, I'm not working this weekend."

"Yes, the shop is closed. But I hadn't given you a way to contact me and I wanted to check up."

"Would you like to leave your number?" I didn't attempt to sound friendly.

"No. I'll stop by the shop again next week." He gave us a nod, not quite frowning but looking displeased. The man walked along the edge of the clearing until he disappeared into the dark.

Luca sent his light bobbing after him. I caught a glimpse of the man, still skirting the clearing. We watched until the curving treelined obscured him from view.

Luca extinguished his light. "Do you usually have customers who act like that?"

"No." I glared into the dark for a moment longer. "Let's go back to the party."

We entered near the couches. Luckily Stella and the others had moved on. I flopped down and Luca perched beside me.

I tore my eyes away from the darkness beyond. "I'm worried he followed me here from the city."

Luca seemed deeply concerned, his brow furrowed and mouth tight. "What was he talking about?"

I recounted the story about the crystal. "I don't think it's even that remarkable of an object, to tell you the truth. It's holding a spell, but not one that enhances earth magic. It didn't seem particularly powerful. And he said tell no one, but didn't seem fussed about approaching me when I wasn't alone."

"It's all strange." Luca tapped his fingers on his knee. "The shop's protected, right? If he'd meant you harm he wouldn't have been able to enter."

"That's right. My uncle laid the protections himself. They're relatively strong."

Luca seemed to relax a fraction. "You'll be all right when he comes by the shop again?"

"Yeah." I felt a rush of affection for Luca simply because he didn't assume I was helpless or unable to handle my own problems. "He's creepy and I don't like that he showed up here with some lame excuse about being someone's plus one, but I can't imagine he's up to anything sinister. And if the spell on the crystal turns out to be dangerous—which I highly doubt—then I'll report it."

"Just be careful." Luca reached out and squeezed my hand.

I nodded, a glowing feeling warming my chest.

"Theodore!" Jason's voice cut through the party chatter and music. He was heading over, mercifully without his fiancé. "I've been looking for you. Oh—and look. You brought your boyfriend."

Jason plopped down on the couch next to me.

I stood, pulling Luca along with me. "Hi, Jason." I towered over him on the low couch. "We were just about to go and dance, so you'll have to excuse us."

His eyes flashed. "Were you?"

Jason thought I didn't like dancing, but that wasn't true. I didn't like clubs, pulsing loud noise and being pressed in a crowd. That wasn't the kind of dancing going on tonight.

I turned to Luca. "You're about to be impressed by my waltzing skills."

"Yeah?" He looked delighted. Excited even.

I pulled him toward the string quartet, leaving Jason on the couch and feeling great about it.

"I'm a good dancer." I pulled Luca into position.

He went easily, following my lead. "I don't doubt it. You're poised and graceful even when you're digging around in the dirt. You'll be a natural dancer."

I let out a hearty laugh. Luca beamed.

He was pretty graceful himself, even if he didn't seem as familiar with all the different steps. We danced for song after song. It was the best night I'd had in ages. Luca's hand in mine. Our chests almost touching. My grip on his waist. His breath against my ear and the sound of the music.

It was gorgeous. Romantic in that effortless way. I wanted to kiss Luca, pull him tighter against me, feel his body move with mine without any space between. But not here. Dancing like this was perfect for now. More wasn't for a crowd, and looking into Luca's eyes I could have sworn he was thinking it too. There was desire and affection there, and even if he wasn't my boyfriend, it seemed real.

WE GOT BACK to my room late. The party was still going but there came a point dancing when both Luca and I decided we needed to get out of there.

I shut my bedroom door and leaned against it, pulling Luca toward me. "I was thinking—"

Luca quirked a brow. "Yeah?"

I swallowed the fluttering feeling rising up inside me, enjoying the sensation instead of letting it distract me or turn into nerves. "I was thinking about kissing."

"Oh." Luca gave me a coy smile, like he'd expected me to say just that. He leaned in closer as he looked down at me, resting an arm on the door above my head.

I nodded with mock seriousness. "We had a good first try this afternoon, but I"—Luca pressed his body against mine— "I've been thinking about it all day." I grabbed the front of his shirt.

He seemed to lose his playful air, letting it be replaced with something more raw. "So have I, Theo."

I tugged on Luca's shirt and he closed the distance between us, covering my mouth with his. I groaned with how good it felt. My heart pounded. I swept my tongue over his and savored the feel of his rough stubble on my cheeks. Releasing his shirt, I draped my arms around his neck so I could sink my fingers into his hair.

Everything felt so right. His kiss. The way he'd looked at me all night. The way he talked to me and seemed to care so deeply about everything around him.

Luca cradled my jaw with a delicate hand, rubbing his thumb back and forth as his lips worked against mine. The hand above my head came to rest on my hip. A small gasp escaped me and Luca made a satisfied, almost purring noise in response.

"Stars above, I like kissing you," he groaned, pulling back just enough to get the words out.

"Me too." I held him tight. "I swear this kiss is better than I ever remember them being."

Luca's eyes flashed with heat but he shifted further from me, not closer.

I loosened my hold on him, disentangling my hands from his hair and allowing him space.

"What are we doing, Theo?" Luca's voice was almost a whisper.

I'd have said *kissing* as a joke, but I detected a hint of vulnerability in the question. Luca's mouth had settled into a serious line rather than an easy, lusty grin.

He still had his hand on my cheek, running his thumb along my jawline. I let my eyes futter closed for half a moment and just enjoyed the feeling.

"I think we might be about to have sex. If that's something you want?" I looked at him as I spoke, my cheeks flushing but not in a way I was embarrassed about.

Luca rested his forehead against mine and took a ragged breath. "Yes, Theo. That's something I'd like very much."

"Perfect. I'll make sure you more than like it." I ran a hand up his side.

Luca straightened, pulling back even further and releasing his hold on me. I let my hands fall too. His face was set in an unreadable expression, eyes blazing.

"What does this mean?" Luca sounded even more vulnerable than before.

"I—" Surprise made me falter. I hadn't expected him to look for meaning in this. But then, why not? Because he'd said, ten years ago, that he was only into casual sex, or because he told me on a blind date gone horribly wrong that he wasn't looking for a relationship. That wasn't the whole story and I knew it. The Luca I'd spent the weekend with seemed like a person looking for connection.

"What do you want it to mean?" I asked, turning the question back on him.

"I don't know." Luca blinked like he was lost for a split second. Then looked down, avoiding my eyes. "Only to acknowledge that it does mean something. We may not be together, but that doesn't make this casual. Not to me."

My chest twinged in understanding and rapidly increasing affection. "It means something to me to. I like you. And you're right, we might not be boyfriends, but that doesn't mean there isn't something real here."

My pulse thudded in my throat as I waited for his reply.

Luca looked up and smiled, bright and unrestrained. "I'm not saying we have to redefine our arrangement, now's probably not the time, but can we agree to see where this goes? See what adding this"—he grabbed my hand, pulling me off the door and into his arms—"does to us?"

"Yes," I breathed.

Still, he hesitated. "You should know, I'm not good at relationships." Luca sounded as if he was admitting a fault, his voice quiet and unsure. "I wonder if things are going so well this weekend only because I can tell myself it's not really happening, there's no risk of failing."

I laid a soft kiss on his lips. "I get that. It can't go wrong if there's nothing going on. But if we want to see where this goes we have to accept the risk too."

Saying it out loud, I couldn't deny that it scared me. Agreeing to see where we went, acknowledging that taking this step wasn't meaningless, and aiming for a relationship, was what I wanted. But it would have been easier to indulge in physical attraction without talking about it, to get part of what I needed without having to worry.

"I want to try." Luca wrapped his arms around me. "I like you too, Theo."

Happiness buzzed around in my head and sent a shiver down my spine. I couldn't ask for more than that. If we were on the same page that had to be a good sign, even if we were both afraid of the risk.

We kissed until we were breathless. It was like we'd unlocked something new by admitting there was emotion behind our actions.

Luca nudged me back so he could run his eyes up and down my body. "You always look so stunning,"

I glowed, feeling as good about myself as I did on my best days. "I like the way you look at me."

"I can tell." He reached for the first button on my waistcoat. "May I?"

"Yeah, we've got a lot of buttons to get through."

Luca laughed deeply and there was no mistaking the delight in it, even though it was a silly thing for me to have said. He undid my waistcoat, not exactly slowly but not like he was in any particular rush. He slid it off my shoulders and I took the opportunity to get rid of his suit jacket.

He pulled at my shirt, untucking it from my waistband. The deliberate, jerky movements and feeling of sliding fabric made my breath hitch. Luca left the buttons alone, instead dipping a hand under the shirt, skimming my hip and palming my lower back. His touch was hot on my skin, his eyes focused on mine.

He grabbed my belt and pulled, bringing me closer. Luca's hand trailed lower, brushing over my erection but not rubbing me with the kind of pressure I was starting to ache for.

I began undoing my shirt, fingers fumbling. Luca watched every inch of my chest as it was exposed. My stomach fluttered with a combination of pleasure and mounting nerves.

I wanted this to go well. There was more to lose now if it didn't.

"See—stunning." He traced a line up my torso.

"You're pretty gorgeous, yourself." I gripped his biceps and he grinned. "Should we maybe get close to the bed?"

We were still by the door, all the way across the large room. As I glanced over my shoulder my stomach flipped uncomfortably.

"If that's where you'd like to be." Luca ran his fingers back down my chest.

I supposed we didn't *need* to go to the bed. "What do you want?" I sounded uncertain, nerves officially drowning out my more pleasurable feelings.

Luca looked up from where he was touching me. "I'd like to take you to bed, Theo. I'd rather that, than against the door."

I would too, and maybe that was boring, but why should it matter? It shouldn't, right? Or was he implying against the door would have been good, but the bed was fine if I wasn't into it? I was starting to over think, anxiety and doubt creeping up on me when I hadn't expected it to. I'd thought I'd come past this uncertainty with Luca.

Trying to push the feelings away, I grabbed his hand and led him across the room.

Once we were at the bed I dropped Luca's hand. I shrugged off my shirt and got rid of my belt. Shoes and socks were next, but I struggled with the knotted laces. Was I taking too long? Was it obvious I was nervous? I fumbled with the button on my pants, all my feelings of arousal gone. I was sure they'd come back. I'd be able to banish my worry once we got going.

"Hey." Luca touched my arm and I looked up at him. "What's up?"

My nervousness hit an agonizing peak. Was I acting weird? *Shit*. I was. I hadn't even been looking at Luca as I'd continued undressing. Maybe he'd wanted to unbutton my pants. Or maybe he'd wanted me to attend to his clothes.

It was like my easy confidence had evaporated. I studied Luca's face for hidden thoughts. He seemed fine, maybe less sultry than before. Perhaps he hadn't been thinking anything. But he hadn't taken his shoes off, hadn't undressed at all while I'd been quickly getting all the annoying bits of clothes out of the way. Why hadn't he?

My hands trembled.

"Am I messing this up?" I hated voicing the worry almost as much as I hated having it in the first place.

"No, you're not messing anything up, Theo." Luca sounded reassuring. That wasn't good. He should sound aroused, not like he had to comfort me.

"Are you sure?" I cringed and had to look away.

Luca sat down on the bed next to where I was standing. "Yes, I'm sure. But I think something's happened just now."

I sat next to him feeling increasingly upset with myself, worried everything was doomed. "Is having sex on the bed boring?" *Curse everything*. It was like I couldn't help myself. What a dumb thing to say.

"No." Luca sounded patient. I looked at my hands instead of at him. "I'd never think sex with you—anywhere—was boring."

So I was being ridiculous. I *was* messing this up. Probably completely blowing it. Why had I interrupted us to say we had to come over here? If we'd stayed by the door we'd probably be naked and sweaty already.

Why had I said anything? Why was this happening?

I tried to stop my thoughts but couldn't. My confidence wasn't coming back. I'd psyched myself out and fucked everything up.

"Theo—" Luca's voice was soft. His hand brushed my knee.

I scrambled to try and figure out what had gone wrong and how to save it, only I kept getting stuck trying to analyze every detail of what Luca had said and done. "Why didn't you take off your shoes?"

"Um—? I was getting to it. Here—" Luca hesitated, then kicked them off.

Why was I focusing on that? It didn't even make sense to me.

I flopped back on the bed and covered my face with my hands, fingers poking under my glasses to better cover my eyes.

After a long moment Luca laid down next to me, but not too close. "What's going on, Theo? You can talk to me."

"I don't want to talk. I want—I wanted to be having fun with you right now."

"Yeah, but I'm feeling like we need to talk a bit before that happens."

I looked at him. He was propped on an elbow, looking kind and full of open understanding. I couldn't help wondering if he was really laughing at me even though I hated the thought, knew it was bullshit and not true. Luca wouldn't do that but I couldn't push the notion away.

"I haven't done this in a long time." I sounded miserable and gave up hoping that I'd come out of this looking any kind of good.

"That's okay. I'm not expecting you to do anything you're not comfortable with. Are you nervous?" Luca reached out and touched my fist where it was clenched in the duvet.

"No. I wasn't nervous before. You saw. I was—" Confident, but I stopped myself from saying the word. It would mean admitting that now I was insecure. "I don't know what happened."

It was a truth that only made the whole situation feel worse.

We lay in silence. Luca was probably waiting for me to decide what the fuck was going on.

In one quick roll I turned from my back to my stomach. It brought me into Luca's space and I tucked my face in the crook between his chest—still clothed in his dress shirt—and the bed.

His arm came to rest lightly on my bare back.

"We're not having sex tonight are we?" My question came out muffled.

"No, I don't think so." Luca rubbed my back.

I tried to fight the feeling that I'd ruined everything.

"Do you want to talk?"

"I just don't know what changed," I said into the bedspread. "I couldn't stop thinking."

"What were you thinking about?" Luca's hand began massaging the tension in my shoulders.

I let out a breath. "Ridiculous bullshit."

"I'm going to have to disagree with that. Your thoughts and feeling aren't ridiculous. They matter."

But I didn't want them to matter. That was part of the problem. They were mostly irrational worries. And I knew where they'd come from.

"I haven't been with anyone since Jason." I decided the night couldn't get any worse, so I might as well not hold back. "It's not like I haven't wanted to. I just always blow it. Usually things don't even get this far."

"You didn't blow it, Theo. I don't see it like that at all." Luca sounded stern and maybe a bit offended, so I didn't argue.

I told myself to accept what he was saying. I had no reason to think he'd lie.

With my face firmly planted out of sight, I went on, "It's just, I have all these worries. And I know they don't really make sense, but when they get a hold of me I can't push them away."

Luca moved his massaging to my other shoulder. "Does that sort of thing happen to you often?"

I thought for a moment. "No. I think about stuff and worry, but it doesn't send me into a spiral I can't get out of. Only when it's—um—like this, I guess."

"Do you mean when it's to do with sex, or relationships in general?" Luca didn't sound judgmental. It was like he was trying to understand something completely normal.

"I'm not sure. I haven't had a lot of opportunities to find out." I had to tell myself not to be embarrassed about that, and somehow managed it.

When I considered everything that had happened just now with a bit more perspective, I felt calmer. More myself. I breathed more easily even though I was half smothering myself with the duvet.

My glasses dug into my face. "I think some of the things Jason said to me got stuck in my head and I can't get them out. It's like these things I only ever worried about here and there, or used to easily dismiss, have become sharp and stuck in my gut no matter how much I don't want them to be there. And then I doubt everything."

Luca's hand stilled. "What the hell did he say to you?"

His anger made me feel better. It reminded me that this wasn't all my fault. That this problem didn't stem from some flaw of mine.

"I don't really want to recount it word for word."

Luca paused. "No, of course not."

I squirmed so that my face was tucked more into Luca's chest than the bed. "I started worrying that I seemed boring to you. That I'd given myself away as this undesirable sort of person, and that messed everything up. Then worrying I was acting weird only made it worse, like a feedback loop."

"Do you doubt that I like you?" Luca sounded startled. "You aren't boring. I would never think that."

"I'm sorry. I know. I mean, I don't doubt when you say you like me, or that I'm stunning, or that you like spending time with me. I don't. But at the same time"—I hesitated, taking a breath and rolling so that I was looking up into Luca's face—"Jason said he liked me too. He liked my herb picking and book collecting. But then later, he admitted it was all a lie. He'd thought I was kind of pathetic and acted like he'd been doing me a favor by dating me. And I know that's on him. Not everyone is that kind of asshole. But I'm afraid of it happening again. Afraid of finding out everyone has these secret judgments hidden while they pretend the opposite to my face. I trusted Jason and the extreme switch in his opinion caught me so off guard. I don't think I'd be able to see it coming if it started to happen again because I don't know what to look for. So I'm always wondering—is it happening now?"

Luca pulled me into a hug. "I'm sorry, Theo. What Jason did was fucked up. Of course you trusted him. He should never have betrayed you like that."

"I don't know how to get over it," I whispered.

Luca nodded, his head moving against mine. "Does it feel like this is helping at all? Like, if you start worrying I'm judging you, do you think mentioning it would help?"

"I don't know. Just now, every time you reassured me it made it worse. Not because you did anything wrong, I just couldn't stop worrying it was all a lie. That's why pretending was nice. It *was* a lie so there was no space left for worry. But I want to see where something real goes. If you still have any interest in that?"

"Yes, I'd still like that. Nothing has changed in a negative way. I like you, Theo. And knowing what's going on with you is a good thing."

Maybe knowing he understood would help more than Luca reassuring me. I had to sort this out for myself. This wasn't something he could fix for me, but knowing he was aware of what was going on in my head, and knowing he accepted it, might make a difference.

I breathed in the smell of Luca's cologne. Tonight wasn't a disaster. Luca liked me, and he'd been vulnerable with me. Luca had said our kissing meant something when hiding behind the situation would have been easier. That told me he cared. He'd been showing me he cared all weekend. I could trust someone who cared. I just had to trust myself, which was a hell of a lot harder.

12

LUCA

e tucked into bed, Theo now in his pajamas.

He folded his glasses and put them on the nightstand before rolling to face me. "Can I come closer?"

I made a space for him under my arm. "Yes, come here—" I was about to say *babe* but that was our agreed fake nickname and I didn't want to confuse things.

Theo tucked into me, his head on my chest. It felt nice, so right and comfortable even when the rest of the night had me concerned.

"When you said you were worried that your siblings secretly agreed with Jason, do they know everything you've just told me?" I kept my voice quiet, hoping it wasn't the wrong thing to say now that we'd moved on from our earlier chat.

"No," Theo said, and some of the tension left my body in relief. "All they know is that he was the one to end it, and that I found out Jason had been judging me the whole time. I didn't say about what, or how harsh his judgments were. And I know my siblings don't believe truly nasty things about me, but they have opinions about everything. I've always wondered what they're really thinking. After Jason, it got worse."

"I can imagine it would have."

Theo shifted his weight, moving in tighter against me. "If I'd told them everything, Stella never would have invited Jason, right?"

It broke my heart that he was asking. "No, I doubt she would have. I don't know her well, but they all strike me as people who are ultimately on your side."

Theo was quiet for a long time and I wondered if he'd fallen asleep. My mind started to drift. I nodded off only to blink awake.

"Thank you, Luca," Theo whispered.

Maybe he thought I was asleep and wouldn't hear. I squeezed the arm I had around him. "Of course."

A STRANGLED SOUND woke me up.

Theo was thrashing in the bed next to me, having another dream. This time I reached for him without hesitating as I said his name, trying to gently coax him awake.

He whimpered but didn't otherwise respond. I shook his shoulder more forcefully. He still didn't wake up.

"Theo." It came out close to a shout.

He didn't wake. His eyes darted around behind their lids in frantic, jerky movements.

Something didn't seem right. Was it possible this wasn't your usual type of nightmare? Could it be some sort of magical issue? The thought made me panicky, not knowing what to do.

I shook Theo's shoulders and called his name again but he still didn't wake up. He kicked and flailed, a pained look on his face.

I twisted around to grab my phone from the nightstand.

The grimoire app would be able to tell me how to deal with magically induced dreams, but it wasn't going to give me a quick and easy answer. First, I'd have to figure out what was going on, what kind of magic was at work, then figure out how to counter it.

I had no idea why Theo would be suffering from magical nightmares he couldn't wake up from, but I couldn't think of any other explanation for what was happening to him.

As I typed in the app's search bar, Theo gasped. I looked up in time to see his eyes fly open.

I dropped the phone on the bed. "Are you all right?"

"Huh?" He was breathing heavily, looking around until his eyes found me.

"You had another dream. I thought—" My pulse pounded.

"Was I screaming?" Theo looked more frightened, and a lot more confused, than last night.

"No, just whimpering. But you wouldn't wake up."

He ran a hand through his hair then reached for his glasses, his breathing slowly returning to normal. "What do you mean?"

I described it to him. "Has this ever happened before? Last night just seemed like a dream but this, I don't know." I was at a loss.

Theo frowned, sitting up in bed. I was on my knees facing him and had to resist grabbing him and pulling him into an embrace.

"I don't have a lot of nightmares, no." Theo's brow creased in concentration. "Never twice in a row like these last nights. Though, I'm pretty sure I had one last week, now that I'm think about it. I'd mostly forgotten it by morning. I don't remember what last night's dream was about either."

"What about this one?" I picked up my phone. "I wondered if it might be magic."

Theo's concentration sharpened in alarm. "Like a curse?"

"I don't know. I have no experience with those sorts of spells. I was trying to look it up."

"I don't really remember what this dream was about either. Maybe the woods. Or that guy—" His voice trailed off.

"The customer?" I was surprised. The encounter with the man had been odd, but not frightening. "Could the crystal he gave you have been cursed?"

Theo shook his head. "No. I'd have detected that easily. The spell on it seemed simple. Though it was concealing something, I'm pretty sure."

"Concealing?"

Theo bit his lip. "Yeah, but the concealment—if that's what it is, I haven't checked—didn't seem strong in itself. I'd have sensed if the spell was complex, like a curse would be."

I nodded in agreement as something else occurred to me. "A simple spell wouldn't affect you this far away."

"No, it wouldn't. Maybe it wasn't magic. Maybe I was just in a deep sleep. I woke up on my own after all."

"That's possible." I didn't know if worry was the only thing making me think otherwise. "Will you tell me if the dreams keep happening?"

Theo blinked in surprise. "I—um—guess I could."

I tried to ignore the awkwardness brought on by my presumptuous request. "I just thought—I don't know—in case it is magic. What if it gets worse?"

He wasn't my boyfriend. There was no expectation I'd help him with this, not at the see-where-things-go stage of getting to know each other, especially when the dreams might not even be a real problem. But being over-invested from day one and trying too hard was typical of me. It seemed like I couldn't help acting that way.

I could be cool and disconnected in every other aspect of my life, but when I fell for someone I was the opposite. It tended to put guys off.

"No, that's a good idea," Theo agreed after considering for a moment.

I didn't say anything else. Maybe he was humoring me, but I hoped not. Surely Theo wouldn't see caring too much as a bad thing after everything with his ex. Unless he preferred the smooth, flawless version of me to my more needy side.

With all this on my mind, it took me a long time to fall back asleep.

13

LUCA

*W*ork was hellish on Monday.

I was swamped, and while no one said anything about me taking half a day off, or being unavailable over the weekend, they didn't have to. The implication I'd misprioritized was there. Maybe it was just bad timing, but we always seemed to be busy. Something always came up. The expectation that I'd give all my time to work had been clear when I'd been granted my promotion to senior associate. Work came first. It wasn't negotiable, so I couldn't act like any of this was a surprise.

Theo's mom had asked if I enjoyed my job and I'd basically lied. I didn't enjoy this, and maybe I never had, at least not in the way I thought she'd meant. I used to get satisfaction out of my success, every win had felt good, every step up was proof I'd done something right. That wasn't the same as enjoying any of it, and now I was just exhausted. Success meant I was expected to do more, keep it up, and there was nothing satisfying about that.

At five o'clock I texted Marci, asking if she was free later. I wasn't sure exactly what time I'd get away but I needed something other than my empty home to look froward to.

I arrived at her place at quarter to nine. She lived in one of the more subdued Victorian style homes, compared to others in the neighborhood. Marci had picked it for its view and flat roof, in order to accommodate her need for a roof-top balcony.

Marci greeted me at the door in slippers, a ragged sweater, and leggings that looked like sleepwear. "You know it's Monday right?"

"If it's too late I can go."

We both lived in the Mission so it wasn't far to my place.

"I'm not trying to get rid of you, Luca. I'm just surprised you've sought me out outside our usual Saturday drinks." Marci closed the door behind me and walked up the stairs to her living room.

I followed. "I'm not that rigid, am I?"

She made a noncommittal sound.

Fine, we both knew she'd basically forced her friendship on me most of our lives. It had taken her decades to finagle me into the relationship we had now. It wasn't that I hadn't liked Marci when we were young. We'd gone to nightly Witch-school together as kids and I'd considered her my academic rival.

My parents had always expected the best of Aria and me, and when I began to outmatch my twin in school they'd made it clear I was expected to out-do all my classmates as well. However, Marci was infinitely smarter than me and there was no measuring up to her cunning. Even with my boosted magical link to my stars I couldn't compete; access to raw power was only part of the equation. When I was young it ate me up. All my magical achievements in high school were essentially failures when you came from a family who believed that if you weren't the best you weren't good enough.

Aria had begun to pull away from our parents' stifling expectations when we were teenagers, but I hadn't had a rebellious bone in my body. I'd wanted to be the best, make them proud, and I'd seen Marci as the one preventing my parents from seeing how good I was. Which was ridiculous. I knew that now.

It had been much easier to be friends with Marci once I'd moved away from home. I sorely regretted how I'd tried to compete with her in our younger days. She'd only ever wanted to be my friend and I really could have used it back then. I'd spent my childhood chasing affection as much as success and never seemed to get the former without the latter, at least not from my parents.

The ironic thing was my parents now adored the fact that I was buddies with the most promising Witch of my generation. They loved Marci and how well her friendship with me reflected on the family.

We were halfway up the stairs when a pounding started up at the front door. The buzzer sounded, the faint ringing coming from the apartment.

Marci stopped ahead of me and looked back down the stairs. "Who could that be?"

"Should we just ignore it?" I asked. Whoever it was pounded on the door again.

Marci unlocked her phone and opened her security app. The camera outside showed a white guy who appeared about ten years older than us, but if he was a Witch that gave away little about his actual age. He scowled as he banged on the door again.

"What the hell?" Marci frowned at her phone.

"Recognize him?"

"Yeah." She looked up at me. "He's that contractor I was telling you about."

"The one you had to call security on?"

"The receptionists only had to mention security and he left, but I haven't heard from or seen him since."

I looked back down at the door. "Him showing up at your place isn't a good sign."

"No." Marci's attention went back to the man on her phone screen. "But the protective spells on this building are almost impenetrable. I hired a specialized team of Witches to put them in place."

"Yeah, I know." I eyed the man as he checked the time. He seemed impatient, as if he'd had an appointment with Marci and she was late. "But what if he comes back while you're going out? The spells won't help then."

Marci made a frustrated sound almost like a growl. She turned and marched upstairs. I followed.

Her office was located at the front of the house. Marci went to the window and opened it, sticking her head out. "Excuse me," she called down into the street.

"Marcella," the man called back. "Why didn't you open your door?"

"Why are you even banging on it this late at night?"

"What other choice did I have?" the man called. "You're ignoring me."

"Mr. Miller, you no longer work for me. There's no reason for you to be showing up at my home. Your contract is over, and if you think that, after harassing me, you're going to get more work or a recommendation from me, you're seriously mistaken."

"Do you know how it looks, working for you and not getting a reference? I haven't been able to find a new contract." Anger tinged the man's voice.

"That's not my fault," Marci replied, staying calm even as she talked out the window. "You didn't deliver the work I hired you to do, or give any reasonable explanation for the lack of progress. It doesn't actually seem like you did anything while I was paying you. Now leave my front steps or I'll have to call the Authority and report you." Marci pulled her head back inside and slammed the window shut.

I peered outside to see the man walking away. At least he was leaving. "What had you hired him to do?"

Marci shut the curtains. "Some development for the grimoire app update. And the rest of the team have said his only contributions were thin excuses about how he would be working over the weekend to catch up, only to find no evidence he'd actually done so. Really, I should have cut his contract short. Come on." Marci pulled me out of the office, our arms linked. "I'll deal with him in the morning."

"If you need anything, let me know."

Marci smiled at me and patted my hand. "Thank you, Luca, but I have a whole company at my disposal. It'll be fine. I don't need to add to your worries."

We made our way to the living room and I pushed the man from my mind. Marci was right, she was better equipped to handle him than anything I could provide.

Marci's home had much more character than mine. Her style was eclectic. Art lined the walls, and the mismatch of furniture in the living room made her house cozy in a way I hadn't been able to achieve with mine.

"Have you eaten?" Marci asked as she curled up amongst the many pillows on her couch.

I lay back, boneless in an armchair. "Yeah. I had something delivered to the office."

There was a silence that I enjoyed with my eyes closed. I had half a mind to kick off my shoes and fall asleep.

Marci had other ideas. "So, how did your weekend go?"

I picked up my head to see Marci smiling at me with glee. All I'd told her was that Theo had invited me to Tahoe for a weekend with his family. I hadn't admitted how badly the blind date had gone, or the fact that my presence on the trip had been part of a ruse.

I considered keeping the fake part of it quiet. If things were turning real with Theo, I might be able to get away without Marci ever knowing how it started. But I needed her advice.

I scratched my stubble-lined chin. "The weekend was complicated."

She gave me a bemused look. "Well, meeting the family on the second date was an odd choice, but it had to be a good one, right? Or he wouldn't have asked you to come."

I explained the whole thing, busying myself turning an embroidered throw pillow in circles to avoid looking at Marci. As I talked, I stayed away from Theo's problems with his siblings and Jason. It wasn't for me to tell, and I didn't know if Theo had shared any of it with Marci, but there was one fact that couldn't be avoided.

"I cannot believe Theo has been pretending to have a boyfriend for months and I knew nothing about it." Marci looked aghast at being kept out of the loop.

"I'd say it's a good thing he didn't feel the need to lie to you."

"True." Marci reconsidered, frowning slightly. "But why do something like that in the first place? It's not like him."

"You weren't this confused when *I* mentioned wanting to lie about having a boyfriend."

She waved dismissively at me. "Yes well, you're ridiculous, Luca. It wasn't surprising. I'd just never thought Theo would feel the need to keep up appearances. He's such an honest person."

A twinge of hurt jabbed at my gut. Did Marci see me as someone overly concerned with keeping up appearances?

I tossed the throw pillow aside. "Theo is honest. And I don't actually want to talk too much about his need for a fake boyfriend. If you want to know, ask him. What I was getting at was—I might have gone on the trip as a favor, but while we were there things actually went really well between us."

"I bet they did." Marci looked down her nose at me. "I told you, you two would be great together."

"You were right. We hit it off." I didn't sound too happy about it. Preoccupation with the risk of it not working out was starting to overshadow my good feelings.

Was I really what Theo desired in a partner? I wanted to be good to him, especially after what had happened with Jason, and while there was no risk of me being a jerk to Theo, I didn't know if I could be everything he deserved. I hadn't figured out how to be a good boyfriend yet. I needed to get it right this time.

"So you've stopped faking it?" Marci looked marginally hopeful.

"Yes and no."

She threw one of her pillows at me. "*Luca!*"

I caught it before it hit me in the face. "Yes, we've agreed to see where we go for real, but the need to fake it for our families hasn't gone anywhere."

Theo and I hadn't discussed our fake boyfriend arrangement on the car ride home as we'd intended. It almost felt like we hadn't needed to after admitting to liking each other. Except I still didn't know how long we needed to keep up the lies. Would Theo want me to visit his family again? It was too soon in our real relationship for that, but we couldn't go back on lying to them now, and we couldn't 'break up' if our real relationship might last.

The situation was messy, to say the least.

Marci studied me, another pillow in her hands. "You're going to make him meet your dad, aren't you?"

I felt a wave of guilt. That had been the original plan. One Theo had agreed to, even insisted on. I didn't have the same hang-ups about lying to my parents that I had about lying to

Theo's family. My father was being an overbearing asshole and disregarding what I wanted in favor of his own agenda. I didn't owe him honesty.

But Theo shouldn't have to put up with my father. He deserved a good start to dating me. Normally, I'd never consider subjecting him to my parents this early on. They weren't the kindest people, and Theo didn't need more judgment in his life.

"I'll tell my father I've been seeing someone, and if that isn't enough, we'll see." I pulled out my phone. "I don't want to let lying to my father mess this up." But I couldn't take it if he tried to push another well connected Witch on me.

"There's a simple solution to that." Marci set her pillow aside, apparently deciding not to throw it at me. "Tell your dad the truth."

I ignored her. I *had* tried to tell my father the truth, he just hadn't listened.

My thumb hovered over my phone screen. "Is it too soon to message Theo?" It had barely been a day and a half since I'd seen him.

Marci's frustrated attitude disappeared. Out of the corner of my eye I caught a hint of a soft smile. "Message him if you want to, Luca. Don't worry about too soon, or whatever. Just do what you think is right."

"I don't really know what to say." I flipped my phone over so the screen wasn't staring at me.

I didn't want to be overbearing, contacting him the second we weren't together. Then again, if I didn't message him soon enough he might think I was losing interest. I needed to hit the perfect balance.

This was the part of dating that I wished were simpler. If only there was a set of standard things to do, proven to work. Then I wouldn't get it wrong.

I was good at following rules and procedures. Knowing

exactly what was needed and doing it flawlessly. That was part of what made me good at my job. It was the only way I could be successful, but that sort of formula didn't exist in dating.

"You'll figure it out, Luca." Marci got up from the couch and headed toward the kitchen, patting my shoulder as she went. "Want some tea?"

14

THEO

Tuesday morning was quiet at Graywoods.

The day before had been relatively busy, with my typical weekend customers all coming in now I was back, and I'd felt great settling back into my routine. I had the mushrooms and moss I'd collected drying out back, and had done several tea services. All my favorite parts of the job.

This morning no one had come in and it was almost lunch time. This wasn't an unusual occurrence. I liked that the shop was quiet. Graywoods was situated away from most other shops in Noe Valley in order to attract as few random Mortal customers as possible. We were around the corner from a few restaurants and a cafe, but on my street the only other shop was Quill's Antiquarian Books. The rest was residential.

Neither shop got much foot-traffic but Witches knew where to find us. Quill's was another Witchy business, and both of our buildings looked like they could have stepped out of a historical photo. The front room of the bookshop sold rare Mortal books, while the back room was all grimoires and magical history. The owner, my friend Jacob Quill, had been running the place for about eighty years.

Working next to a bookshop was perfect for me. There were weeks when I wouldn't even leave the block, between delivery food and ordering all my books from Quill's. Jacob didn't typically stock Mortal new releases, I was his exception. I'd much rather support his shop than anyone else. He liked the quiet too, so we were perfect neighbors.

However, this morning the quiet was less than ideal. Instead of enjoying the serenity of the shop as I normally would, I was on edge. The back of my neck kept prickling. It was almost as if I doubted I was alone.

Unease was making me restless, so I left the counter and did a circuit of the shop, even poking my head out the front door and scanning the street. There was nothing to see. No one watching or lurking anywhere in sight. The Victorian buildings lining the street looked as welcoming and comfortingly familiar as ever. Not that I'd expected to find anyone, but I was hoping proof I was alone would trick my brain into abandoning the odd feeling plaguing me.

I ducked back into Graywoods, the uncomfortable sensation still nagging at me.

Back at the counter I turned my attention to finishing the analysis of the crystal. I wondered if the small quartz was where my unease was coming from but didn't see how it could be.

The crystal was less interesting than I'd first thought. It didn't even look as mysterious as it had that first night the man had dropped it off. It was magically dyed a shimmering almost-black color, an alteration that turned out to be aesthetic only. It didn't even seem to swallow the light as I'd previously sworn it had. In the daylight the thing was pretty unremarkable.

I'd gotten as far as confirming there was a concealing spell cast on it this morning. I took out my phone and opened the grimoire app. If I was going to uncover the crystal's essence and see if it had unique magical properties due to any other spells that may have been cast on it, I needed to undo the concealing spell placed on it first. I didn't normally have to do this kind of counter magic, so I had to look up instructions on the app.

As I scrolled through the list of search results, a shuffling sound came from the front corner of the shop.

I looked up, blinking after focusing on the crystal at close range. "Hello?"

There was nothing but silence.

The bell hadn't rung so there shouldn't be anyone in here, and there were spells in place to keep out mice and other pests. I put the crystal down as my unease deepened. Which was a ridiculous reaction. I didn't know why I was so in my head about weird feelings today. I'd probably imagined the sound.

But there it was again.

I pushed my glasses further up my nose and strode to the front of the shop to check the aisles and the corner where I thought the noise had come from. There was no one there, just like the last time I'd looked less than ten minutes ago.

I was more annoyed than scared. What was freaking me out about being here alone? I loved this kind of time to myself surrounded by herbs, having the chance to read, explore new ingredients, or play around with potions and tweak difference essences. I often went hours without realizing any time had passed, or full days without missing talking to people at all. I liked quiet days over busy ones, but everything was backward this week.

There was one explanation: I was lonely.

It felt like the only thing that fit, little that I liked it. The paranoia of thinking someone was watching wasn't my usual MO, but perhaps my brain would rather send my worry in that direction than get too close to something personal.

I liked my alone time but that didn't mean I always wanted to be alone. Today felt like one of those days when I wasn't choosing solitude but had no other option. It leached the joy out of everything, and I couldn't help thinking how often I was by myself.

Back at the counter, I picked up my phone. The grimoire app greeted me. I swiped it away and considered texting Luca. It wasn't like I missed him or anything. Two days apart was nothing, and wasn't why I was feeling off. I didn't want to make this about him when it wasn't.

I just wanted to talk to *somebody*.

Maybe the busy weekend full of family—and okay, Luca too —was too much of a contrast with this solitary day, even though my family gave me mixed feelings.

I missed my uncle. Running the shop with him had been even better than doing things solo. He'd been the perfect company, mostly quiet and introverted like me, but he'd always known when to speak, or when to share something with me. He'd seemed to be able to sense when I needed to talk. We'd been in tune like nothing I'd ever had with anyone else.

I loved my parents and my siblings, but my Uncle Theodore had always had a special place in my heart. If he'd still been alive when Jason had broken up with me, I'd have told him everything, down to the last insult Jason had thrown, and my uncle would have known just what to say to help me deal with it.

Instead I'd barely told anyone what had happened, and kept most of the details to myself.

Great. Now that I'd let my mind go down that road, there was no denying I was feeling lonely, despite whatever the weird sense of being watched was about.

I pulled up my text messages. Bypassing Luca's name, I clicked on my chat with Marci. I felt guilty for avoiding her after the blind date. Pushing away one of my only friends was a dumb move.

I typed out a message: *your app is saving me again!* And pressed send.

Marci didn't reply instantly. She was probably busy running her Witchy tech company.

I sent another message: *We should catch up soon.*

The unsettled feeling plaguing me didn't go anywhere. If anything it intensified. Which wasn't rational. Marci not replying within a minute didn't mean anything, and I hadn't expected her to anyway. But I felt weirdly empty.

Fuck, maybe I did miss Luca. Spending a full weekend with him had gotten me used to his company much quicker than any normal start to a relationship would have. We'd shared a lot, and my sense of who Luca was felt much more solid than it had on Friday. I didn't even feel as bad about our failed attempt at sleeping together as I'd have thought I would. It hadn't been an ideal night, but it wasn't mortifying to look back on either.

I felt close to Luca. Cared for when I was with him. Safe to show him who I really was, worries and less than perfect bits included.

But—I had to remember—we hadn't actually been dating for six months. I didn't need to text him the second I was feeling moody, and should probably go slow as far as sharing things and trying to incorporate him into my life. My loneliness today was about me, not about Luca, and I needed to deal with it myself. Looking forward to seeing him again soon should be enough for what he and I were to each other.

I set my phone down on the counter, clicked back to the grimoire app, and picked up the crystal.

The concealment didn't seem strong, so I selected a basic counter spell, grabbed a few candles from the shelf behind me, and gave it a try. My crystal rings flashed as I recited the incantation, magic sparking in the air around me. The spell came off without a hitch.

Now that the crystal wasn't hiding its secrets from me, I had another look at it, reaching out with my magic and giving it a thorough feel. I didn't detect any power other than the earth magic it naturally possessed. It was as if the concealment spell had been hiding nothing.

How strange.

The crystal wasn't special after all. Other than it's dyed coloring, it was no different from any other quartz originating from Southern California. I could detect its essence and origin now, but those general details were all that had been hidden. The man was bound to be disappointed by that.

The bell above the front door jangled. I looked up and smiled. "Why, hello."

"Good day, Theo." Jacob Quill returned my grin. He was older than me but still a relatively young Witch, about one-hundred years old, and always dressed in knit sweaters he made himself.

"How's it going?" I put the crystal down, my mood lifting.

"Excellent, thank you." Jacob eyed the black quartz as he approached. "I'm not interrupting, am I?"

"No, no." I waved a dismissive hand. "Just finished removing a concealing spell."

He leaned against the counter, a wrapped brown paper package under his arm. "That's not your usual fare."

I shrugged. "Right? Had to look the incantation up on the app. At least I can't say I'm bored."

"I'm glad you aren't too busy." Jacob set his package on the counter, covering it with a white hand clad in flashy crystal rings. "Your latest order arrived this morning."

"Oh, *yay!*" I pretty much squealed.

Jacob chuckled. "I have to say, I'm continually intrigued by your selection. Buying books for you has exposed me to so many new authors, and that's saying something."

I blushed as I slid the package across the counter.

Having a friend next door was ideal. We both liked to stick close to home, so it was nice to have someone nearby. Jacob and I mostly spent time together in each other's shops, making his bookstore feel like an extended home. I had a feeling he saw Graywoods the same way.

Seeing Jacob helped my lonely day. I should have thought to seek him out myself, and made a mental note to do so next time, rather than wallow.

I ran my fingers around the edge of the package. "I finished that murder mystery, if you still wanted to borrow it?"

"Oh, yes. It was good then?" Jacob's expression was serious, his well-manicured mustache framing his not-quite-frown. He respected my book recommendations, something I took pride in.

"The suspense was great, and if you want to be a bit freaked out but not horrified, it's the book for you."

He nodded. "I'll take you up on the offer to borrow it, then. Thank you, Theo."

I ducked into the back to grab the book. There was a small shelf by the reading chair and I hadn't yet moved my recently finished books upstairs.

I handed Jacob the book along with cash to cover my new purchases.

He slipped the money into the murder mystery. "Anything new with you these days?"

"Not really." I often felt boring when people asked me this, and my answer was almost always no, but Jacob got me. I imagined his personal life was a lot like mine, and his enquiries never felt like an interrogation, or like he was passing judgment.

"You had a weekend away. That's something." Jacob sounded genuinely interested, encouraging.

"Oh, yeah." I picked up the crystal, fiddling with it mindlessly. "Just seeing family."

"Right, your mother's birthday." Jacob tapped the book I'd lent him as recognition lit his face, probably remembering me mentioning the party during one of our other chats. "I could have sworn I'd seen a handsome man come by on Friday. Thought you might have something exciting going on."

"I'm not sure yet," I admitted, averting my graze. "We'll have to see where it goes."

"The start can be the most fun, you know." Jacob's smile was evident in his tone so I looked up. "You deserve it, Theo." With that, he picked up the book and departed.

I unwrapped my package, finding two contemporary romances and a fantasy novel. I cracked open the romance that promised high heat and low conflict.

The day was looking up.

15

LUCA

My week got progressively worse.

One of our largest clients had gotten in touch to say they were considering moving to a new firm for representation, and the partners were in a panic. I'd been a major part of bringing them on board with us to begin with, so it became my responsibility to fix.

The client wanted a smaller firm, one that could provide more individual attention to their needs. Suddenly my week was booked with dinners and meetings to try and win them back. I had to come up with a strategic plan, and it wasn't like I didn't have other shit to do.

I was in my office chewing on the end of a pen, phone pressed to my ear. I stared off into space, not even registering the view of the surrounding skyscrapers. I was hitting the point where I had so many competing deadlines and demands on my time that I was unable to do anything, and part of me didn't care.

Let the client go if that's what they wanted. No one was going to congratulate me if they stayed. That was the expected outcome, anything less would be a disappointment.

To top everything off, my father was the one on the other

end of the phone line. He'd greeted me by saying how disappointed he was that I wouldn't be seeing Herold again. He'd had the nerve to tell me I needed to try harder next time. As if I'd been rejected. As if someone not liking me meant I'd fucked up, and meant I was *obviously* flawed.

He treated me as if not clicking with someone was a personal failure.

One of the things that I hated most about my father's whole set up scheme was how he acted when his chosen Witches weren't the one for me. I had to deal with his disappointment when the dates were something I'd never wanted in the first place. I should have been able to brush it off, but part of me felt like the failure was real, even though I knew that was bullshit from any angle.

Maybe it was because I'd been unable to make romance work when I'd actually tried, with men I'd genuinely liked. It wasn't the same, but the way my father reacted to me rejecting his set ups made me feel like shit about my dating life as a whole.

"You're making it hard to keep finding options, Luca," my father scolded.

I gripped the phone tighter, dropping the chewed pen to my desk. "You can stop looking. I *told* you I don't want any more set ups. I've been seeing someone."

"You don't have to sound angry about it." My father sniffed. "And since when are you seeing someone? Why haven't I heard about this?"

"Because I don't need to tell you everything. Saying I didn't want to be matched up should have been enough. I don't have to tell you the second I go on a date with someone."

"True." He paused as he considered. "So it's serious then? That's why you waited to mention it?"

"Yes," I growled, even though I felt bad for lying. Not for my father's sake but for Theo's.

"This is great, Luca. Tell me about him. What district does he work in? What's his position in court?"

I ground my teeth. "Now's not a good time. I'm at work. I'll talk to you later."

"You're right. Of course. I won't keep you."

I lowered my phone from my ear to end the call.

My father's voice wafted up from the device. "I'll expect an introduction soon, Luca. Text me his credentials."

I hung up.

"Fuck." I tossed my phone to the side.

Unlike Theo's family, there was no way my father would let me get away with delaying an introductions for six months.

My phone buzzed.

I reached across the desk for it. My father had sent a calendar invite for dinner this Saturday. For three. Typical, he never asked, he always assumed.

I considered telling him Theo wasn't free this weekend. But maybe it was better to get this over with. We'd done the fake thing for his family. Once we got through this dinner we could get into regular dating.

An email notification popped up on my computer and phone screens simultaneously. Then another. I swiveled my desk chair around so I couldn't see the computer and swiped to my text chat with Theo. I'd wanted to message him about something not to do with our fake boyfriend agreement, only I hadn't thought of anything good yet.

Not wanting to say the wrong thing held me back. I wanted to get it right. There wasn't room for making the wrong move, but now I'd have to tell him about the dinner.

As I stared at the screen a text popped up. It was from Theo and instantly went to *read*. I jolted in my seat. He might deduce

I'd been staring at the app. I tried to not worry about coming across as over eager. Surely Theo wouldn't be the kind of person to be annoyed by that.

The message said: *Hey, how's your week going?*

Part of me felt foolish for not being able to come up with a simple message like this, or for considering it myself and then lacking the courage to send it. The question felt so natural when Theo asked. I didn't know why I was so hesitant to reach out as he had. As if he'd somehow see I didn't know what I was doing.

Marci would tell me this wasn't something I could get wrong, but I begged to differ.

I messaged back: *I was just going to text you.*

Haha perfect, Theo replied.

My week has been a mess actually.

Theo sent me a very sympathetic looking emoji and I smiled. He followed it up with: *Any way I can help?*

Not really. Work's been a beast, I typed. *I think I need another day off.*

Can't you take one?

I hesitated.

The answer was essentially no. At least not right now. I'd just taken time off. Besides, I couldn't ignore the real issue. I needed more than a day.

There was no rush to progress my career, not as a thirty-one-year-old Witch. One of the partners here hadn't even gone to law school until he was fifty. Our newest paralegal was a Witch who had a thirty-year career as a schoolteacher behind her. We lived the equivalent of multiple lifetimes. I could gather achievements slowly, take a break and come back in a couple decades. But that wasn't what my parents had been training me for.

When I was growing up the idea of being the youngest Witch to lead a firm or to gain a seat on a Judicial Committee excited me. Now it didn't matter, except for the fact that my father would take any deviation from our plan as a failure on my part, and it would feel like failure to me too, no matter how much I didn't want it to.

Success had always been expected, not celebrated, and after thirty years it had made me increasingly bitter.

Our parents had been unreasonably harsh on Aria when she'd taken her life down a different path. I knew that making her feel like a failure for that choice was unfair and manipulative of them. I'd never considered Aria that way, or changed my opinion of her because she abandoned her legal career, but at the same time, I couldn't escape the feeling changing my direction now would cancel out everything I'd gotten right. I couldn't seem to extend the same grace I gave Aria to myself. My success defined me. I felt like nothing without it.

None of this was something I could convey in a text to Theo.

Maybe later, I said. *How's your week?*

Pretty much the usual.

I wanted to ask if he'd had any more dreams, but that felt like the wrong move. Theo said he'd tell me if he had any more, and if he didn't want to mention it, it wasn't exactly my business.

Instead I said, *I want to come by your shop but don't think I'll be able to escape the office during sociable hours any time soon.*

The three little texting dots popped up and disappeared a bunch of times, making it seem like Theo was writing a long message.

What about Saturday? Was all that came through.

I'd likely be at the office all day, and not free until the evening. I typed: *My father asked to meet you actually. He wants to go to dinner Saturday. I was talking to him just before you texted.*

There was a long pause. Just enough to leave me wondering if I'd fucked everything up and Theo wasn't going to reply.

Then a message came through: *Yeah. No problem. Gotta return the favor. Lol.*

Someone knocked on my office door.

Thanks, I typed quickly. *I'll fill you on the details soon. I think I'm getting called into a meeting, so I have to go.*

He texted me saying bye and attached a waving hand emoji.

I said *bye* as well, but couldn't help a nagging feeling I'd done something wrong.

16

THEO

By Friday evening I'd finished the steamy romance and the fantasy. The second romance was taking me a bit of time to get into, but it wasn't the book's fault.

My suspicious feelings hadn't been quelled. I still felt like I wasn't alone in Graywoods, and only seemed to relax when customers were in the shop and I could attribute any sense of another presence to them.

At least today had been on the busier side, lots of customers and good conversations. I'd even met with a local teacher who worked with high-school-age Witches. She'd wanted to know if I'd be interested in doing an earth magic seminar for her advanced students. It wasn't my usual sort of work but I was excited about it. I'd agreed on the spot. Teaching young Witches was a very respected position and I was chuffed that someone thought I was worth seeking out.

Sadie was a Witchy teacher back in Tahoe. I messaged her about the school I was planning to drop in on and she seemed pretty thrilled for me. She got liberal with emojis when she was excited. The whole thing was exactly what I needed to boost my mood.

Yet my mood remained largely unaffected.

I was filling in the end of the day organizing the jars of mushrooms for sale, making notes about which types, and from which regions, I needed to replenish stock. Local ones I'd forage myself but if I wanted anything further afield I ordered it from other apothecaries.

I was near the front of the shop and glanced out the window. The streetlights popped on as I scanned the street. The only person around was a woman walking her dog across the street. Other than that, I saw no one.

My skin crawled.

"I'm sick of this," I grumbled to the empty shop, forcefully putting down a jar with a loud *thunk*.

I took a breath, trying to relax as I turned back to my notebook. At least the mysterious crystal man was due back any minute. It had been too much to hope he'd come in early. With my luck he'd show up as I was trying to close, like he had last time.

I counted my last row of mushroom jars, noted the quantity, and closed my notebook. My phone buzzed back on the counter where I'd left it. It seemed unreasonably loud in the quiet shop.

My inventory task was done for the week, so I retrieved the phone and stowed my notebook on the shelf behind the counter. I was expecting another text from Sadie since we'd been talking not long ago, but it was Tobias.

I wasn't unhappy to hear from him, but Tobias hassled me the most out of my siblings. Not that he was mean, I just wasn't sure a text from him was what I needed to close out my weird week.

Tobias ran Landon Apothecary in Tahoe with our parents. He'd moved away after finishing school, only to come back when Stella was born. He hadn't wanted the two of us young ones to miss out, or grow up without the whole family around.

He'd even lived in the house with us while Sadie had been across town. Tobias had loved playing with Stella and me when we were kids, and due to his age it had almost been like having another parent, but in the best way.

He was a good brother, so it wasn't surprising when his message said: *miss you Little Theodore!*

I had time to feel bad for my initial negative reaction before he followed it up with: *So is Luca coming to solstice? We've seen him now. No point hiding him anymore.*

I groaned out load.

I wanted Luca to come to Winter Solstice, and not as more proof I had a boyfriend, or because I knew Tobias was going to harass me about it for the next three months. I thought Luca would love the celebration. It was the kind of magical event he'd seemed to yearn for when I'd reminisced about growing up in a fairy tale.

Solstice would be romantic. Spending the day and long night together in the snowy forest. It would be an ideal date. A special time with a partner. And three months from now wasn't entirely too soon for Luca and me to be doing something like that for real.

But I wasn't sure.

I certainly couldn't commit now and tell Tobias Luca would come. What if we broke up? For real. Or I guess never progressed to that kind of *real* in the first place. Luca still seemed to be focused on the fake boyfriend thing, and maybe that was because we hadn't yet convinced his dad, but we hadn't talked much. Not like I might have hoped after how open we both were last weekend. Our only communication had been to bang out details for the dinner with Mr. Belmonte.

I messaged Tobias back saying I'd let him know about Luca later, leaving things vague.

I checked the time. The crystal man better be coming in

soon. I'd stay open a bit late and wait for him, but that was more out of a desire to have his business behind me than kindness.

I clicked back to my texts with Luca. He'd sent a bunch today. All at odd times like he was doing it in between meetings or other things. I'd say Luca was nervous about presenting me to his dad. He'd sent a long text—like almost embarrassingly long, except I didn't care, it was exactly like something I'd do—explaining all about his parents' expectations. The whole situation with his family trying to marry him off against his wishes sounded weird and not okay. Hearing about it made me uncomfortable on Luca's behalf.

His parents did not seem remotely like mine.

Luca had forewarned me that his dad was judgmental. Even though Luca had already broken the news that I wasn't some Witch-lawyer, he seemed to expect his dad to view me negatively at dinner. I could see why Luca was worried about bringing me into a judgmental situation, and I tried to tell him it was fine, as well as could be done over text.

I was proud of what I did at Graywoods, and Luca's dad's opinion wasn't going to affect me. Jason hadn't made me unable to deal with judgment. I could deal just fine when it wasn't sneaking up on me from someone I trusted.

The shop was getting dark, so I turned the lights on with a flick of my wrist and a flash of my crystal rings. When rereading Luca's texts got old, I turned back to my book. The shadows in the shop did nothing to keep the sense I was being watched away. I looked up from the page so often, reading was almost pointless.

By six the man still hadn't shown. Figured. This whole thing was a pain. But the fact that he'd sought me out at a party on the other side of the state only to ghost me today was suspicious. None of it made any sense. If the crystal was uninteresting and had no particular power, what was the deal?

Again I wondered if the quartz was the source of my unease, even though I'd inspected the thing several more times since Tuesday, and was confident there wasn't anything off about it.

I ordered some dinner, deciding to wait down in the shop until it arrived in case the man came by. Abandoning my book, I wiped down the already clean counter and teapot display.

I considered having a cup, and would have if doing a tea service alone hadn't seemed so melancholy. I used to have tea all the time with my uncle. We'd brew it for each other, and while there was no reason I couldn't make myself a magical cup of my perfect tea, it lost some of the comfort without anyone else here.

In the end my food came, and with no sign of the man, I retreated up to my apartment.

I woke in confusion sometime in the middle of the night. My breathing came fast and sharp, my muscles tense and cramped. My heart pounded in fear.

I untangled myself from my blankets, struggling to remember what I'd been dreaming about. Nothing came to me other than darkness and horrible feelings. Another nightmare. Maybe that wasn't surprising after the downer of week I'd had, except bad dreams weren't usually an issue for me, even when I was depressed.

I'd had a low period after Jason. Not surprisingly. But nightmares hadn't been a part of that. I barely remembered having any in my adult life before the last couple weeks.

I lay in the dark staring up at the blurry ceiling as my breathing and heart rate returned to normal. There were too many weird things going on, and they'd all started after the mysterious man dropped off the crystal. Alone in my room, I was sure it was all connected, even if there was no proof.

What if the crystal had given me some sort of magical affliction? I had zero experience with curses. Maybe I'd missed some sign the quartz was dangerous. What if the dreams got worse and worse? It had taken me longer to calm down this time than after any of my previous dreams. Even the paranoia I was feeling in Graywoods could be a symptom of something.

I needed someone else to look at the damn crystal. I'd still be surprised if I'd missed anything as big as a curse, but didn't know what else to do. Having someone double check would put my mind at ease, if nothing else. And if it wasn't the quartz causing all my problems, I'd talk to my therapist about how I'd been feeling. I should probably do that whether the dreams were a magical issue or not.

Luca had seemed so sure it was more than a nightmare last weekend. He'd been worried. I hadn't been then, but now I starting to worry myself. I could text him. Luca had asked me to tell him about any more dreams, except I didn't see how bothering him about it in the middle of the night would help. Surely he'd be sleeping.

I rolled to my side and hugged a pillow, burrowing into the blankets, and found it hard to get back to sleep.

THE NEXT MORNING my midnight worries seemed less urgent. I didn't have any watched feelings up in my apartment, but I couldn't say I was my usual relaxed self. It left me uncertain. Bad dreams might just be bad dreams. I'd still get the crystal checked out—unless the blasted man came and picked it up—and mention things to my therapist. One way or another I'd work things out.

Therapy felt more important than looking into the crystal as I got ready for my day. My therapist was a Witch, so I wouldn't have to hide any aspects of the situation from her. We could discuss the possibility this had to do with magic.

But I could dwell on all that later.

I was meeting Marci for an early morning coffee and hurried down the stairs, bypassing Graywoods for now, and exited directly onto the street. Marci had been kind enough to offer to meet me at the cafe around the corner, so I wouldn't have far to go since I had to be back at Graywoods in time to open.

Jacob was out and about already, watering the flowers in the planter boxes lining his shop windows.

"Morning," I called as I locked up.

He put his watering can down. "Theo. How are the books treating you?"

"Good. I'll have finished the last one by Monday."

"You're keeping me in business, reading at that rate." Jacob shook his head. "That murder mystery had me up last night."

I cringed. "Oh, no."

Jacob laughed. "Not like that. I couldn't put the damn thing down."

My smile returned. "Thank goodness. There's a bit I'd love to discuss, but I've got to run." I gestured off down the street.

Jacob picked up his watering can. "I won't hold you back from your big day."

"Ha." He was teasing me but it was kind of true, and he only said it because outings were big news for him as well as me. "I've got dinner out tonight too," I admitted.

Jacob raised his brows. "With the handsome man?"

I blushed like the hopeless romantic I was. "Maybe."

Jacob gave me an approving nod. "I won't expect to see you back until morning then." He added a mischievous smile.

"Oh my god." I turned and hurried off around the corner, my whole body flashing hot.

I wasn't bothered by Jacob's teasing; it always seemed to come from a place of cheering me on. I just needed to get better at peering out my windows so I'd know the moment he started seeing someone. Then I'd return the favor.

When I arrived, Marci was already at the coffee shop, sitting outside with a plate of pastries.

"Theo!" She bounced up from her seat to hug me.

I hugged her back. "Did you run here?"

Marci was in activewear, her earbuds discarded on the table. "Yeah. Though, I don't know if I'll be running home. There's a cake in there I might have to buy on my way out."

I laughed.

"Sit." She pointed to the other chair as she returned to hers. "I've already ordered your tea."

I wasn't much of a coffee person and always had at least two cups of black tea in the morning. "Thanks."

"No problem." Marci began to cut up the pastries so we could share. "Figured you'd need the caffeine ready and waiting when you got here. Luca told be all about your weekend."

"Did he?" My insides churned uneasily. "What did he say?"

"It's all right, Theo." Marci put down the knife and squeezed my hand. "It was all good things, I promise. Though, he did mention you needing a fake boyfriend."

"Oh." My stomach sank.

A server brought out my tea and Marci's coffee just then. I latched on to the distraction and took the lid off the pot to check the brew. Then replaced it to let it steep longer.

I fiddled with the teaspoon in the sugar bowl. "Why did you set me up with Luca anyway?"

Marci put her coffee down. "Because you two are good for each other."

She sounded matter of fact rather than evasive, even though it was a vague answer. It was as if Marci believed finding the right person was that simple. Part of me wanted to hear all the things about Luca that Marci liked and thought were specifically good for me, but really I should find that out for myself, from Luca directly.

I crossed my arms and looked at Marci. "You knew he wanted a fake boyfriend from the start, and didn't mention that when you set up our date."

She frowned. "Luca had been entertaining that silly idea, yes. But it wasn't what he really wanted. Not by a long shot. You know I wouldn't have set him up with you otherwise. Even if you somehow ended up telling silly lies of your own."

"Sor—"

"Don't apologize, Theo." Marci smiled warmly, the morning light glinting off her crystal crown. "You can tell whatever lies you want. I'm choosing to take it as a sign you and Luca were even more meant for each other than I could have imagined."

My face heated. "Maybe, I don't know." I checked the strength of my tea again. It needed more time.

I wasn't surprised Marci hadn't asked why I was lying about being in a relationship. She'd always been respectful of my boundaries and happy to let me share or not share things as I needed. I'd known her almost since I'd started working at Graywoods, back when it was both my uncle and me. I met Marci at the shop—naturally—since I didn't like going out. Marci had already been a regular customer of my uncle's and had seemed thrilled to meet me.

She'd known me through my whole relationship with Jason, though I hadn't shared much with her. I'd wanted to hide the details of the break-up from everyone for a long time, out of embarrassment and other mixed feelings. Now I didn't see why I should.

As I fixed my tea with milk and a dash of sugar, I told Marci all about my relationship with Jason, exactly how it ended, and how it tied into me lying to my family to try and escape their constant assessment and critique of my life.

"Have you tried to talk to your brother and sisters about how they treat you? Told them what you don't like?" Marci asked.

Our drinks and most of the pastries were gone. I crunched a napkin. "They don't treat me badly."

"But they're still pressuring you and monitoring you in a way you're not okay with. They don't have to be completely awful for you to ask for things to be different."

"That's true, I guess." I couldn't imagine how the conversation with my siblings would go. I suspected it would hurt Tobias' feelings. I didn't want that, but really it shouldn't stop me. Not if the alternative was increasingly avoiding my family and hiding my life from them.

"It's not like you have to do it today," Marci assured me. "But it might lead to a better outcome than pretending Luca is your boyfriend."

"Having a fake boyfriend didn't really change anything with me and my siblings," I admitted. "At first the lies helped. They stopped hassling me about getting out there, and I stopped worrying about them judging me for being single. I really needed the space. But it didn't completely work. They just started bugging me about new stuff. Apparently my life needs lots of improving, and the whole thing where they suspected I was lying made me feel worse."

"It makes me glad I'm an only child." Marci popped the last bit of croissant in her mouth.

I chuckled and reached for a piece of cheese Danish. "Sorry I avoided you after the blind date."

Marci waved her hand. "It's fine. I should have realized Luca would have already blown it with you in some past life."

"College isn't a past life."

"Isn't it?"

I checked the time. "I'll have to go soon. But we should hang out more. If you want, I mean."

"Of course I want to. Stars above, you're as antisocial as Luca. I don't know how I keep finding Witches like you two to force my friendship on."

Was Luca antisocial? Thinking about it, I realized all my assumptions that he liked to go out to fancy bars or go clubbing and do all the busy city things I disliked were baseless and stemmed from the Luca I thought I'd known in college.

Maybe getting Luca to take a chance on that blind date had been as much work for Marci as it had been for her to get me there.

I smiled.

"You aren't forcing friendship on me." I assured Marci. I suspected she knew that, she just liked to be dramatic.

I'd always resented people saying I needed to get out more and be social, but Marci wasn't like that. She wasn't trying to change me, or push me to do things I didn't want. She just wanted to see me more. And I wanted that too. There was no way I'd be meeting Marci at all the trendy clubs she liked to go to, but she wouldn't expect it. Committing to hanging out with her more was me not isolating myself when I should be turning to my friends, not me giving in to pressure to change.

Speaking of turning to friends, that reminded me. "Do you know much about curses?"

Marci's eyes went wide at the abrupt shift in topic. "They're not really my area of expertise, no. But I studied a bit of curse breaking and counter magic as I was putting the grimoire app together."

I told Marci about the crystal and she insisted on following me back to Graywoods to check it out, boxed up cake in hand.

As I opened the shop, Marci examined the crystal. "It doesn't seem like anything's cast on it. Other than a spell to change the coloring," she called out to me from the counter.

I drew back the front curtains. "I know, right?"

"Maybe we should undo the alteration to its appearance, just in case."

I made my way back to her. "But if the guy comes back and I've ruined it, he won't be happy."

Marci put a hand on her hip. "So? Who cares about him?"

"He's a *customer*." I was metaphorically clutching my pearls. "There's no law against being weird and maybe a bit creepy. I'll complain about him but I'll still serve him like anyone else." Until there was proof the crystal was dangerous, that is.

"So reasonable." Marci narrowed her eyes at the crystal. "I'm pretty sure I can undo the physical change and put it back again. He'll never know."

"In that case, go for it." I silently asked the stars not to let this be the moment the man returned.

Marci checked a few spells on her grimoire app, then reversed the spell changing the crystal's color. There was no grand reveal. No hidden magic jumped out. We both inspected the now clear quartz, finding it exactly the same as before, magically speaking.

"I don't think this is your problem," Marci said after she returned the crystal to its blackened state.

I sighed. "Oh, well. Mental health was always more likely anyway. I'll go see my therapist about paranoia next week."

Marci put a hand on my shoulder. "Let me know if it gets worse, or if you need anything, okay?"

I agreed and we hugged goodbye. Before departing she left

me a piece of cake, which I dug into as soon as she was out the door.

By closing the man hadn't shown up, but all in all it had been a good day, uneasy feelings notwithstanding.

17

LUCA

Being apprehensive about dinner didn't stop me from looking forward to seeing Theo. I wanted to show him some of my real feelings, even if dragging him out to see my father was *so* not the way to do that.

I'd told my father to be openminded when I'd let him know Theo wasn't the kind of partner who'd get me in with Witches running any of the judicial districts. The man had said he would, and gone as far as to say he'd *never* discount someone I liked solely based on their occupation. All evidence pointed to that being total bullshit, but I hoped his assurance meant he'd keep up appearances in front of Theo and act accepting.

I rang the buzzer to Theo's apartment, leaving the rideshare I'd booked waiting at the curb behind me.

After a moment the door opened. Theo gave me a sweet little smile as his eyes swept over me. "Hi."

"Hey." I ran a hand through my hair.

Theo was wearing the same tweed jacket he'd had on for our blind date, this time paired with a forest green sweater. It looked soft, like cashmere. He adjusted the jacket. "You really didn't have to pick me up. I could have met you there."

"Then I wouldn't have been able to give you this." I brought a dried rose out from behind my back.

Theo's eyes widened in surprise. "Is this the one from our blind date?"

"Um—yeah." I was still holding the rose. Theo hadn't reached for it, and I couldn't tell if his surprise was positive or not. "It wasn't our best night, I admit, but I thought it would go well with your shop. Since it's dried."

The gesture had seemed romantic in my head, but maybe regifting something from a past date wasn't the right move.

Theo's brow crinkled like he was trying to add things up. "You saved it?"

"I did." I looked down at the rose, not one hundred percent sure why I'd saved it. I hoped Theo wouldn't ask.

"Thank you." Theo reached out and delicately took hold of the stem. "Here, I'll put it away before we go."

I followed him into the stairwell and through to the back of the apothecary shop. Theo grabbed a small vase—he seemed to have plenty of them around—and carefully placed the dried rose inside.

"I like flowers." He placed it on a small bookshelf next to an armchair in the back room.

I remembered Tobias implying something along those lines, and knowing Theo liked flowers was the main reason I'd given it to him. "Next time I'll get you one that doesn't come with so many mixed memories."

Theo turned away from the shelf, adjusting his glasses. "I don't know." He attempted a casual shrug, which was ruined by his pink cheeks. "This has the makings of a pretty good memory."

Relief hit me. Maybe the rose hadn't completely missed the mark. "I think you're right."

I moved closer as Theo reached for me, and our arms came

around each other. I brushed his jaw with my thumb before placing my hand at the nape of his neck and pulling him into a kiss. I kept it soft and short, but while our lips touched I was completely absorbed in him.

Theo's arms tightened around my middle. Something light in my chest fluttered.

"I want to start again," I murmured. "Re-do all our failed first dates and replace them with a better one."

"We could." Theo kissed me. "But those dates still led us here."

"True. I like that thinking." I pulled back. "Tonight isn't going to be the do-over date I wanted, anyway. It's next on the list, promise."

Theo's eyebrows rose. His smile looked eager. "There's a list? Lucky me."

I chuckled. "You're making it sound like the list is this cool thing, when really my life is so busy I can't function without an itemized schedule."

Theo's joy shifted to concern. "Sounds like your week didn't get any better."

It took physical effort not to sigh. "No. It's been the week from hell and it isn't even over. In saying that, we should probably go."

Theo seemed reluctant, but now wasn't the best time to get into my work complaints. My date seemed to come to the same conclusion because he didn't say anything as we made our way toward the side exit.

Theo locked up behind us before grabbing my hand. "Maybe I can help make your week better. Even if this isn't our do-over date."

Stars above, he was sweet. It made me bold enough to say how I felt and not worry whether it was the right or wrong thing to do.

I squeezed his hand. "You already have. Just seeing you has made my day."

Theo radiated pleasure at my words.

We rode over to dinner in silence. I'd been at the office all day and used the down time to rest my eyes, my head tilted back against the seat.

As we got out of the car Theo linked his arm with mine. "Don't worry, Luca. This will go fine. Then we can forget about your dad."

"Preferably for a good decade or so, but I'm afraid he has a way of making it impossible to forget him." I paused, then said more seriously, "Thank you for doing this, Theo."

He blinked rapidly. "Of course."

We found my father waiting at a table. He stood, draped his folded cloth napkin over the back of his chair, and shook Theo's hand as I made introductions. My father had white hair and brown skin, and was dressed in a pristine suit as if he'd been at the office all day, even though he was retired. He wasn't a man of many smiles, but then neither was I in the normal course of my life.

Around Theo it seemed to be another story. I was always grinning like a fool.

We all took our seats. The restaurant was overly fancy. Something casual would have taken the sense of pressure down a notch, but neither of my parents were big on comfort.

"I'm sorry Deirdre couldn't make it." My father picked up his wineglass, his napkin returned to his lap. "She's out of town at the moment."

"That's all right." Theo gave my father an understanding smile.

"If we had any idea Luca was in a relationship, we'd have invited you out before now." Father looked between us, displaying pleasant curiosity. "How long *have* you two been together?"

"Six months." I picked up my menu, hoping the lack of eye contact didn't give away my lie. Theo and I had agreed to keep the story the same between our families, to lessen the chance of slipping up.

"*Six months*," my father repeated as if he'd been caught off guard, even though I was sure I'd mentioned it when I'd told him Theo was an apothecary.

"Like I said"—I glanced over my menu—"I've never kept you updated on my dating life. It only made sense to mention having a boyfriend after a period of time."

Father turned to Theo, who was examining the label of the wine bottle sitting open on the table. "You didn't mind Luca going on all those other dates while you were together?"

A deep, frustrated anger gripped my chest.

Theo's eyes flicked up, sharp with attention. "No. And as I understand it, Luca never agreed to any of those *dates* in the first place."

I was surprised by his bluntness. Yes, I'd filled Theo in on the issue I had with my father, but I hadn't expected him to take a stand on my behalf.

Father was also taken aback, the neutral lines around his mouth turning downward. "I don't know what you mean."

Yes, he did. But if he didn't admit it he could pretend it wasn't true.

"I told you repeatedly I didn't want to be set up." I picked up the wine and poured a glass for Theo and myself.

"So no, Mr. Belmonte, I didn't mind. Other than for the fact that Luca kept finding himself in uncomfortable situations he hadn't asked for." Theo picked up his glass and smiled at me. "Thank you, babe."

"You're welcome." I sounded a bit dumbfounded.

Having someone back me up in these infuriating conversations with my father meant more to me than I'd have thought. I hadn't gone into detail about how my father's set ups made me feel, but Theo seemed to have picked up on how horrible I found the whole situation.

"Please, call me Marcos." My father addressed Theo, ignoring everything else we'd had to say.

Theo gave my father a tight smile.

We discussed the menu. I wasn't particularly hungry despite my long, exhausting day. Sitting here was making me angrier than I'd anticipated. I resented concocting this lie and putting on a performance for a man who wouldn't listen to me, or even acknowledge me unless it suited him. It felt like too much effort expended on his behalf. I'd thought a fake boyfriend was the perfect plan, only now it was hard to remember why.

Telling Theo what had been going on with my father, and seeing him angry about it, validated all the feelings I'd been trying to ignore. None of this was okay, and I'd known that, but having my father constantly act like I was the unreasonable one made me doubt myself when I shouldn't have. Seeing all that clearly, through Theo's eyes, made me want to go back in time and make my objections heard much more forcefully than I had done.

I didn't need to act like the reason the set ups should stop was because I was taken. I shouldn't have to be 'claimed' by someone for my father to stop trying to manipulate my life.

After we ordered, my father turned pointedly to Theo. "So you're an apothecary. What an interesting occupation."

Maybe it was just me, but the man made the word *interesting* sound unbearably condescending.

"It is interesting." Theo spoke earnestly, not reacting to the unkind tone. He talked briefly about taking over Graywoods from his uncle. His love of his job shone through every word. I could have listened to him go on all night.

"I've heard of Graywoods, though I haven't been." My father leaned forward in his seat. "So tell me, what will you do next?"

"Next?" Theo's brow wrinkled in puzzlement.

My father sipped his wine. "What else is there to do in the apothecary field? I've been so entrenched in the legal world I'm afraid I'm a bit ignorant of other magical vocations."

"Um. Some apothecaries concentrate on cultivating magical ingredients, rather than selling them. Some go into teaching." Theo glanced at me.

Before I could speak my father cut in. "But is that progression? I can't imagine growing sage is much better than selling it?"

Realization dawned on Theo's face and the friendly edge left his voice. "It isn't about better. Apothecary positions aren't hierarchical. There's no trading up for power. It's a field of knowledge, sharing what we know with the community, and learning new things about earth magic."

"Well, it all sounds very noble." My father smiled. I doubted Theo mistook his words for a compliment.

"I think it's great." I narrowed my eyes in my father's direction. "Really fascinating. I love hearing about what Theo does. There's so much more to earth magic than I realized."

My father cocked his head. "Shopkeeping interests you?"

I clenched a fist under the table. "Theo's way of interacting with magic interests me. And yes, Graywoods does to. I think it would be really cool to run such an iconic establishment, not to mention rewarding."

Theo's hand found mine under the table. His fingers curled lightly around my clenched ones. I wasn't able to relax but he held onto me anyway, rubbing my fist with his ring clad thumb.

The food arrived. I picked at mine, focusing a little too much on the wine.

My father seemed to have bought our ruse. He accepted the fact I'd been dating someone in secret, waiting to present them when it was serious. I should have been thankful for that. It meant the plan was working. But I found myself increasingly frustrated, spikes of anger hitting me acutely.

This dinner made it seem like I was trying to gain my father's approval. Asking him to endorse my relationship with a man like Theo, rather than someone like the Witches he'd set me up with. I hadn't considered this aspect of my lie when I'd concocted it on Marci's balcony, but wanting something real with Theo made it hard to dismiss my father's judgment. I shouldn't need his approval, and wished he could have just been happy for me.

"Well this was lovely." My father stood from the table at the end of the meal and shook both of our hands. "Once Deirdre is back we'll have you two over to the house."

I buttoned my jacket. "I'm not sure when I'll be free. I'm going to be even more busy than usual in the coming weeks."

My father crossed his arms. "Yes. I heard one of your clients is jumping ship. I can't believe you let that happen. After everything you worked for, there's no slacking now, Luca. Once one goes, others will follow."

I didn't know what part of that statement to be angry at first. I saw red, blinded by unfairness. Nothing was ever good enough.

"It'll get sorted out," was all I managed to say.

My father nodded, his assessing gaze sharp as glass. "Good."

18

LUCA

I booked a rideshare home and didn't unclench my jaw the entire ride. The parting text my father sent as we moved through the city only made things worse.

I was being a bad date, ignoring Theo, but this hadn't been a real date and I couldn't figure out what to say. I was upset about too many things.

We were spending too much time not really dating for two people who wanted to be together. What if meeting my father this soon put Theo off? It would be understandable, but I'd much rather fail at a relationship with him, trying my best and screwing it up, than soiling it with lies to unreasonable people for misguided reasons.

Using Theo to lie to my father had been a mistake. But still, he'd stood up for me. Done way more than I'd asked of him.

We reached my house and I got out of the car, thanking the driver.

"This is a beautiful place," Theo said from beside me.

I turned to him, keys in my hand, realizing I'd made another mistake. "I didn't even ask if you wanted to go to your house instead." I'd just booked the car and gotten in, assuming he'd follow, distraction making me presumptuous and inconsiderate.

Theo placed a comforting hand on my arm. "It's okay."

"No, it's not." I gestured to my three story Victorian, which was more flamboyant than Marci's. "I didn't even ask if you wanted to come home with me. Or if you wanted to be done with the night and see me later." Or *not* see me later.

"I'd have said yes to coming home with you, Luca." Theo grabbed me by the shoulders, turning me to face him. "I think you could use some company."

He was right. I tried to collect myself and stop fretting. We climbed the front steps and went inside, entering into the living room one level above the street and first floor garage.

Theo looked around the room with obvious interest. "Wow. This place is great, and I'm not just saying that." He slipped off his shoes and went over to the fireplace to inspect the painting I'd hung above it.

I almost smiled. "Thanks. I bought the house after my last promotion. It's a bit big, though. I tried to get my sister to move in with me but she fell in love instead."

Theo snorted a laugh. "How rude of her."

My grin won out. "I know."

Theo turned away from the painting, coming back over to where I was standing by the door. "The chore part of the night is done. How about a drink or something? That way we can relax."

"I might have had my share of drinks at dinner." I wasn't drunk, but would be if I kept going.

"Tea then?" Theo looked hopeful.

I led him to the kitchen. "No tea, but I think I have hot chocolate."

"You know, that might actually be better."

There was an unopened container of cocoa hiding amongst my dried goods. I heated milk in a pot with a quick spell as Theo rooted around the remaining cupboards looking for marsh-mallows.

"Jackpot!" he cried, kneeling down on the floor and pulling a bag of jumbo marshmallows out of the back of the pantry.

"Those are way too big." I poured milk over top of the choco-late in one of the mugs.

"No. Look." Theo covered my hand with his to stop my pour-ing. "Just leave room." He finished serving, leaving a good inch of space between the liquid and the mug's rim. After stirring, he plopped one enormous marshmallow in each cup.

I poked one of the marshmallows, watching it bob. "Perfect."

"Told you." Theo picked up a mug and blew on it, his glasses fogging up slightly. "So is this a hot chocolate on the couch kind of night, or a hot chocolate in bed night?"

"I didn't realize there were categories." I was smiling widely now, unable to help myself around him.

Theo took the distinction seriously as he explained. "Hot chocolate on the couch is your every-day hot chocolate. Like when you just need something sweet. Hot chocolate in bed is when you need ultimate comfort."

"In that case, I'll show you up to my room." I picked up the other mug.

Theo looked at me in understanding. "Yeah, I thought you might need some comfort."

I turned away and led us to the stairs, my chest aching. Theo and I might not have been together for six months, but it didn't feel like we were at the beginning of dating either. This felt like a relationship. One with support, where both parties cared and were invested in each other.

It was what I wanted.

I'd never gotten to a place with a partner that felt like what Theo and I had, even though I'd been with people longer than the week he and I had been doing whatever *this* was. I'd happily skip the get-to-know-you dates where I always worried about seeming too interested or not interested enough. Maybe that was the bit I was bad at.

I hoped that meant I could make this work.

My room was on the boring side, decoratively speaking. It had modern furniture, a large bed and a view of the street. I hadn't put up any art in here. No pictures or knickknacks beyond a few candles. I didn't spend a lot of time in my room, other than to sleep.

Theo set his mug carefully on one of the bedside tables. "I'm concerned about the lack of pillows here."

"What do you mean? There's four."

"Yeah, but if we're going to get cozy with our cocoa we need more cushioning."

"Okay." I handed Theo my mug. "I'll raid the guest room."

I returned with four more pillows.

"Better." Theo arranged them on the bed. "Hop on up, Luca." He patted the mattress.

"Why don't we get into pajamas first? Wouldn't that be cozier than climbing into bed in a suit?"

"Only one of us is wearing a suit. But I won't stop you if you want to undress." Theo smiled, then looked away. He picked up his cup and took a sip of his hot chocolate, getting melted marshmallow on his nose. He wiped at it, then licked it off his finger.

I turned toward my dresser. "Actually, I bought these." I pulled two pairs of pajamas out of the top drawer.

Theo was at my side in an instant, his hot chocolate abandoned on the nightstand. "What do you mean bought these?"

"At lunch the other day. I thought you might want something to sleep in if you ever came over and—um—I got some for me too." I awkwardly held out two pairs of flannel pants and cotton T-shirts.

"You bought us pajamas?" Theo crooned, his eyes wide with happy surprise.

"They're not matching or anything." I'd bought green for him and blue for me.

Theo kissed me, his hands tangling in my hair. I dropped the pajamas on our feet and pulled him in tight. Theo tasted like chocolate and red wine. His lips sweet and soft, his kisses hungry, almost frantic like they'd been that day in the woods.

"I didn't think you'd be quite this happy," I said with a breathy laugh when he released me.

Theo's cheeks were flushed from the kiss. The color deepened. "Come on, let's get changed."

We stripped off our clothes. I didn't find any signs of nervousness in Theo, like I had the night we'd almost hooked up. He seemed relaxed as he casually shed his clothes, and kept darting interested glances my way.

He couldn't seem to stop smiling.

Once we were in the pajamas we climbed into bed and tucked our legs under the covers, situating ourselves amongst the pillows piled against the headboard. Theo passed me my mug and cradled his. We sat snuggled together, shoulder to shoulder as we sipped our hot drinks.

Theo made a content sound. "Comforting, right?

Stars, it was so much more than that.

I let out a ragged breath. "I don't know the last time I felt like this."

"Like what?" Theo asked in the softest voice.

"Upset and then fully taken care of." I stole a sideways glance at him.

He put an arm around me, his expression tender. "Cocoa is magic."

I rested my head on his shoulder. "It's not the hot chocolate."

Theo squeezed me. "I know."

I basked in his company, so glad he was here with me. I wanted to ignore all the reasons I was upset but couldn't quite manage it. "I'm sorry about tonight. My father wasn't kind to you, and it wasn't fair of me to ask you to put up with that."

Theo put his empty mug aside. "We aren't actually at the point where we need to think about each other's parent's opinions. So don't worry about it."

"Maybe. But at the same time, I want you to be my boyfriend. And now you know that if this lasts, you'll have to deal with my shitty parents eventually. I can't just act like tonight doesn't matter because it was built on lies. The result is real. And I'm so fucking mad that my father would treat someone I cared for poorly. *He* didn't know we've only just started seeing each other, which only makes his attitude worse." I paused. "He sent me a text when we were on the ride home."

"What did it say?" Theo asked cautiously.

"He said I could do better. That bluntly. As if that was a thing that was even remotely okay to say to me. It's so disrespectful to you. It made me want to turn the car around and scream at him. Nothing is ever good enough. I've delt with that shit my whole life and I don't want you to have to deal with it too. I want to be good to you, Theo, and this isn't being good to you." Especially when he was comforting and supporting me. Doing all the right things.

"Fuck your dad." Theo was venomous, his features arranged in pure outrage. "His actions aren't your fault, Luca, or a reason for me not to want to be with you. If we're together, I'll deal with him alongside you. You shouldn't have to put up with the way he treats you either, you know."

I looked at the melted marshmallow smeared all over the inside of my cup, not sure what to say to that. I took a sip. "I don't know how to get him to stop being this way."

Theo took a moment before saying, "Have you ever

confronted him? Or would you want to? And I don't mean for my sake."

My gut twisted. "I've tried, but I always fall back on avoidance—ignoring the problem—when he doesn't listen. Marci said I need to talk to him properly." But sometimes I wondered if that was even possible. Did it even matter what I said?

"Yeah, Marci is smart." Theo tightened his arm around me. "She told me to do the same with my siblings, and I know she's right. Even if I don't want to have that conversation with them, I think I might have to."

"I can be there with you when you do, if you want." I didn't think the offer was overstepping like I normally would have. We were being honest and nothing felt like the wrong thing to say, as long as it was true.

"Thanks, Luca. I'll be there with you, if you decide to confront you dad."

"Deal." I put my mug aside and enveloped Theo in a hug. "Can we forget about it all for now?"

He ran a hand through my hair. "Absolutely."

19

THEO

*L*uca and I sunk down into the bed, snuggled amongst
the pillows and wrapped up in each other. He clung to
me in a way that felt desperate.

"I'm afraid I like you more than I should," Luca whispered in
my ear.

Butterflies fluttered, not just in my stomach but in my chest.
A purely happy tingling started at the base of my skull and radiated out in every direction. "How is that possible?"

"I don't know." Luca nuzzled my neck. "Seeing where things
go has never felt like this."

"It hasn't for me either."

Luca propped himself up to look down at me. "Can I just
start calling you my boyfriend for real? Can we be together and
forget about lies?"

"Yes." I sounded breathless, winded like we'd been kissing
hard or sprinting uphill.

I'd always been the kind of person who fell hard and fast,
and my trust in Luca had grown rapidly, even in spite of all my
consuming worries. Maybe pretending to be together had taken

the intimacy between us and pushed it to the next level, but that didn't mean what we were feeling wasn't real.

Luca trusted me to take care of him and clearly wanted to look out for me. There was no room for hidden judgments anywhere in that dynamic.

Jason had never been like Luca was with me. I hadn't realized how much had been lacking in that old relationship until I had something to contrast it with. Thinking about it now, I'd never felt fully safe or relaxed with Jason—he'd been dishonest with a lot of the people in his life and I knew it—but I hadn't realized what was off between us at the time. Never suspected he'd be as two-faced with me as I'd seen him be with others.

There was none of that with Luca. He said how he felt even when it wasn't easy. He had trouble standing up to his dad but didn't pretend one thing in front of his father and talk shit later. He tried consistently and honestly. It wasn't his fault if his dad disregarded him. Luca wasn't lying to his dad to project an image—which was what Jason had done in countless situations with people he told me behind closed doors he didn't like. Luca had lied to his dad out of desperation, and he'd felt guilty lying to my family because lying wasn't something he did as if it were nothing. How could I not trust him, knowing that?

Most importantly, Luca accepted me without trying to change me, and I believed it was all genuine.

Luca ran a hand through my hair. "I'll figure out how to be the perfect boyfriend for you, Theo. I want to get this right."

I traced along his jaw with a finger. Was he that worried about the dinner with his dad? He was getting all the things that mattered right. "You don't have to be perfect, Luca. Just be you."

It looked like the idea freaked him out but he didn't argue, he just leaned down and kissed me.

I wrapped my arms around his neck and pulled him closer.

Luca shifted, settling between my open legs. This close feeling was its own kind of magic. I loved connecting physically with my partners, and being with Luca like this set my pulse thumping.

I liked him so much. I wanted to express it, share all my sentimental and lusty feelings. I kissed Luca hard, pressing my body up into his.

"Does this feel good?" Luca murmured between brushes of his lips.

"So good." I wrapped a leg around his hip to prove my point.

Luca kissed me deeper, his tongue in my mouth. His movements were thorough, purposeful, like he wanted to find every possible shape our mouths could make together. He kissed me until I almost couldn't breathe.

His hands stayed in my hair and on my face, not roaming my body. He seemed in no hurry to make his touches overtly sexual, even with such a scorching kiss. Still, my arousal grew. I wanted to move and find the friction we both surely needed. However, I was enjoying this too, taking our time and kissing like nothing else mattered.

Slowly Luca's hands traveled away from my face and down my body. "This okay?"

I clung to him. "Yes, don't stop."

As Luca touched me, I gave in to my urge to move beneath him, rolling my hips with a groan. Luca responded in kind, sending pleasurable shocks through my body.

"Can I touch you too?" I asked when his lips traveled down to my neck.

"Yes. You can touch me however you like, Theo." Luca's voice was deep and raspy. He nipped my neck gently. "Though I could kiss you all night and still not have enough."

I ran my hands down his back and cupped his ass, encouraging him to press into me with all his weight as he rolled his hips. Our bodies moved together, our breathing a chorus of gasps.

"Can we keep doing this, but like, with less clothes?" My request came out more awkward than I'd intended, but the worry I'd sound dumb was so short lived I didn't even have time to care.

Luca sat back on his knees and pulled off his shirt. "How's this?"

"Great." My face went hot. "Here. Um." I squirmed, pulling my shirt off too, knocking my glasses off kilter in the process.

A hint of nerves tinged the edge of my arousal as I set the glasses right. I wasn't as smooth or effortlessly alluring as I hoped I could be, but Luca seemed to like me just like this.

His eyes raked over me. "You're so fucking lovely, Theo."

I tried to respond, but all that came out was an eager gasp as Luca ran his hands up my stomach and chest. He settled back on top of me, kissing lower than before, exploring my newly exposed skin. He circled a nipple with his tongue. I squirmed.

"You're sensitive here?" Luca turned to my other nipple.

"I guess—" I sucked in an involuntary breath.

"Do you like it?" Luca looked up and caught my eye. His curls tumbled around him face, the stubble on his chin brushing my sternum.

I nodded. "Yeah." My face was even hotter than before. I'd never been able to help my reactions.

"What else do you like?" Luca lowered his lips back to my nipple, this time covering it and sucking before flicking it with his tongue.

"Um—" I breathed, my whole body now feeling hot. Talking in bed wasn't usually my thing, and while I wasn't rid of my embarrassment at saying what I liked out loud, it didn't stop me wanting to tell Luca.

I wanted to give him all my secrets, my confidences. I wanted him to know everything about me in a way I hadn't with anyone else. There was no holding back. He could have my awkwardness when he treated it like something good.

Maybe I was bolder, too, after a time of self-reflection. Being alone the past few years hadn't been bad. I'd learned things about myself. Now, with Luca, I could do and say everything I'd always wanted.

I sank my fingers into Luca's curls and closed my eyes. "I—I like your mouth. I'd like it anywhere on me. I like how you make me feel."

Luca made a deep, needy sound.

Maybe I hadn't said much, or been very specific, but I found his reaction encouraging. I let him hear how much I liked what he was doing with his tongue. "I'd—*oh yes*, that—I'd like anything with you, Luca."

"Can I strip you?" Luca looked at me briefly before getting back to kissing my chest, slowly moving lower.

"Yes." I lifted my hips. "As long as you get naked with me."

He chuckled and yes, it was maybe a silly way for me to ask, but Luca seemed to love it. He sat back, this sexy smoldering look on his face, and pulled my pajama pants and boxer briefs off in one single motion.

Luca gave my body one long look, from my erection up to my eyes. "I like looking at you."

I suddenly didn't know what to do with my hands. Did I even have to do anything with them? I was on fire and squirmed, fisting the bedsheets. I swallowed. "I like you looking at me too," I whispered.

Being this vulnerable wasn't something I was always into. Someone staring at you naked could feel like an assessment. I often preferred being busy and getting on with it, not lingering. But I didn't want to rush this.

Luca was looking at me like it was its own act, like a touch or a kiss. It was something he could give me to show how he felt.

I lay there, lips parted, and unable to look away from Luca's deep brown eyes. My breathing turned shallow. The tension reached a peak and I couldn't take it. I reached down and stroked myself in one leisurely motion.

Luca's gaze dropped. I expected him to reach out and touch me as I'd just done, but he shifted back, taking off the rest of his clothes. He settled on his knees, cock at attention, and copied my slow deliberate strokes on himself. I watched his magically tattooed hand work, wetness glistening at his tip.

My own movements became less lazy and more purposeful. Luca noticed. "Do you want to come like this, Theo?"

"Do you?" I bit my lip as my pleasure mounted.

Luca leaned forward, his body hovering over mine, holding himself up with one hand. Our noses brushed. The tip of his cock touched my shaft. "I asked you first." Luca gave me a sly smile before tugging my bottom lip gently between his teeth.

He released me without leaning in to kiss me as I'd expected. It left me stammering and desperate to answer his question. "No —n-not like this. I need you to touch me."

Luca's hand joined mine on my dick, stroking slowly. I let go and touched him instead. Luca groaned and rocked his hips, thrusting into my hand.

I felt bold watching him slowly unravel. His eyes fluttered closed as he hovered above me. "Your turn to tell me what you want, Luca."

He shuddered. "I want you in my mouth."

I sucked in a breath. "Yes, I want that too." I let go of Luca and he slid down my body.

He kissed my stomach, my hips, my inner thighs. Luca kissed all around the place where I wanted him most. Then he took my cock in his hand and looked at me. "I've been wanting to do this for a long time."

Luca's eyes seemed to blaze. I wasn't sure what to say.

"I'm glad I waited until now, Theo. I wouldn't have wanted us any other way." Luca swirled his tongue around the head of my cock.

I made a desperate sound that was only partially fueled by his mouth on me. My heart pounded at Luca's sweetness, at knowing this moment meant something to both of us.

Luca wrapped his lips around me, taking my cock inside him, and sucked.

I let my head drop back onto the pillows. "Oh *fuck*, Luca."

He hummed and took me deeper. His hand left my shaft to give some attention to my balls and I spread my legs wide, knees bent. Luca's hands followed the invitation as he sucked me, letting his fingers explore between my legs.

"So good." I tangled my hands in Luca's hair. It was like his earlier request to hear what I liked had released something in me. I babbled when I was usually quiet. "Yes, that. Please."

Luca traced my rim as I'd indicated and freed his mouth. "What else? Tell me."

I picked my head and looked down at him. "I like getting fingered."

Luca's attention shifted to my face. I had a moment of worry that I'd been too forward, gone too far. It was embarrassing to say something so lewd when I usually avoided giving direction.

"Hearing you talk like this is so fucking hot, Theo. I love it." He licked my tip, not breaking eye contact.

"It's only for you." The words escaped and I could almost blame it on being distracted by physical sensation, but I wanted him to know this was special. That he was giving me the space to talk like this and explore.

"Thank you." Something in Luca sounded raw. "You have no

idea how much I like it." He looked down and took me back into his mouth.

A finger returned to my hole, touching lightly. My body went taut in anticipation. Luca's mouth left me too soon, and I gasped at the tease. He summoned a bottle of lube out of his bedside table. It came flying through the air and landed on the bed beside us.

"Love that," I laughed. Magic was so convenient.

"Just wait." Luca sounded devious and wickedly sexy. Then a slickened finger pressed between my legs.

It wasn't long before I was babbling again, this time saying *oh my god* over and over. Luca told me how amazing I was like this. How much he liked it, and how much he liked me. His finger circled and circled. As he finally pushed in, he took my cock back into his mouth. Luca sucked me with purpose as he stroked inside me, and I got lost in it until I came with my hands tangled in his hair.

Luca hummed deeply, his lips leaving me with a wet pop. He kissed my inner thighs, taking his time as I caught my breath and blinked away my dizzy lightheaded pleasure.

"Curse everything, that was amazing," I said in a winded puff.

"Oh, Theo." Luca placed an open-mouthed kiss on my stomach.

I brushed back his hair so I could see his face better. "Now, what do you want?"

"Anything you do to me is going to send me over the edge." He gave me a rueful grin. "You choose. Tell me what else you need tonight. I like hearing what you want."

I reached for him. "Come up here."

Luca crawled up my body. We kissed, tasting like chocolate and sex. I was relaxed and possibly drunk off my orgasm. Whatever it was, I kept talking as I had been before, my loose-lipped lustiness not shutting down now I was satisfied. I was more comfortable with Luca than I'd been with anyone.

"If you're into it, I'd love it if you fucked me," I said between kisses. My pulse thudded in my ears as my skin heated, joy and lusty feelings coursing through me. I felt powerful and confident. Together with Luca, anything was possible.

20

LUCA

I'd never seen Theo blush so fiercely. He had this unique mix of confidence and bashfulness that, when combined, made everything between us feel so important. It was intoxicating.

I'd never had sex like this. Sure, I'd had great sex and didn't think feelings were essential to a good time, but I'd never felt so strongly for someone and been able to see all those feelings returned with equal intensity. Theo's feelings shone in the way he looked at me, the way he touched me, the way he talked to me.

I could feel Theo taking risks, trusting me, and I was quickly becoming addicted to our specific kind of intimacy. I wanted more of Theo. I wanted him to say filthy things, and I wanted to see the small look of shock on his face afterward. I planned to fulfill all his desires so he knew I liked all of this as much has he did.

I wanted to be fully open with Theo so he knew he could be that way with me. For him, I'd throw cation to the wind. I couldn't be afraid of failure when he gave me everything despite his own fears.

I curled around Theo, shifting him on his side so I could hold him from behind, and kiss his neck. "I've never heard a more perfect request."

"Yeah?" Theo sounded surprised and deeply pleased. He snuggled back into me. "How about you tell me what way you want me. So I can hear you talk all sexy too."

I smiled, gripping his hip and pressing myself against his ass. "I'm going to wait until you've recovered from that last orgasm, get you hard, and fill you so I can hear more of your sweet little noises." I rolled my hips, rubbing against him.

Theo whimpered.

"How does that sound?"

"So good." He squirmed against me.

I ran my hand from his hip to his thigh. "But first let's just lie here and enjoy feeling each other. I like being naked with you."

A breathy sound escaped his throat. "You like talking in bed, don't you?"

"I do." I kissed Theo's shoulder.

"I never have." He ran his fingers over my arm where it was draped across his chest. "But I'm liking it with you."

"Me too." I hugged Theo tighter, even wrapping a leg over him and clinging. It wasn't meant to be a sexy gesture, but there was room for all the mushier emotions between us, too. I kissed behind his ear. "You're the best boyfriend I've ever had."

Theo laughed, sounding pleased. "It hasn't been that long."

"No, but I'm going to make it last." It was a promise I was determined to keep.

It really felt like we could do anything. My problems weren't solved and neither were his, but surely we could manage it together. I'd make this work out no matter what.

I kissed Theo's neck, running my hands over him. I explored his arms, his wrists and slender fingers, each ring he wore. I mapped out his chest with my palms, finding the spots that made him sigh and squirm. I rolled his nipples between my finger and listened to his gorgeous moans.

By the time my hands traveled down past Theo's bellybutton, his cock was swelling. I stroked him until he was fully erect then grabbed the lube.

Theo hitched one of his legs up as my hand delved between them. I started slow, circling until he begged me to enter him. I kissed him, sucking what would probably be a hickey into his neck, listening to his gasps and muttered swears of pleasure.

"I want to worship you," I whispered in his ear, feeling distantly ridiculous at the sound of the words, but also like nothing had ever been truer.

"Luca, please," Theo whined.

I summoned a condom from the bedside drawer and rolled it on, lubing up with increasing clumsiness as my excitement mounted. I lined up with his entrance. Theo pushed back as I pressed in, moaning into his shoulder.

"Luca," Theo panted, releasing the most desperate sound I'd heard all night as he took me fully inside him.

I rocked my hips slowly, lost in the consuming feeling of him. "Theo, baby, you're so good."

He whimpered needily. I draped an arm across his chest, holding us tight together, and thrusted, keeping it slow and measured, biting my lip trying not to get carried away too quickly. Theo moved with me, and after admitting he didn't usually talk during sex, he had a lot to say. Mostly, *more*, and *please*, then *don't stop, Luca*. All Theo's inhibitions seemed to melt away as he begged me to fuck him.

"I got you, baby." My pace picked up, granting me a chorus of *yeses* from the stunning man in my arms. I moved my hand to Theo's dick and stroked him until he cried out, his pleasure spilling onto my hand. I lost myself in him after that and my own orgasm crashed into me.

We were both panting and sweaty. I buried my face in the crook of Theo's neck.

"I like it when you call me baby." Even breathless, Theo's words sounded painfully sincere.

"Yeah?" I kissed along his shoulder, wanting to call him all the endearments.

As Theo caught his breath, he seemed to hesitate. "Can it be your private nickname for me?" His question came out quiet.

My chest swelled, full of affection. "Of course it can, baby. I'd like that."

Theo sighed and his whole body went boneless.

We lay together a while before cleaning up. Theo slipped his boxer briefs back on before crawling under the covers, so I did the same. A yawn overtook me. I scrubbed a hand over my face and smiled.

Theo turned on his side and looked at me. His glasses were smudged and his cheeks still flushed. "You can call me babe in public, too, if you want. As long as it's real."

I grabbed his hand. "Everything between us is real, you know."

Theo's smile lit up my whole world. "Yeah, it is, isn't it?"

21

THEO

*L*uca and I had coffee and tea at a bakery in his neighborhood the next morning. Sunday was a free day for me, so I'd have been down for a lazy morning in bed and maybe brunch by noon, but Luca had to go into the office.

"If I go in early I think I can get out by the afternoon," he explained as we left the bakery.

"You can come over after, if you want."

As Luca sipped his to-go coffee, the morning sun caught in the natural highlights in his tousled hair. He'd ordered a second latte to take to work. He lowered the cup, revealing a wide smile. "Yes, I do want."

I linked my arm with his. "You're sure you have to go to work? I mean—this isn't just me being needy—you mentioned you're stressed. Maybe you should take a full day off."

Luca's smile dimmed. "At the moment taking time off would stress me out more than going to work."

I didn't like the sound of that. It was a weekend and shouldn't be considered time off, but it was Luca's job and he knew how to handle it best.

We kissed goodbye and Luca hopped in a rideshare to head downtown. I opted to walk home. It wasn't far to Noe Valley and it was mostly downhill. Besides, it was a nice fall morning and I was in an excellent mood.

Graywoods was cozy and closed up when I got home, the front curtains drawn just as I'd left them. I didn't see Jacob around. Quill's was also shut on Sundays, so I went directly up to my apartment. Normally I might do some tidying in the shop, or sort out any loose ends, but I'd done a lot of that Friday night when I'd stayed late waiting for the mysterious crystal man.

A prickle of unease ran through me as I passed the side entrance to the shop. I shook it off and kept going up the stairs. Maybe I needed a break from work too, to see if my paranoid thoughts caught up to me outside Graywoods.

I occupied myself cleaning the apartment, doing laundry and corralling all my stray mugs. Once the living room was looking respectable I had the urge to go get the dried rose Luca had given me. It would be nice to have down in Graywoods so I could see it while working, but I'd rather have it up here.

Popping in to get something wasn't the same as working, so I figure grabbing the rose wouldn't disrupt my not-at-all-scientific experiment investigating the strange feeling I'd been getting—which hadn't bothered me since arriving home. Not that I was surprised. If loneliness was the root of my problem, I wouldn't expect to feel uneasy today. I was having a perfect alone-and-enjoying-it day.

I unlocked the door to Graywoods' back room and turned on the lights with a flick of my wrist. The feeling that I wasn't alone hit me with force and the hairs on my arms stood up.

Okay. Maybe I'd psyched myself out, avoiding the shop and wondering if the feelings would come back or not. I tried to center myself, but something felt very wrong. I swore someone was standing behind me.

When I turned there was no one. "Hello?" I called out.

Nothing greeted me but silence.

I scanned the store room. Everything looked just as I'd left it. The rose was still in its vase. My drying mushrooms were all laid out. The extra stock was neatly organized.

There shouldn't be anyone here. Graywoods was protected with magic, spells that locked the place better than keys, and kept anyone intending harm out whether the doors were open or not. I knew all this and still couldn't get the feeling I wasn't alone to abate.

I drew back the curtain sectioning off the back room and stepped into the shop. I gasped and sagged against the counter in shock. "No, no, no. *No!*" I looked frantically around.

The place was trashed.

I gripped the counter, wishing in vain that this was a dream. I didn't know what to do. Destroying the shop shouldn't have been possible. The magical protections!

I called up my magic and reached out to examine my surroundings. The familiar hum of the security spells didn't greet me. Someone had broken through my uncle's protections. That meant they were powerful, more so than me.

The feeling I was being watched hit me anew.

"Fuck." I tried to collect myself as I looked quickly around the shop. Someone could very well be in here with me.

All the shelves were still upright, which was good because they weren't broken, but bad because I couldn't see more than the center aisle and front door. The merchandise had been thrown from every shelf. Glass glittered on the floor. Potions dripped down their displays. Herbs and broken candles were everywhere, but none of that was immediately important.

I strode out from behind the counter and quickly walked to the front of the shop, checking the aisles as I went. I saw no one, just more destruction. I heard no rustling or movement beyond my own noises.

I was able to check most of the shop from this center position, but there were a few corners I'd have to circle back to. When I reached the door I drew back the curtains, letting in the natural light. The openness exposed what was going on in here to the street, not that there were a lot of pedestrians, but if there was a chance I was about to find someone lurking I'd rather not feel like no one could see what was happening.

The front door was locked, which surprised me. Why would the vandal have broken Graywoods' spells and then locked up behind themselves? And the locked door had to mean they were gone, right? They wouldn't lock themselves in. So then why was my skin crawling?

I checked the rest of the shop, up and down every narrow aisle, poking into every corner no matter how small, all while trying not to step on anything that might be salvaged.

No one was here.

By the time I got back to the counter I was breathing hard. My chest twinged. My fear was mostly gone, but something worse was taking its place. Graywoods was supposed to be safe. This was my haven, where everything in my life was right and exactly as I wanted it to be.

Why would someone do this?

They hadn't robbed my shelves, just destroyed everything. I checked the register in case cash was all they'd been after. Every last coin was accounted for and I'd cleared the safe out back yesterday.

The drawer under the counter was locked, but that meant nothing. So was the front door. I unlocked it and found my iPad and the nuisance of a crystal right where they were supposed to be.

I'd half expected the crystal to be gone. The damn thing was useless, so someone stealing it made little sense, but everything had started after it had showed up. However, it was here, mocking me and the conclusions I'd drawn.

Why had someone broken in? Just to ruin everything I loved? I looked desperately around for what felt like the millionth time and something that I'd missed before caught my eye.

A pitiful wail started in the back of my throat. It was a strangled, almost inhuman sound. The teapot was gone.

I lunged to the other end of the counter as if hurrying would do damn thing. The pedestal was empty. The ceramic cup and ornate teapot were nowhere in sight.

I searched the shop again, moving broken items around and getting on my hands and knees. I searched the back room, which appeared untouched by the thief. I even tried summoning the teapot, but it wasn't here.

I slumped on the floor behind the counter and pulled my legs to my chest. My eyes burned. Uncle Theodore's legacy was gone. The part of this job that gave me the most joy had been taken. It felt cruelly personal.

I rubbed at my damp eyes with the end of my sleeve. I was still in yesterday's clothes, the green sweater I'd worn to dinner, but all the good feelings of last night felt far away.

I pulled my phone out of my pocket and called Luca. As the phone rang my heart slowed down, almost returning to its normal pace. Just the thought of hearing his voice was comforting.

He didn't answer. Luca's voice on the recorded message didn't sound soothing at all.

I had to fight the hopeless feeling that swelled inside me. I knew it was an irrational reaction. Luca was at work, he could have been in a meeting or have had his phone on silent. Him not answering had no meaning beyond the fact he couldn't pick up the call.

But I needed him, and it hurt to be alone on the floor in my ruined shop with him out of reach. A sob escaped me.

Someone banged on the front door and every muscle in my body tensed.

"Theo! Hello? Theo!" a muffled voice called from out on the street.

I wiped my eyes and got up.

Jacob was peering in through the front door's glass panel, his eyes wide with concern. He spotted me amid the destruction. "Oh my goodness, Theo! Are you all right?"

The sight of my neighbor was a small relief. I went to let him in.

Jacob was carrying a paper bag filled with what looked like produce. "What in the stars happened?"

"I—I don't know." I surveyed the shop helplessly. "I found it like this."

Jacob put a reassuring hand on my shoulder. "Have you called the Authority?"

"No—um—I guess I should." I pulled my phone back out of my pocket. I had to look the number up. At least they had a branch in the city, and said an investigator would be out within the hour.

"When did this happen?" Jacob asked as I hung up the phone. He'd placed his groceries on the ground out of the way of the nearest shattered glass.

"I don't know." Stars above, I felt as useless and scattered as everything in the shop. "I was out last night and didn't even look in Graywoods when I first got home. Did you hear anything? See anything?"

Jacob stroked his mustache as he thought, frowning deeply. "I was in last night but didn't hear or see anything out of the ordinary. Maybe there were a few more people walking around than usual this morning, but it's hard to imagine this happening in daylight."

"True." I sounded as miserable as I felt. "But Witches could have broken in under a cloaking spell. You mightn't have seen even if you were looking."

"I hate to think someone was trashing your place while I was clueless next door." Jacob looked pained.

"I'm just glad nothing happened to you." I was suddenly relieved to not have been here. What if I'd heard something and come downstairs? The break in could have turned dangerous.

Jacob waited with me for the magical Authority to arrive. We decided against cleaning up, so the officials could have a look at everything as it was. With nothing to do but wait and wallow, time stretched unpleasantly.

The bookseller left me briefly to make tea at his place, bringing it back over to share. I was quiet, concentrating on the hot liquid in my cup and feeling awful that I might never taste Graywoods tea again. The shop would never be the same without it.

"It will be all right, Theo." Jacob seemed at loss for how to comfort me beyond tea, but he was trying.

The Authority investigators turned up at last. Two women in identical dark suits and sunglasses stepped out of either side of their black car in perfect unison, almost like a scene out of a movie. It all felt surreal.

One investigator questioned Jacob outside while I detailed everything to the other. She did a magical inspection of the building, confirming my protections had been obliterated, and that whoever had done it hadn't left a magical signature behind to give themselves away.

Before long Jacob was sent home. He told me to call if I needed anything.

When he was gone the two women turned their full attention on me.

"Do you have any idea who could have done this?" the one who'd introduced herself as Ms. Clark asked.

"No one I know." My voice was strained. I opened the drawer and pulled out the black crystal, telling them all about it.

Ms. Clark picked up the quartz. "It doesn't have any sort of spell cast on it, other than to change its appearance." She must have been inspecting it with her magic, and she would know. Picking apart spells and scoping out their purposes was what paranormal investigators did.

Clark handed the crystal to her partner, Ms. Ellis.

The second woman did her own inspection. "There's nothing dangerous about this, but if the man comes back, try and get some information on his identity." She handed the crystal back to me.

I frowned. "Yeah, okay." As if I hadn't already tried to get the guy's name.

"We'll report your magical teapot stolen." Clark didn't look up as she typed something on her phone. "And be on the lookout for any hint of it on known black market trading sites."

"Is that all?" I couldn't help being disappointed.

Ellis put her sunglasses back on. "Unless there was a tracking spell cast on the item—one that hasn't already been broken by the thief—there's nothing more to do right now."

They left me in the shop with the business card of a Witch who cast protections for a fee, in case I needed help re-upping my security.

I grabbed a broom.

22

LUCA

Theo had called me almost two hours ago and I'd missed it.

As I stepped out of the office I called him back. It went directly to voicemail. Maybe he'd forgotten to charge his phone after a night away from home.

I assumed Theo hadn't been calling to cancel our plans to meet up, and made my way over to his place, stopping on the way to pick up some food. It was closer to dinner time than I'd have liked but I hadn't been able to get away sooner. The senior partners had been in the office and I hadn't exactly been able to tell them it was a bad time to catch up.

The lights were on in Graywoods when I arrived. That seemed odd since Theo had said the shop was closed today. I tried the front door and found it unlocked. Still, I knocked before opening it all the way, to announce my presence.

Theo's head popped out from behind a shelf. The closer I looked the more I noticed Graywoods didn't look like it had last time I'd visited. The shelves I could see were bare and an odd assortment of things was piled in the middle aisle.

Theo's supersized expression sagged in what looked like

relief once he realized I was the one at his door. As I entered I noticed his face was red and blotchy, his clothes untidy. Was that a stain of something on his knee?

"Luca." Theo sounded pained as he approached. His eyes were red.

"What's wrong?"

He glanced around the shop, looking lost, before returning his focus to me. "I—I tried to call."

"I'm sorry. Work was busier than I'd anticipated. What happened?"

"You don't have to apologize. Just—" Theo lifted his arms and dropped them hopelessly. "The shop got broken into." With a sigh he turned and made his way toward the counter.

I followed. "Oh, shit."

The place was a mess but it looked like Theo had already put in a considerable effort cleaning. Ruined merchandise had been swept into piles on the floor and not a single shelf had anything left on it.

Theo turned to face me, sagging against the counter. "They stole my tea."

Theo seemed like he was about to cry. I dropped the food on the counter and pulled him into a hug. My gaze fell on the empty stand that had housed the shop's legendary magical teapot. Theo and I hadn't really talked about Graywoods tea, however it seemed like the kind of thing he'd not only adore, but value for its principle alone.

I ran a hand through his hair. "Theo, what can I do to help? Tell me."

"This." He hugged me tighter.

We stood like that until Theo was ready to tell me what had happened. He kept his face tucked into me as he spoke. I took in the mess of the shop. Stealing the tea was no reason to trash the place. It made me angry. Theo was so kind. No one deserved this to happen to them, but Theo least of all.

"So the Authority aren't doing anything?" I asked in frustration when Theo had finished his recount of the afternoon.

"No." He sounded hopeless.

I clenched my jaw, thinking. "There has to be something more we can figure out."

Theo pulled away from me. "I know, but I can't seem to come up with anything. Graywoods tea might be gone forever." He wrung his hands, the idea clearly distressing him. "I know the spell to activate the teapot and brew the tea, but I can't recreate the magical items themselves. The tea set is where the magic that detects your prefect tea is held. If it's gone, it's gone. Uncle Theodore didn't even create it by himself. It was a joint effort with his partner. And even if he'd left notes on how they'd done it—which he didn't—it wouldn't be the same."

"I know. That kind of magic doesn't seem like something you can recreate, at least not in the exact same way."

Theo blinked and a tiny smile broke through his sadness. "You're right. It can't be recreated with the same undercurrents of personal magic left by the original Witches, even if the spell itself could be redone."

He seemed pleased I understood, but of course this would be a big deal to Theo, and not a problem that could be solved by replacing things. I knew him well enough to get that. Magical details mattered to him.

An idea struck. I pulled out my phone. "Maybe I should call my sister."

"Why?"

"She works for an investigator. Just because the officials aren't doing a whole lot, doesn't mean we can't ask someone else to try."

Theo perked up. "I didn't even think of calling someone privately. My brain is a mess right now."

It was understandable and I was glad to help. Aria answered my call on what felt like the last possible ring. After a quick chat she promised to talk to her boss right away and get back to me. I hung up hoping they'd be able to pass on some tips, or even recommend a local PI.

Theo rummaged around in the bag I'd brought. "You got us burritos."

My stomach growled. "Yeah, but they might be getting cold."

"We can fix that." Theo smiled fully for the first time since I'd arrived. "This is exactly what I needed."

I chuckled. "Good. I'm pretty much starving after skipping lunch so, I figured it couldn't hurt."

Theo reheated the food with a quick spell and we ate. He seemed to be giving his full attention to the burrito, eating small methodical bites, every so often closing his eyes, chewing blissfully.

I could watch him do anything. His many crystal rings caught the light as he pulled back the foil wrapping his food. I couldn't help thinking about how those fingers had felt on my body, how they'd tangled in my hair. My eyes slid to the hickey on Theo's neck. He'd declined to heal it with a spell this morning. I really, *really* liked that.

Theo caught me staring at the mark and his cheeks flushed. I reached out and brushed the heated skin with my thumb.

There was a knock on the shop door.

Theo practically jumped, clearing his throat as he swallowed his food. "Everyone keeps scaring the hell out of me today. Who could that even be?"

I put my burrito down and turned toward the front.

Aria waved from the doorway. "Brother, so good to see you."

Theo gave me a sideways look of confusion. "I thought you said she lived in SoCal."

I frowned at Aria as she stepped inside. "Hello, sister. Not that I'm not glad to see you, but what—?"

Two more people entered the shop behind her. A woman I didn't recognized and a man I did. My frown deepened.

"I gave your sister a lift," said Mr. Bickel, a slender white man in a vintage suit and bow tie. He had the unique ability to teleport, explaining the group's sudden appearance. "If you'd like our help with the break in, we're happy to look into it now."

I looked from Bickel to Theo, this was his call.

"Um. Thank you. Yeah." He put his burrito down and wiped his hands.

"I'm Aria." My sister stuck out her hand to shake Theo's. She introduced the other woman, Juliet Herrera, her boss and the PI I was hoping might have advice for us.

"Edwin Bickel. Juliet's magical chauffeur." Bickel shook Theo's hand, smiling. His expression was unsettlingly genuine for a guy who was permanently—not to mention famously—grumpy.

"Oh, right. Nice to meet you." Theo seemed throw off, making me think he'd heard of Bickel, or at least of his powers. The guy was a legend after all.

"Sorry we've interrupted your dinner." Juliet gestured to the burritos. "Shall we give you a minute?"

"We can examine the broken protections while you eat," Bickel suggested.

"How very considerate." My comment came out sounding sarcastic and everyone looked at me.

Bickel was being considerate, but I was thrown off by his friendly attitude and not exactly happy to see him. I'd been thoroughly humiliated by my father the last time I'd been around the guy. My father had implied I was a more eligible match for the powerful Witch than the boyfriend Bickel already had. Bickel had seemed pissed off about the whole situation and —for entirely different reasons—had ended up shouting at me outside court. But maybe Bickel had forgotten his frustration with me. He blinked at my snarky words, almost as if he were confused.

Theo touched my arm, recapturing my attention. "Let's finish eating."

Juliet and Bickel stepped back and discussed examining the broken spells between themselves.

Aria poked into the bag of chips sitting on the counter. "May I?" A chip was in her mouth before I nodded. "So what's up, Luca? I feel like I'm missing a lot." Her eyes landed on Theo.

I took my time chewing. "This is my boyfriend, Theo. Marci introduced us."

"Oh my *god*, boyfriend? Since when?" She gaped at me.

I rubbed my neck. "Um." Theo and I shared a look.

Aria frowned, her eyes narrowing. "It's not a hard question."

"It's a new development," I said truthfully. "We've just started dating but I've told our parents we've been together for months. So don't blow my cover."

Aria looked intrigued. "I mean, I wasn't planning on stopping by the family home on this trip, but don't worry. I'll happily back up any lie you want to tell them, Luca."

"Thanks. I'll explain later."

My twin seemed happy with that and let Theo and me eat in piece, though she stole most of the chips.

When his food was finished, Theo balled up his discarded tinfoil with an air of satisfaction. "I feel way more functional now."

He seemed more himself too. Despite looking disheveled, Theo had an authoritative air as he explained to the newcomers everything that had happened. You could hear the pride he took in running Graywoods in every word, and his despair about the break-in seemed to morph into determination.

Theo brought out the crystal he'd told me about at his mom's party. Juliet and Bickel examined it.

"There's nothing cast on this to explain the unsettling feelings you've been experiencing in the shop," Juliet said as she placed it back on the counter. "Unfortunately, I don't have much more to say about the broken protections than what the Authority told you, but that doesn't mean we can't figure out something. Why don't we help you clean while we try and come up with a plan?"

Theo looked between the three of them. "You really don't have to."

"No, but we're offering." Aria gave Theo one of her genuine smiles.

He hesitated.

Juliet gestured to the mess. "We might find something useful. It would be good to look for anything that could help us figure out who did this."

"Okay. When you put it that way." Theo grabbed a broom that had been propped up behind the counter. "I really appreciate it."

Bickel frowned at the broom. With a wave of his hand, all the shattered glass in and amongst the various piles of things on the floor vanished. "No need to risk cutting ourselves if we're digging around for clues."

"Um. Thanks." Theo sounded awed. Vanishing wasn't a typical magical ability, but one related to Bickel's teleporting.

The powerful Witch didn't seem to be showing off, which only made the trick more annoying for its impressiveness. "I can also cast new protection spells on the building," Bickel offered Theo as he continued to baffle me by being a nice guy. "I've the advantage of almost unbeatable magical strength, so whoever did this won't be able to get back in again."

Theo considered. "What's the cost for your services?"

"Nothing." Bickel shrugged.

"Seriously?" Theo's awe seemed to be growing, his green eyes widening.

I couldn't help being suspicious. "Why would you offer to protect Graywoods?"

Bickel met my stare and his cheeks went ever so slightly pink. "Luca, I think I owe you an apology."

I faltered. "Really?" I mean, I was annoyed he'd yelled at me, but the situation had been high stress for him, and offering an apology wasn't in line with the indifferent personality Bickel was known for.

He clasped his hands behind his back. "Yes. I'm sorry for taking out my anger on you when you were only trying to help. I should have said something sooner." He frowned. "You're Aria's brother, I'd like for us to be able to get along."

I glanced at my sister. "Why?"

"Edwin and I are friends now." Aria made a face like she found this fact annoying, but I could tell she was actually pleased. It was a classic Aria move. "If you come down for Christmas with the Mortals like I've been trying to get you to do, then you'll be seeing a lot of him. So you might as well try and get along."

"Oh." I'd almost forgotten about the invitation. Most Witches didn't celebrate Christmas, but Aria's Mortal partner Owen did. I'd missed their celebration last year due to work. "I might be doing solstice with Theo."

Theo beamed at me. "We could probably fit both in."

"I can always give you a lift, if that would help," Bickel offered, seeming eager to make it all work.

I couldn't fault that. If he was really friends with my sister, I'd be interested in spending more time with the two of them to figure out how they'd managed to get along. The last time Aria, Bickel, and I had been in a room together she couldn't stand him.

"Thank you Mr. Bickel, that would be great," I said awkwardly.

He smiled. "Please, call me Edwin."

Theo leaned in to whisper to me as everyone turned to cleaning up. "What great friends."

"Yeah, my sister's found some good people." I wondered if they would ever be my friends too. Like my childhood rivalry with Marci, there was no reason to hang on to not liking Edwin.

From the look of it, Aria seemed to have gotten over her hatred, the three of them all giggling at something on the far side of the shop. Aria was trying to resist smiling and failing. I'd missed my sister and wished she didn't live so far away. Work made it too hard to visit her.

Theo nudged my shoulder. "You should join them for Christmas."

"Would you want to come with me?"

"Hell, yes." His eyes flashed. "But I'm warning you, solstice is going to make it a hard act to follow."

We made quick work of the shop. Most of the items were too ruined to be sold, but we placed what we could back on the shelves. Theo was going to salvage anything usable out of the crushed ingredients for his own spells and potions, so we sorted everything that couldn't be sold into containers for him.

"What's this?" I reached under a shelf and grabbed a large silver coin. Only it wasn't a coin. There were no markings on it, it was completely smooth.

Theo took it from me, turning it over in his hand. "I've never seen this before."

Edwin came tentatively over to us. "Can I take a look?" He'd removed his hat and jacket and looked more approachable for it. The lack of scowl helped to.

Theo handed him the metal disk.

Edwin closed it in his fist, likely doing a silent examination. "There's a spell cast on it."

I exchanged a glance with Theo. The kind of magical assessments investigators did were tricky and took a lot of practice. I'd done an introductory class more than ten years ago, but that was as far as my knowledge went. There was no way I'd be able to examine a magical object and figure out what it did. At least not without a lot more training.

A crease in Edwin's brow was the only sign he was doing anything more than staring at the piece of metal in his hand. After a long moment he looked up at us. "I'd say this has been the cause of your uneasy feelings, Theo."

"Really? So it *was* magic?" Theo sagged in relief, but only briefly. "Where would it have come from? Did someone drop it by mistake?"

Juliet joined us in the narrow aisle.

Edwin handed her the piece of metal. "It could have been left unintentionally, but I don't know how likely that is. The coin, for lack of a better term, seems to have been created solely to carry a spell that mimics a sinister presence. All the feelings you were getting, of not being alone, or being watched, was your response to the spell. It seems like the kind of thing a person would carry around intentionally, in order to leave with whoever they were trying to mess with. Surely they'd notice the loss if they dropped or misplaced the coin and could no longer feel its sensations."

"So you think someone left it here deliberately?" Theo looked at the coin as if it had betrayed him. "But what does that have to do with stealing my tea?"

"I don't know." Edwin looked at Juliet.

"I'm not sure either, maybe nothing," Juliet said after examining the coin. "It's not like this coin made it easier for the thief to break in. It might not be related, but I can still take a closer look at it. If you don't mind me taking it home?"

Theo didn't mind at all. He seemed glad to have it gone, and to have an explanation for the unease he'd been feeling at work.

I'd had no idea he'd been worried something was wrong. He hadn't mentioned it to me, but then, I'd been swamped with my own work and hadn't talked to him much over the last week. We were only at the beginning of our relationship, despite how the intimacy felt, and there was still a lot we both didn't know about each other.

"Could the coin have given Theo strange dreams?" I asked.

Everyone looked at me, Aria peering through the empty shelf separating this aisle from the one she was standing in.

"I've been having nightmares," Theo explained, running a hand through his hair. "But we don't know that they're a magical issue. I thought *maybe* it was all connected—the dreams, the feelings in the shop—but then, I thought the crystal was my problem and was completely wrong about that. I only ever felt watched at work. The dreams happened even when I was in Tahoe for a weekend."

"You weren't wrong about a spelled object being the cause of your unease," I reminded him.

Theo turned to Juliet. "Would you be able to tell from the coin if it were giving me weird dreams?"

She rolled the coin between her fingers. "I can't detect anything that would affect your unconscious. And I'd say this spell doesn't have a very large range, so there's no way it could have affected you while you were out of town."

"That's good at least." Theo gave a strained smile.

"If there's a chance the coin being here isn't a coincidence, maybe it can help us find the thief. I can pick apart the spell and see where it leads." Juliet sounded optimistic and I hoped she was right. We'd found no other clues, magical or otherwise, as we'd cleaned the shop.

Theo agreed with Juliet and with that tentative plan in place, he and I wished the others a good evening. They teleported back to Southern California, Juliet promising to let us know as soon as they had results.

Edwin's new protection spell was in place and Theo seemed at ease as he locked up and closed the front curtains.

I felt a pang at the sight of the almost empty shop. "Why don't I help you restock the shelves with what you have in the back so you're ready for tomorrow?"

Theo came up and kissed me. "Thank you, Luca. I'd appreciate it."

"It's all right." I'd only done what anyone would have in the circumstance, but Theo acted like me being here made all the difference. I kissed him back, more deeply than he had done. "We'll get to the stock in a minute. I think you need a little attention first."

Theo's arms wrapped around my neck. "Yeah, okay."

23

THEO

Up in my apartment I made a pot of tea to share with Luca. It wasn't Graywoods tea but it was a nice herbal blend good for the end of the day.

Stars above, what a day.

Luca and I both added liberal amounts of honey to our steaming mugs and settled on my couch. As we let our tea cool, Luca eyed my bookshelf with interest.

"You've got a good collection of books."

"There's more in my study. These are all fiction." It wasn't my entire fiction selection, only most of it.

"Can I borrow something?" Luca eyed me sideways. "I haven't read in ages."

I smiled widely. "Sure. What caught your eye?"

He ran a finger along the shelf closest to us. "Nothing in particular. I can't say I recognize any of the titles. I want something fun. Fast paced and upbeat."

Excitement stirred in me. I loved sharing books and it had been a while since I'd recommended anything to anyone other than Jacob. "Can I pick a book for you?"

"Yes, please." Luca seemed excited too, his eyes intense and bright.

I got off the couch, bringing my tea with me. Part of me was exhausted but I wanted to end this day on a good note. I'd have wallowed if I'd been alone and was glad to have Luca here with me, helping and getting my mind off everything, being my boyfriend in all the ways I wanted him to be.

I took my time considering the titles, gently sipping my tea. Eventually I grabbed a few books off the various shelves and handed them to Luca. "See what you think."

He read the backs carefully. I drank him in. His slightly serious expression, the dark stubble lining his jaw, the tattoos on the back of his finger as it skimmed the text.

I'd noticed his sister's matching tattoos on her knuckles. I was looking forward to seeing her again, and was thrilled that Luca had asked me to join him when he visited her. I liked that Luca was making plans for us. It made me feel like we were on the same page.

Luca rearranged the books into a particular order, maybe in accordance with his preference. He tapped the top book. "How are you feeling about opening Graywoods tomorrow?"

I sagged into the couch. "As fine as I can be. After depleting the back room's reserves there's a halfway-decent assortment of items to sell. And there's no reason I can't be open for advice. I just—it's going to be hard if anyone comes in for tea."

"I could call in sick from work and help you out." Luca continued tapping the books. "I know I can't do anything about the tea, but I could keep you company if you want."

I put a hand on his restless fingers. "You don't have to put your whole life aside for me."

"I know." Luca's gaze turned imploring, his words earnest. "I'm not, it's just a day. Besides, I want to be a good boyfriend."

I paused. Luca had mentioned more than once that taking time off was stressful—he didn't even feel he could have his weekends free—and yet he was suddenly okay with ditching tomorrow?

"You are a good boyfriend." I squeezed Luca's hand. This wasn't the first time he'd said something like that, either. "Really, tomorrow will be fine."

Luca frowned slightly, as if me declining his offer worried him.

I shifted on the couch. "Is there some other reason you don't want to go to work?"

"What?" Luca gave me a startled look and ran a hand through his hair. "No. I need to be at work. I've got a lot to do. Only. This is more important. I want you to know I'm here for you."

"I know you are." I pulled Luca into a hug, the books sliding onto the couch cushion. "You've helped me so much today."

"Yeah?" His voice was soft in my ear. For whatever reason, Luca seemed to need reassurance. I got that, seeing as I worried a lot in relationships, I was just surprised Luca and I had this kind of insecurity in common.

"Yes, Luca. And if I need anything, I promise I'll ask. Don't worry about going to work or being busy. I like you as my boyfriend just as you are."

I HAD ANOTHER NIGHTMARE.

Luca had stayed the night and gotten up early to head home and change before work. I fell back asleep after he'd left, only to wake up gasping in fear.

Juliet and Edwin had said the coin couldn't have caused the

dreams, but if the coin had been the source of my paranoia—rather than my feelings being solely to do with mental health—the dreams didn't make sense. Having bad dreams as part of depression or some other change in me was one thing, but if my other symptoms were explained away by magic, where were the dreams coming from?

Graywoods was bleak that day. I had to recount the shop's vandalism over and over as each customer asked why the place was so empty. Even with the things I'd pulled out of the back room, I had to send most of my patrons away empty handed.

I managed to put through a bunch of stock orders and would have most of my key items back on the shelves by the end of the week. However, specialty ingredients were what Graywoods was known for, and it would take a lot longer to replace all the unique specimens I'd collected.

The empty pedestal looked sad on the counter. I wasted a lot of the time staring at it, but couldn't bring myself to put it out back.

The mysterious man didn't come to collect his crystal, not that I was really waiting around for him, or expecting much from the situation anymore. He'd paid for my time and the quartz wasn't dangerous. If he never came back, oh well.

I was relieved when five o'clock hit. Of course that meant the bell above the door jangled, signaling the arrival of a last minute customer.

I summoned the last dregs of energy I possessed.

"*Theodore!*" Tobias barged into the shop and rushed to the counter.

Soon I was in his arms, being spun around in a crushing hug. When he put me down I noticed Stella and Sadie with him. I fixed my glasses, which had been knocked off center. I was at a loss for what to say.

"I think we surprised him." Sadie beamed, satisfaction written all over her face.

"You got me." I crossed my arms.

Tobias ruffled my hair. "Don't sound so annoyed, we're here to inject some fun into your week."

He meant well, but the comment pissed me off. My life was fun. I liked doing quiet things. I didn't need Tobias or anyone forcing activities on me. *That* wasn't fun.

Stella grabbed a lone candle off a nearby shelf. "What's going on with the shop? Where is everything?"

I pushed past them to close the curtains and lock the door before any more nuisances could come barreling in. "It got broken into."

A chorus of gasps and shocked exclamations filled Gray-woods. My siblings expressed their sympathy and I recounted the story of the trashed shop yet again, my temper getting short.

"Why didn't you tell Mom and Dad?" Tobias asked.

"I'm an adult. I don't need to call my parents to come help me."

Tobias frowned. "All right. That's not what I meant. Something this big just doesn't seem right to keep from the rest of the family. If Landon Apothecary got broken into, we'd tell you."

"I'm not keeping it from anyone." I gestured jerkily around the shop. "I've been busy. Had a lot to deal with between reporting the incident and cleaning up."

Tobias flinched at the loudness of my voice, looking hurt. "Why are you getting so angry at me?"

"He's not." Sadie stepped between us. "This has probably been really stressful."

But I was mad at Tobias. All the things I hadn't said to my siblings scraped at me nerves.

"It's a good thing we're here." Stella elbowed Tobias, as if trying to remind him of their purpose. "We're going to take you out, Theo."

"I don't want to go out."

Stella gave the other two an exasperated look. "Come on, Theo. Sadie and Tobias are here for the week. It won't kill you to *do* something. Spend time with us."

I shoved my glasses up my nose. "What's that supposed to mean?"

"Look," Sadie said calmly, like she was trying to be the peace keeper. "We've obviously caught you at a bad time."

"And who's fault is that? You could have said you were coming. I talked to you both on Friday. Why not mention it?" I glared between Sadie and Tobias.

"We couldn't have anticipated Graywoods getting robbed." Tobias raised his brows at me like he thought I was being ridiculous.

"Just come out with us for the night, Theo," Sadie insisted. "It will get your mind off everything."

They were acting like I never left the shop. Which wasn't true. Maybe I'd isolated myself to an extent but I was sorting that out, seeing Marci more, and for the most part I *liked* being a homebody and was happy to avoid most people.

If my siblings had invited me to dinner normally, called and said they were coming and wanted to see me, everything would be fine. I'd have been happy to go. Instead they were making a big deal out of everything, like they thought I was some weirdo who had to be tricked into doing things and be dragged outside. Like they thought the quiet life I led was boring and needed fixing. As if a night out was an intervention instead of something they thought we would all enjoy.

I hadn't become fixated on people secretly judging me just because of Jason. My siblings had always been part of the issue. I hadn't started wondering what they were thinking after my horrible break up. I'd always wondered, and then Jason had proven my fears, making me concerned about Tobias, Stella and Sadie's comments in a way I hadn't been before, worrying until it had consumed me. But my fear of judgment was easy to get a handle on when I was treated respectfully. Luca had shown me that. I'd been anxious about what he thought of me before I'd gotten to know him, but as we spent time together he'd never acted like my siblings or Jason, and my trust in him had solidified.

I wasn't the problem. My worries weren't some flaw I needed to fix or get over. They weren't completely unfounded or unreasonable. Not in the way I'd been thinking before. My anxiety about being judged came from how I was treated. As soon as I felt safe with someone, as soon as I knew they wouldn't treat me that way, my worry abated. But I'd never stop worrying what my sibling thought when they constantly implied being myself wasn't good enough.

My life wasn't perfect. It's not like anyone's was. Maybe I was lonely sometimes, but my siblings weren't helping me or being supportive about that. They didn't act like they cared about what I needed. Not like Luca or Marci, or even Jacob, whose teasing comments felt friendly when he only ever commented on things I knew he and I had in common, like we were on the same side.

"We're going to karaoke." Stella grinned. "My office goes once a month. It's a blast."

"Yeah, you're doing a duet with me." Tobias mirrored Stella's happy yet devious expression.

"Your office?" I rounded on Stella, the last of my tolerance snapping. "Is Jason going to be there?"

"Yeah, probably." She shrugged. "What the big deal? You see him enough. It's been years."

"So what!" I shouted. "I don't care if it'd been decades. I don't want to see him. Ever again. I fucking hate him. He was awful to me. He said I was pathetic, and shit on everything I loved and shared with him, laughing at me behind my back the whole fucking time. And you keep shoving him in my face. Fucking stop it."

I took a heaving breath.

Stella's eyes were wide. "Theo—" The word came out small and sad.

"Just don't." I closed my eyes, trying to pretend I wasn't tearing up because of Jason *again*. My problems might not have started with him, but he'd hurt me infinitely more than my siblings ever had.

"We had no idea," Sadie said.

I didn't open my eyes. "So what. I shouldn't have had to tell you. I don't need to share every single piece of my life with you." And I didn't like sharing my life when I worried how they'd view it. The whole thing with Jason and my sibling felt like an endless loop.

Someone touched my elbow. I blinked through unshed tears to see Tobias.

"We're sorry, Theo," he said.

"Fine." I cleared my throat. "Whatever. Can you just leave now? I'm not going out to karaoke, that sounds like a personal nightmare. You all should *know* that I'd hate something like that. Regardless of Jason."

"We can do something else," Stella offered. I didn't think I'd ever heard her so tentative in my life.

"I'm busy, actually." I removed my glasses and wiped my eyes. "I have a book to pick up from next door and have been meaning to talk to Jacob about this one murder mystery."

"Theo," Tobias whined, a hint of exasperation returning to his voice.

"What?" I glared at him, jamming the glasses back on my face. "My evening isn't good enough? You think I should be doing something else? I don't care." I headed for the front door.

The three of them were quiet as I showed them out of the shop. I locked up behind us, feeling guilty for lying about having plans, but not for anything else.

I kept falling back on lies even though I knew it wasn't helping me. I should have been able to say I didn't want to go out tonight for no reason beyond wanting to stay home, but I knew my siblings wouldn't listen, and I knew they'd judge my choice. I didn't want to deal with it. Tonight had been enough of an argument, I was dreading the bigger conversation the four of us needed to have.

"Can we see you tomorrow?" Sadie asked when we were all out on the sidewalk.

I shoved my hands in my pockets. It was cold and I'd left my jacket in the shop. "I don't know. Text me later."

I turned and walked to the bookstore, thanking the stars that Quill's was open late most nights of the week. Jacob wanted to be available for people who worked nine-to-five and it was usually when I visited his shop.

I didn't look back at my siblings as I entered the warm, softly lit room. Beautiful, rare editions of Mortal classics greeted me. Jacob wasn't in the front section of the shop, but I knew he'd pop out of the back soon. He didn't have a bell, the noise was too obtrusive for him. He used a silent magical alert instead. Jacob had told me once that he liked the effect of appearing mysteriously as needed for his Mortal customers.

Sure enough he drifted out of the back room a minute later. "Theo." Jacob sounded wholeheartedly pleased to see me.

I smiled. "Are you free for a bit of book chat tonight?"

"Always." Jacob pulled back the curtain behind his counter and we entered the back of the bookshop.

Grimoires lined the shelves. This room was actually larger

than the front, with a reading desk in the far corner and a set of armchairs right at the back. I settled in a chair as Jacob fixed us tea, heating the water in his delicate china pot with a spell.

I accepted the cup he handed me. "I'd like to put another order in too, if that okay?"

"More than okay." Jacob smiled. "Can't wait to see what you're reading next."

I couldn't help thinking how much happier I was here than I could have been with my family, and that made me sad.

24

LUCA

*S*even thirty hit and I gave up on the research I was trying to complete for an upcoming case. I reached into my pocket and pulled out my phone. My stomach flipped but I wasn't sure what was making me nervous. Was it wanting to see Theo, or was it work?

A voice in the back of my head said it was too much too soon to spend a third day in a row with Theo, that I was being too eager. Needy. An equally loud nagging was making me uncomfortable for wanting to leave the office when I knew I should stay for another hour and get things done.

The way to alleviate both of these concerns was obvious, but I didn't want to stay at work. Everything had gotten on my nerves today. Every person that came to talk to me added to my stress, every email I received pissed me off. I didn't want to be here at all.

I knew I was only leaving a bigger pile of tasks for tomorrow but couldn't seem to face doing anything about it. There'd be more work regardless of how much I got done tonight. I'd never catch up or get ahead.

My phone buzzed in my hand, my father's name lighting up

the screen. I sent him to voicemail. Hearing from him was the opposite of what I needed.

I stared out my office window.

For some reason I thought of Theo's mom. How she'd kissed me on the cheek when we'd met, hugged me every day I'd been in her house, and how the only thing about my job that seemed to interest her was whether I liked it or not. She had been so warm and caring.

I hoped, now that Theo and I were actual boyfriends, that I'd get to know her better. The weekend away had been dominated by Theo's siblings but there was something about his parents I was almost drawn to, despite having spent so little time with them.

A voicemail from my father popped up on my phone.

I couldn't remember the last time either of my parents had hugged me. Even thinking back to my childhood I couldn't remember that kind of affection. Not that I'd never been hugged, just that it hadn't been a normal part of our relationship. Before now I probably wouldn't have thought anything of it. So what? As an adult, I didn't particularly want hugs from my parents. It wouldn't feel natural.

It struck me how conditional both my parent's love was. How they used their approval and limited affection to manipulate me. Thinking there was a right and wrong way to do everything had been engrained in me since before I could remember, but not everything in life should feel like that.

I shouldn't feel like there was a right or wrong way to date. I was considering holding back from Theo because, if I got it wrong, I was afraid he'd take all his affection away. Like my value was in what I did and how well I did it, rather than who I was.

It was a misplaced fear. I knew Theo wouldn't treat me like that. There were reasons we might not work out, but one wrong step wasn't going to make him hate me. He'd give me space to figure out how to be a good boyfriend to him.

I messaged Theo to see if he was free and left the office. I wanted more of him in my life and less of everything else that had taken up so much space until now. It could be that simple if I let it.

I was waiting for the train when he replied. Theo said he'd love to see me, and to meet him at the bookshop next to Graywoods. I smiled down at the message like a besotted fool. For the first time since arriving at work that day I relaxed and felt happy in a completely uncomplicated way.

See, I didn't need to worry about presenting myself perfectly to Theo. He wasn't interested in someone who was aloof. He didn't value status or appearances more than he valued me. He wanted attention and romance, someone who cared about him and accepted him. It was what I wanted too, and even when I got carried away—offering to skip work to keep him company—it didn't put him off. He'd told me it was too much and didn't seem to have held it against me.

Marci was right, Theo and I were good for each other. Maybe I could actually do this. I didn't need a strategy or a good boyfriend formula if Theo was going to give me room to be myself.

I hopped on a bus after getting off the train and before long I was approaching the bookshop. Soft light emanated from the front window display, spilling onto the street. I entered a room well-stocked with old books. No one was in sight, but before I could text Theo and ask, a Witch popped out from behind a curtain.

"Why, if it isn't the handsome man." He gave me an apprecia-tive look.

"Um." I really had no idea what I was supposed to do with

his comment. The guy wasn't bad looking himself, but saying so didn't feel right.

"And he's modest." The guy sounded pleased, like he approved of my non-answer. "Come on, Theo is out back."

With some relief, I followed him behind the curtain.

Theo waved to me from an armchair, a cup of tea in his other hand, and what looked like the remains of sandwiches set out on the coffee table in front of him. He introduced me to the man who'd greeted me, Jacob, the owner of Quill's.

The bookseller grabbed a third chair from behind a nearby desk and offered me the other armchair. I settled in, the companionable dynamic between the two men apparent. It was enough to put me at ease after the strange greeting.

"Tea?" Jacob lifted the pot in offer.

I accepted even though I almost never drank tea. I had a feeling I was going to be having a lot more of it now Theo was in my life.

Jacob had only just finished pouring me a cup when his head snapped up, at attention. "Now who could that be?" He glanced over his shoulder toward the curtain blocking the front of the shop. "Excuse me, you two, I'll be right—"

Before he could finish, someone pulled back the curtain. A poised man stood in the doorway. He was a Witch dressed casually in jeans and a trendy jacket, and seemed surprised to find the three of us.

I was surprised too. It was the man I'd seen through Marci's security camera, banging on her door.

"You have guests. So sorry, Jacob." The man—Mr. Miller if I remembered correctly—gave the bookseller an apologetic smile.

"Not a problem at all, Dean." Jacob jumped up, looking eager to greet his unexpected guest. He ushered him over to us and introduced Theo and me.

"The apothecary." Dean nodded to Theo. "I've heard a lot

about you." The man's eyes travelled to me. "Seems your date went well."

"*Shush*." Jacob swatted at the other man's shoulder, going red.

"As if Theo doesn't know you're a terrible gossip." Dean smiled at Jacob, a distinctly flirty edge to his tone. Jacob's blush deepened.

"Maybe Luca and I should leave you guys." Theo set down his teacup. He didn't seem fazed to hear Jacob had been talking about him with this other Witch, but knowing this Dean guy had been harassing Marci, I didn't like it.

"You don't have to go." Jacob glanced between everyone, not sounding entirely convincing.

"Actually"—Dean put a hand on Jacob's shoulder—"I was hoping to catch you alone."

"O-oh." Jacob stuttered, seeming flustered yet undeniably pleased.

And that was our cue to leave.

Out on the sidewalk, Theo smiled, practically skipping his way next door. "Oh my god. There is totally something going on between them. This is great."

I looked back at the bookshop. "Is it?"

Theo nodded before turning to unlock his door. "Yes, and not just because I can tease him about *this* as much as he does with me."

That caught my attention, distracting me from Dean. "Jacob teases you?"

Theo shut the door to the stairs behind us and began to make his way up to the apartment. "Not in a bad way. We're friends. Jacob's quiet like me, so whenever there's something going on with one of us, it's worth noting. He seemed really happy to hear things were going well with you and me. The look he gave me when you texted tonight." Theo smiled over his shoulder at me. "You should come hang out with us again when Jacob isn't so *busy*."

"Sure, sounds great." I followed Theo into his apartment, happy he wanted me to get to know his friend, even if it seemed a little strange that Jacob had told some other guy about Theo's and my date. If Theo wasn't bothered by Jacob's behavior, that was all that mattered. However, I couldn't keep my thoughts on Dean to myself. "I recognized that guy."

"Oh?" Theo stopped on his way past the living room.

"Yeah. He used to work for Marci's company, but he's been harassing her since his contract ended."

"What?" Theo's eyes widened in shock.

I pulled my phone out of my pocket. "He showed up at Marci's house at nine pm. I was there. She wasn't too worried, but he doesn't seem like a great guy." I shot off a text to Marci. She hadn't said anything about Dean to me since I'd been to her house.

Theo continued up the next set of stairs and I followed. He stopped in his bedroom, next to his desk. The room was much tidier than it had been the first time I'd seen it. "Jacob deserves some romantic attention, but if Dean's the kind of guy to harass people, then he can't be good for Jacob."

"No, but he probably has no idea. Dean seemed way friendlier tonight than when I saw him last."

"I bet." Theo scowled, probably at the thought of anyone bothering Marci. "I'll tell Jacob what you said."

My phone vibrated. "It's Marci. She said she hasn't seen or heard from Dean since that night at her house. So that's good at least." I was glad the harassment seemed to have stopped.

"Yeah, that's a relief," Theo agreed. "But Jacob should still know what kind of guy he is before he commits to anything." He pulled out his own phone and typed out a long text. He stared at the device, waiting for a response. "He must not be checking his phone right now."

"He'll get the message. Dean didn't seem dangerous or anything, so I don't think we have anything to worry about other than Jacob knowing who he's dealing with."

Theo nodded. "Yeah, I just wish I wasn't giving Jacob bad news."

"Up until this whole Dean thing, it seemed like you'd had a good day," I said, changing the subject, not wanting Theo to get down about Jacob's potential crush not being the right guy for him. "You were practically glowing with happiness when I got to the bookshop."

Theo turned to me. "Actually, my day kind of sucked. But this evening is really, *really* looking up." He slipped his arms around my waist and pulled me close.

I leaned in to kiss him. "I couldn't agree more."

Theo didn't waste much time before he was untucking my shirt and undoing its buttons. I pulled his sweater over his head, followed by the shirt underneath. The hickey I'd given him had faded and wasn't so noticeable now. I kissed the spot and Theo shivered.

He tugged me toward the bed, his eagerness drawing me in completely. I discarded my pants, then helped Theo take his off. He lay back and arched for me as I ran my hands over him. I trailed kisses over his body, up his neck, and nibbled gently on his earlobe, earning me many gorgeous little gasps.

"Tell me what you'd like, baby," I breathed in his ear.

Theo whimpered and didn't say anything right away. I continued to kiss him, everywhere but his mouth, giving him all the time he needed to respond.

He sunk his hands into my hair. "I'd like to suck you off." He paused. "And then maybe you could, you know, do the same for me?"

I pulled back and looked down at him. He was bright eyed. "I'd love that, Theo." I moved off him into a kneeling position and Theo sat up. "You're always welcome to tell me what to do, by the way."

"*Oh,*" he breathed, clearly liking that idea. "You're going to kill me, Luca."

"Kill you?" I reached out and traced his lips with a finger. "Do you want me to stop?"

His tongue darted out to caress my finger. "No."

I slipped my finger into Theo's mouth. He sucked it eagerly, his eyes fixed on me. "Look at you," I murmured.

Theo's gaze dropped and I let my finger slide from his mouth. "You make me feel so sexy, Luca."

Warm, affectionate feelings swelled inside me. I stroked his cheek and he met my eyes again. "You are, baby."

"It's like everything I do gets you going." Theo trailed a hand up my leg.

I let out a breath. "It does."

Theo's smile twisted mischievously as he gently pushed my hip.

I laid back, letting him settle between my legs and strip my underwear away. "The way you're looking at me right now, Theo, it's like you can't wait to get your mouth on me. It's stunning."

Theo tucked his head, blushing. "I can't hide anything, can I?"

"Do you want to? I love watching you blush and search for the right words."

He looked up. "No, I don't want to hide. I want to show you how good you make me feel." Theo leaned down and captured my mouth in a kiss. He didn't hold back.

I got lost in Theo as his kisses moved down my body. Each of his touches felt purposeful and designed to cherish me, sometimes tender and sweet, other times almost fevered in intensity, like he was losing himself too.

He looked up at me as he wrapped his lips around my cock, his hair tousled, glasses framing his face. Theo took his time, trying different things and driving me wild. It was hard to sit back and take all the pleasure he gave me, to let someone focus on me for so long, but at the same time I craved Theo's affection. I'd let him do anything he wanted, accept any exposing feelings he inspired in me as long as it gave him happiness.

I never wanted to forget the way falling for him felt, like I was opening up to all these wonderful things. "Nothing in my life has ever been as good as you, Theo," I told him with unsteady words.

Theo made a pleased sound as he sucked me, running his hands over my body. It wasn't much longer until pleasure overwhelmed me. I grabbed one of his roaming hands and laced our fingers together, holding him tight as I came down his throat.

Theo bit his lip. "That was fun."

I laughed. "Fuck, I like you, Theo." He beamed and I pulled him by the hand, back up my body so we could kiss.

We stayed in each other's arms, nothing able to intrude on our happiness. I didn't think I'd ever felt quite like this, as if nothing would ever matter as much as the man in front of me. I wanted to give Theo all my feelings and see where our lives led together. I was sure it would be somewhere good.

25

THEO

I woke up pressed against Luca's side, his arm around me. As I stirred, his fingers ran through my hair.

"Good morning, beautiful," he murmured in a deep almost-purr.

I snuggled in tighter, not wanting to get up. Ever. "Morning."

Luca didn't seem to be in a hurry either. He massaged my head and I almost fell back asleep, but as much as I wanted to, I couldn't ignore my responsibilities.

"We should probably get up," I said eventually.

"You're right." Luca stretched. The last time he'd left me on a weekday morning he'd gone much earlier than this. He took his hand out of my hair. "Is it all right if I steal the first shower?"

I agreed and lounged a bit longer in bed as Luca disappeared into the bathroom. I wasn't exactly looking forward to today. My phone showed several missed texts from my siblings. I decided to open them later.

When I got out of my turn in the shower, Luca was gone. It surprised me, and given my mood had already dipped, it left me disproportionately sad. I mean, he probably had to hurry home before work to change out of yesterday's clothes, but he hadn't said bye. Unless I'd missed him calling out?

I got dressed and went down to the kitchen, half hoping Luca would be there. He wasn't.

As I got a mug out of the cabinet, the door to the stairs opened.

"Ah, I really thought I'd be quick enough." Luca came in, carrying a coffee tray and a paper bag.

"You went to get us coffee?" I put my mug down, smiling. This made way more sense than him disappearing on me.

Luca put everything on the counter and leaned in to kiss me. "I got you tea."

"I thought you'd left." I couldn't help saying even though it revealed my insecurity.

Luca looked dismayed, not annoyed with my silly assumption. "Sorry, baby. I thought it would be a good surprise."

I hugged him. "No, it is a good surprise. Treats will always make me smile." I peaked in the bag and found a variety of Danishes. "I don't know why I thought you weren't coming back."

Luca kept his hand on the small of my back. "Something's got you down."

I looked away from the pastries. He was right. Even knowing Luca had done something sweet for me didn't bring my mood back up to where it'd been when I'd first opened my eyes this morning.

"What's wrong, Theo?"

I shrugged, hoping it might help shake off some of my feelings. "I'm not looking forward to work today, like I usually do. But it's not just that." I told Luca about my siblings stopping by last night. "I kind of yelled at them."

Luca frowned. "Do you wish you hadn't?"

"No." I pulled a pastry out of the bag and took a bite. "What I said needed to be out there, and they needed to know how mad I was. I just don't like confronting people. I don't like upsetting them even when I know the alternative will leave me as the hurt one." I had another bite of pastry. "I didn't actually say most of the things I needed to, and now I'm dreading it." I paused. "Do you still want to be there with me when I talk to them?"

"Yes, of course I'll be there." Luca brushed a flake of pastry from my chin.

I bit my lip. "Then maybe we should get it over with. I could text them and ask everyone to come by the shop when I close tonight."

"Okay. Should I plan to meet you then?"

"If that works for you?" I knew Luca didn't usually leave his office that early in the evening. Come to think of it, he'd be late if he didn't get going soon.

"It will work," Luca said without hesitation. "Don't worry about scheduling or timing, Theo. This is important, and I'll be there."

"Thank you." I picked up my tea and had a sip.

We ate the pastries in silence for a few minutes. It was exactly the kind of couple's morning I liked. If everything else hadn't been weighing me down, I'd have been bouncing around with happiness.

Luca checked his phone with an air of reluctance. "I should go." He leaned in and kissed me on the cheek, then seemed to reconsider and kissed me on the lips.

There was that giddy happiness I wanted from this morning. It fluttered in my chest and I kept Luca there with me, kissing in the kitchen long enough that we were both going to be late.

THE DAY TURNED out not to be as bad as the one before. Most of my customers seemed to have heard from friends about what had happened, so I was saved having to explain why the shop had so few things for sale, and no one mentioned the tea.

I spent most of the morning putting together the seminar I was going to give at the school next month, and when the bell above the door sounded, I felt a bit dazed from getting lost in deep concentration.

I blinked, letting my eyes focus as Edwin entered the shop. This time he arrived without Luca's sister or Juliet. "Hi," I called out, glad to see him.

The man returned my smile. "How are you doing today, Theo?"

I shrugged. "Fine enough. I'm guessing you have some news for me?"

Edwin took the strange metal coin out of his pocket and placed it on the counter. "I do, though don't get your hopes up too much."

I had been, and tried to quell the sense of growing relief I felt, thinking that one of my problems was about to be solved. I adjusted my glasses.

Edwin tapped the coin. "Juliet and I both had a look at this. She sends her apologies, she was busy today and couldn't make the trip with me."

"Oh, that's okay. I was only expecting a phone call, to be honest."

"Ah." Edwin paused, seeming vaguely uncomfortable. "I suppose that would have been sufficient. I have a lot of free time these days and figured I'd just stop in."

"I appreciate it," I assured him.

He seemed relieved to hear it, his awkwardness much more noticeable now that the others weren't with him. I found that endlessly relatable.

"I'm sorry I don't have better news." Edwin focused on the coin. "But this was created by a magical manufacturing company that specializes in charmed objects, rather than by an individual. They sell these, and other coins that give off sensations like happiness, or drowsiness. Whoever left this in your shop would have bought it, not created it themselves."

"So there's no way for it to lead us to them." I was disappointed but made myself move on. "Oh, well. I appreciate you checking. It's not like it was *that* likely to lead us to whoever stole my tea."

It was possible everything was connected but that didn't mean it was. The coin probably wasn't related to the theft, even if it was a strange thing for someone to drop here accidentally.

Edwin followed my gaze to the empty pedestal on the counter. "Your mysterious crystal customer still hasn't returned?"

"No." There was a long pause, as if neither of us knew what to say next.

"Seems like we weren't much more help that the Authority after all." Edwin rubbed the back of his neck, frowning. "If anything else comes up, please feel free to call."

"Sure thing," I agreed, but I probably needed to come to terms with the fact that Graywoods tea might be gone for good. I might never know what any of this strangeness had been about.

Edwin half turned to go, only to hesitate. "I hope to see you and Luca at Christmas."

That pushed my worries more firmly to the side. "Yeah, me too. I'd like to get to know Luca's, um, friends." They were all very welcoming, even if Luca had implied they were his sister's friends rather than his.

Edwin seemed to be thinking along the same lines. "I hope Luca does become a friend. I think Aria would like seeing him more, and my boyfriend, Tristan, seemed to get along with him well."

I'd resolved not to close myself off, and this seemed like the perfect chance not to. I seized it. "Why don't you let me know next time you're in town. Maybe we can all meet up."

Edwin blinked as if he were surprised. "I'd like that, thank you."

It was something to look forward to, and made the shop break-in seem less like a total loss if I met some good people out of it. Made a new friend or two.

26

LUCA

*B*eing with Theo made me happy in a way I didn't think I'd ever been. It gave me clarity and inspired me to prioritize the things I cared about, as well as confront the things I was unhappy with. I wasn't going to try to avoid or ignore my problems any longer.

I hated my job, and had for a while if I was being honest with myself. I needed to do something about it. Letting myself take time off and committing to more sociable hours might be a start, but was nowhere near enough. It wouldn't solve the problem. With that in mind, I was planning to talk to one of the senior partners today. Something needed to change even if I wasn't completely sure what form I wanted that change to take.

I couldn't keep pretending that work consuming my life was what I wanted. I shouldn't have to constantly use work to prove myself, trying to earn a place in the lives of the people I wanted to love and respect me.

I'd left my feelings of stress and unhappiness festering for too long. It shouldn't have taken Theo to get me to address them, but for the first time in my life I wasn't worried that my worth lay in getting everything right. I didn't have to be perfect for

Theo, and his opinion of me wouldn't change with my job. He wouldn't think less of me no matter what career choices I made.

It was midmorning and I had done fuck all work. My emails were unanswered. My research for the upcoming case untouched since last night. I wasn't trying to be a bad employee, but confronting my unhappiness made it almost impossible to endure what I'd previously been forcing myself to do.

My phone buzzed. I smiled, assuming it was Theo, but the text wasn't from him. My spark of joy soured instantly. It was my father.

His text said: *I can see what you might like in the apothecary but it's not the time to settle, Luca. You've had your fun dating him, but is he what you want for your future? You've aimed high your whole life, don't let an attractive face distract you.*

I wanted to smash my phone. Was this why he'd called last night? How could he think saying this was okay?

I took a deep breath, needing to focus on one thing at a time, and checked the phone's clock. I'd requested a meeting with Mr. Ellicott first thing this morning and he'd been able to find fifteen minutes to spare, and scheduled it in. I left my office, heading over to his a few minutes early, not wanting to cut into the short time I'd been given.

Mr. Ellicott's office had a wall of solid glass facing the corridor. I could see him on the phone and waited, trying not to hover too obtrusively outside. I was nervous and not expecting this meeting to be easy.

"Has there been a development since Sunday?" Ellicott didn't waste time on greetings as he opened his door.

I entered the office. "No. That's not what I wanted to speak to you about."

Ellicott frowned as I took a seat in front of his desk, not hiding his disappointment in my lack of progress since the weekend. He took his own seat, waiting.

I had no idea what to say. How to begin.

"What's this about then, Luca?" Ellicott steepled his fingers. "You look concerned. It's making me worried."

"Yes." I swallowed. "I am concerned."

Ellicott continued to wait. I was usually more articulate than this.

"Concerned about my position here," I managed at last.

The man nodded. "I understand, but we trust you, Luca. We're confident you'll work things out. Your position isn't in question."

"Oh. Good." I shifted in my seat, anxiety sneaking up on me like it hadn't since I'd been in school, taking final exams.

Ellicott had completely misunderstood me, and in doing so reminded me I was about to disappoint him. I was expected to keep on as I had been. But I couldn't, and admitting it made me feel like I wasn't good enough. All the respect I'd earned here was about to be trashed. I might not value that respect or my position as senior associate more than my wellbeing, but that didn't make it simple to discard these things.

I'd spent my whole life validating my worth through success; changing my frame of mind was terrifying. Everything I knew was screaming at me not do this.

"Is there anything else?" Ellicott glanced at his phone.

"Yes." I turned away and looked out the window. "That wasn't what I meant."

"Luca, you aren't acting like yourself."

I continued to study the neighboring skyscrapers. "I'm not managing well. I think I might need some time off."

"Now isn't really the best time for more days off."

I forced my attention away from the window and met Mr. Ellicott's eye. "It's not something I can time. I can't keep doing this."

"*This* as in your job?" He raised a brow skeptically.

"I don't know. Maybe. I'm not able to keep up with the constant stress. I was thinking, maybe I could take a step back. Return to my previous position as an associate." I'd mulled this over all morning. My previous lower-level position might not be as stressful as it'd been before, if I wasn't trying to work my way up, and might give me enough breathing room. Maybe this was wishful thinking, but I had to start somewhere. It would be better than the situation I was now.

My boss's brow creased in concentrated confusion. "Moving backwards isn't exactly how this works, Luca."

"Then what can I do?" I was getting the impression I hadn't explained myself well, but everything about this made me uncomfortable. I couldn't tell him I was miserable and felt like I'd misprioritized my life. I couldn't tell him I was becoming paralyzed by fear and stress, and was unable to get through the work day.

Mr. Ellicott paused, like he was at least trying to figure out how to help. "I don't think I quite understand the problem."

I tried to explain without saying I hated being here and no longer found value in my success. I focused on stress and long hours, the never-ending tasks and ever-increasing expectations.

"This has come out of nowhere, Luca. You've been a senior associate for two years. You always knew what the position would entail." Mr. Ellicott seemed at a loss, and no more comfortable than I was. He clearly wasn't happy with me. I could almost see him thinking, eyes narrowed, about all the problems I was creating.

"I'm sorry." I looked away, even though I was fairly certain this wasn't something I should apologize for.

"Why don't you take some time to decide how you want to proceed." Ellicott picked up a pen and noted something down on a piece of paper on his desk. "If stepping down to your old role is what you want, we can do that. However, I can't promise the opportunity for promotion will come around again."

I had the vague sense he should be offering more than that. Trying to find some way to help make the position I had manageable, but I'd never really expected that kind of support to be on the table. You could either take it or you couldn't. It was part of why I'd put off saying anything.

I stood. "I'll have a decision for you by Monday."

"Monday?" He sounded incredulous. "You need the rest of the week?"

I nodded, knowing I was doing the right thing for me, but feeling terrible about it. It hurt that the employer I'd spent so many years doing everything I could for didn't seem to care. Yet the urge to not disappoint my boss was almost overwhelming, even when I knew gaining his approval wouldn't help me. This environment being unmanageable wasn't my fault. I wasn't a failure for needing a break or a change. I just couldn't help feeling like one.

I left immediately. Maybe I should have done a bit of handover, made sure my critical tasks for the week didn't get forgotten, but it was surprisingly easy to check out now that everything wasn't trapped inside me.

If this was a disappointment, fine. If choosing to put myself first was failure, then that was what I was. If people wanted to see me that way I couldn't do anything about it, just remind myself not to buy into their judgment.

I crossed the city and found myself sitting idly in Dolores Park, a few blocks from home. I pulled out my phone and called my sister.

"You had the right idea avoiding our parents," I said after Aria picked up.

"Yeah, I know." She sounded smug, as I might have expected. "Why are you calling to tell me that?"

I told Aria everything. Work. Our father. My skewed ideas about why I'd been bad at dating, and why I'd been afraid to try. All the set-ups. Even though the unwanted dates and trying to marry me off had been going on for a while, I hadn't mentioned it to Aria before now. She was irate about the whole thing.

"I'm getting Edwin to teleport me up there. This is bullshit, Luca. We need to tell them that. Loudly."

"It's not that easy."

Her voice softened. "I know. It's not like I've ever been able to handle them."

"Which is why leaving was smart." I crossed the arm that wasn't holding the phone over my chest and tucked my hand into my armpit, glaring at a pigeon.

Aria huffed a dry laugh. "But I didn't mean to leave you too. I didn't realize our parents were like this with you. They always acted like you were the gold standard. If I'd known—do you need me to come up there?"

"I appreciate the offer, but I'll talk to them."

"And when they don't listen?" Aria wasn't being pessimistic, she just knew what I was dealing with.

"I'll stop taking their calls. Figure out maintaining boundaries, or something." I sighed, slumping on the park bench. "Father has been really shitty about Theo. I guess my threshold for ignoring his behavior is a lot lower when it's directed at someone else than it's ever been for myself."

I'd wanted a fake boyfriend so my father would leave me alone. It had been a flawed plan from the start, but being left alone was still what I needed. If my parents didn't like or approve of my life, they didn't need to keep being in it.

"You're doing the right thing, Luca. Not just for Theo, but for you."

I sighed. "Maybe our parents will come around to seeing our side of things when they realize they're alone and neither of their kids want to see them."

"Maybe." Aria didn't sound totally convinced. "And your job? What's happening with that?"

"I'm figuring it out."

I could imagine her narrowed eyes. "I'm holding you to that." She paused. "Have you talked to Marci about it?"

"No." I stared off in the direction of Marci's house; I could just see it from here. "I'll talk to Theo, I think."

"That's great." Aria sounded as soft and mushy as I'd ever heard her. "I know I didn't meet him at the best time, but he seems like a good person to talk to."

"Yeah?" I smiled.

"He had a very sweet vibe. It's what you and I need in our partners."

"He's a lot more than that."

"Of course he is, Luca." Aria was back to sounding annoyed. "He's a whole person. I just can't say much else since I've only met him for like half a second."

"We'll fix that. I want to make this work with him."

"You will Luca, don't worry."

I was trying not to, and for the most part succeeding. Things felt good with Theo. Taking risks with him felt like something we were doing together.

Aria cleared her throat, letting me know I'd been silent too long. "So your job. You're figuring it out?"

"Yes," I promised, even if my plan of attack was far from solid. Would I be happy going back to my old position, or did I need more of a change than that?

Aria made a *humph* sound. "I cannot believe you tried to get me to work there."

"I'm sorry." I spared a moment to be thankful that scheme hadn't worked out, for both our sakes. "I just missed you, Aria."

"Then come visit me for Christmas."

I agreed to that and she hung up, sounding pleased.

WITH NOTHING but a free afternoon ahead of me, I decided to bite the bullet and see my father. Theo was committed to having a hard conversation with his family tonight, so I could do the same.

I took the train across the bay and hopped in a rideshare to my parents' house. They were both retired—despite my father's habit of dressing in a suit and spending most of his time in his home office—and lived in a somewhat grandiose home on a sizable plot of land in the East Bay.

I entered the massive foyer, greeted by familiar magical artifacts and old furniture. My mother was still out of town, so I headed directly to father's office where I found him with several law books laid out in front of him, as well as a notebook and pen.

"Luca." He seemed alarmed to see me. "Is everything all right?"

I entered and found a seat in front of the desk. "No, things aren't all right."

"What are you doing here in the middle of the day? Why aren't you at work?" He took the tone of a parent scolding a child for skipping school.

I ignored his questions. I wasn't here to hash it out over my job. "That text you sent this morning was not okay."

"Text?" My father put his pen down and closed his notebook.

"What does that have to do with you being here in person? You could have messaged me back."

"You can't talk about Theo that way."

"Luca." My father sighed, as if he were about to begin a lecture.

"No." I leveled a cold stare at him. "He's who I've chosen to be with. You need to respect that. You've never respected my wishes when it comes to dating, and I'm not making excuses for how you act toward Theo."

My father frowned. "I've never disrespected your wishes."

"You knew I didn't want to be set up, or marry someone as a career move. And don't pretend you didn't. Why else would you have had to *trick* me into meeting people? I told you to stop it and you didn't listen. So hear me now: cut it out and rein in your judgy opinions about Theo. This part of my life is not your call. You get no say. And if you don't respect that, don't expect to see me around in future because I will choose him over everything else without regret."

Father's face was tight with anger. "Good god, you sound like your sister."

"Thank you." I knew he hadn't meant it as a compliment.

My father let out an exasperated sound. "I'm only trying to do what's best for you, Luca."

"What's best for me is supporting me and accepting the choices I make. I've let you think it was okay to call the shots for too long, but I've had enough."

"Fine." My father pushed his chair back from his desk and stood. "Make this mistake if you have to. Once you've thought about it, figured out what it will cost you, feel free to come back and see me. I will always support you in getting back on track."

I stood to face him. "I have thought about this. I've never been more sure of anything. Once *you've* thought about what I've said, let me know. Don't bother calling sooner."

27

THEO

Edwin had taken the enchanted coin away with him but I was still feeling uneasy. The difference from last week was I knew exactly why. Sadie, Tobias, and Stella were due to arrive any minute.

Luckily, when the bell chimed, it was Luca who entered. "You'll never guess who I just saw." He let the door swing shut behind him.

"Who?"

Luca frowned. "The crystal guy."

"What?" I dropped the sketchbook I was holding, eyeing Luca as he made his way across the shop. "Where?"

"On the street." Luca came around the counter to give me a hug. "I was on the bus heading over here, but I swear it was him I saw out the window."

"Do you think he's coming to Graywoods?" I looked around the mostly empty shop.

"Maybe. He was headed the same direction I was, but I lost him pretty quick. We were quite a few blocks away from here. So, who knows."

I unlocked the crystal drawer and looked at it. "Hm. I guess we'll see. Though he better not come when the others are here."

Luca rubbed my back. "We could go up to your apartment. Talk to your siblings where we won't be interrupted."

Some of my tension melted away. "I'd rather stay in the shop."

"Why's that?"

I turned to lean back against the counter, facing Luca. "Graywoods is my place. It's easiest for me to be exactly who I want here. It's where my insecurities don't rule me. Maybe that's silly, but I need the boost for this."

"It's not silly, Theo." Luca shifted closer, brushing some of my hair back from my forehead.

"You're right. I don't really think it's silly. It's just, um. It's not the kind of thing I've ever admitted to anyone."

Luca gazed at me with warm affection. "Thank you for trusting me to understand."

I smiled a tiny smile. Some people might think my feelings about Graywoods were strange, but not Luca. "I've always wondered if people can tell, on some level. Do you think I'm different here?"

Luca's fingers brushed my cheek. "You do seem to give off a sense of ownership of your shop. As you should. But I've seen you be just as confident and sure of yourself elsewhere. Like in the woods talking about mushrooms. At dinner with my father. When we're alone together."

I glowed. "I think I've felt it too. It's easy to be the Graywoods me when I'm with you."

"It's who you are." Luca leaned in and laid a soft kiss on my lips. "I like the man you've shown me, Theo. A lot."

Something told me he was even counting the things I wished I hadn't let Luca see. I slipped my arms around his waist. "You're so different than I thought you'd be, that night of our blind date."

"Oh?" His brow crinkled. "That can only be a good thing. I hope."

"It is," I assured him. "You've shown me your true self too, you know. It's just, why did you tell me you didn't want a boyfriend that night? It's obvious now I look back that you wanted a relationship as much as I did. You're so caring and really not casual at all."

Luca gave me an embarrassed smile. "I didn't want to admit that I'd blown it with you. I've always lied to myself about what I wanted as much as anyone else. It made it easier to pretend I never wanted a boyfriend than to face not being good enough."

"Oh." I cocked my head, taking him in. "Not being right for someone isn't about not being good enough."

"I know." Luca closed his eyes for a second. "But I couldn't help seeing it that way for a long time. I'm beginning to realize I grew up learning to take rejection and others' disappointment as a personal failure, and let that attitude seep into other aspects of my life."

Luca opened up and told me about the constant pressure he felt to be perfect. How he feared people would only like him if he was a certain way, and how this bled into his work. How the stress of his job had been consuming him for a long time, but he hadn't been able to deal with it. He'd been unable to face change when he saw it as a reason for people to dislike him.

"You've helped me realize so many things, Theo." Luca's voice was thick with emotion. "I needed someone's acceptance so much more than I realized. We both needed someone to see our vulnerabilities and not turn them into something to be ashamed of."

I took hold of his hand and squeezed. "I never wanted you to be perfect, Luca. I just want you to be real."

"Well my life is about to get really messy. I haven't yet, but I think I need to come to terms with resigning from my job. Stepping back like I suggested to my boss today isn't going to be enough. But it's going to be hard to do this even if it's what I want." He tried to smile but it was more of a grimace.

I dropped his hand and hugged him around the middle. "I'll be there for you. However long you need to figure it out. Whatever you do. Just like you've been for me."

"I knew you would be." Luca's smile turned radiant and uncomplicated. "I knew you'd see this as nothing but a good thing. And you've helped me finally see it too."

I tugged Luca down to meet me in a kiss. I may have liked the look of him when I'd bought into his hot flawless Witch act, but I liked this vulnerable Luca infinitely more. I liked him for being the one to push us not to hide behind a fake relationship. I liked him for continuing to put it all out there. He was the most genuine person I'd ever met.

We kissed for what felt like ages. I was keen to keep it going, and would have dragged him upstairs if I weren't expecting people.

Eventually I pulled back. "Maybe walking in on us making out isn't the best start to this chat with my siblings."

"Probably not." Luca looked toward the door. "Seems like they're running late."

"Maybe they've been held up getting here." I hoped they weren't putting me off now I'd said we'd needed to talk. But they wouldn't, right? Not after agreeing to meet me. "Anyway, I don't want anyone else coming in, so I might as well close up." I walked out from behind the counter. "I'll text Tobias and say to call when they arrive."

At the front of the shop I reach for the first curtain, starting to pull it shut. As I did so, I saw the mysterious crystal man out the window. I was shocked. Even after Luca had sworn he'd seen him in the neighborhood, I hadn't actually expected the guy to be on his way here.

But maybe he wasn't. He was across the street and didn't even glance at Graywoods as he continued down the block.

"The man is back!" I called to Luca, not taking my eyes of the guy. "And he's not even coming in. What the hell?"

He crossed the street, coming to this side, but he was past my shop now. I opened the door and popped my head out. The man didn't turn around or notice me as he disappeared into Quill's.

"Maybe he's getting a book before coming to see you," Luca said from behind me.

"I dunno. The way he crossed the street made it seem like he was avoiding Graywoods, not wanting to walk in front of my windows."

Graywoods should have been closed fifteen minutes ago. If the man had needed a book, he still should have come to see me first. It made it seem like he was avoiding coming back for his useless crystal. And maybe I shouldn't have cared. He'd paid. But I needed one of my mysteries solved, and this was currently the only one I could do anything about.

I narrowed my eyes at the bookshop door. "Whatever he's doing, I want the damned crystal gone. Will you wait here while I run next door and ambush him?"

I turned around to find a bemused look on Luca's face. "Sure, I can do that."

"Thanks, be right back." I squeezed Luca's arm and rushed off.

28

THEO

I opened the door to Quill's and stopped short in the doorway, thrown off by the animosity I'd walked in on.

The man was at the counter, talking to Jacob. Or more accurately, snarling at Jacob. "What do you mean you don't know where he is?" he practically shouted.

"Exactly that." Jacob stayed calm, his eyes flicking quickly to me in acknowledgment, then back to his irate customer.

The man's back was to me and he didn't seem to notice my entrance. I carefully shut the door, resolving to lurk here and jump in if it looked like Jacob needed me.

The bookseller seemed to have it covered for now. His voice was stern as he said, "Why do you think I'd know where Dean is? Or that I would tell you? I've never met you before."

Dean? That man seemed to be coming up a lot. I'd talked to Jacob about him earlier. He'd been reluctant to believe the man had a hidden nasty side, but had agreed to ask Dean about his conduct with Marci and see if the man denied it or had his own side of the story to tell.

The crystal man placed his palms on the bookshop counter

and leaned forward in an intimidating fashion. "Don't pretend you two aren't working together. Like he hasn't already filled me in. Now tell me where to find him, or else tell me what the hell is going on."

Jacob crossed his arms, not backing down in the face of the other Witch's aggression. "I don't know what's going on, or what you're talking about."

"The dreams!" the man shouted.

My stomach dropped. *Wait, what?*

"Why the fuck am I having nightmares all the time?" The man pounded the counter. "Ever since Dean hired me for your little scheme, it's been happening. He said the whole thing was your idea." He jabbed a finger at Jacob.

My friend started to look uneasy. He glanced at me again, seeming confused. This time the man noticed Jacob's darting eyes.

I was frozen. What was the guy talking about? Were his dreams like mine?

He turned to see me standing there and shifted his accusatory pointing to me. "This guy. Dean said it was something with your neighbor."

Jacob gave me a helpless look.

"What about me?" I asked the angry Witch.

"I gave you that crystal and ever since I've been having these terrible dreams. I can't figure out how to make it stop."

"And what does that have to do with Jacob?" I felt cold. There was no way my friend was behind any of the strangeness plaguing me, but what if he was? Maybe Jacob already knew Dean wasn't a good guy, and that was why he'd been resistant to my warning.

"Dean said it was a game." The guy glared at me as if any of it were my fault. "I do odd jobs, and one day he asked me to take the crystal to your shop, hide a coin, and that it was all for some game the three of you played."

"A game? Then why did you show up at my mom's party?" It all sounded like nonsense.

"That was part of it." The man shrugged. "Some stupid mystery thing, or something. I was meant to be intimidating. Keep you guessing."

"I have no idea what he's talking about," Jacob cut in, his voiced raised in exasperation.

"You'd lie about it now, wouldn't you?" The man refocused on the bookseller. "Now it's gone wrong and the dream curse got me instead of him. No one warned me there was a risk."

"But I'd never curse Theo." One of Jacob's hands flew to his chest as if he were aghast at the idea.

I believed him, I did, but had a horrible flash of doubt. "Why would Dean curse me? He doesn't know me. Other than you telling him all about my dates with Luca. Why—why'd you really tell him all that? What's going on?"

Jacob shook his head, a bit frantic. "Wait. I know I went overboard sharing, but I was just excited for you, Theo. It was nothing more. And I liked talking to Dean. He seemed interested in me, and my life and friends—I—I don't know. I'd never even suspect a bad thing about him until your text."

"If these two have it out for you"—the man interrupted, directing his warning tone at me—"because who's the fool that thinks this is still a friendly game? They'd have had to trick someone into delivering the curse to you. Otherwise how would they get past your shop's protection if their intentions were bad? Couldn't give you the crystal themselves, could they?"

"*Oh my god,*" I breathed, staring at Jacob in disbelief.

"No." Jacob shook his head, eyes wide. "I'd never do that."

"But I've been getting weird dreams too," I said, feeling hollow.

Jacob seemed surprised by that, his mouth falling silently open.

Except this made no sense. Everyone who'd looked at the crystal had said it was harmless. But then, the man had just admitted to hiding the coin, which hadn't been harmless. Apparently it *was* all connected.

Why would Dean get this guy to do any of this, if Jacob wasn't involved? I'd only met Dean yesterday.

"Did you trash my shop?" I asked Jacob.

He recoiled like I'd slapped him. "No. Of course not, Theo."

I wanted to believe him, but had to ask, "Did you steal my tea?"

"No." Jacob shook his head adamantly. "You can search my shop. My home. Anywhere. I swear on the moon and stars I'd never steal from you." He seemed close to tears.

I refocused on the still unnamed man. "You. Did you break in and rob me?"

He looked dumbfounded.

"It has to be Dean." Jacob sounded strangled. "He—he's lied saying I had anything to do with this. You were right about him, Theo, but I swear I had no idea. Not about your friend Marci, or any of it."

I had the urge to pull at my hair in frustration. "But why would he do this?"

"I don't know, Theo."

"Well this is shit," the man said. "You two are totally useless. Call Dean and get him over here. He's avoiding me and I need these dreams gone. Do something about it."

"Or you could fuck off," Jacob growled, finally seeming to lose his patience.

It was the wrong move. The man called up his magic with one swift motion of his ring-clad hand. He barked an incantation and the shop plunged into complete blackness. The street outside was no longer visible, even though the streetlights should have shone through the windows. It was like we were cut off from the whole world. I couldn't even see my feet.

Someone grabbed my arm, twisting it painfully. I yelped in surprise and the man snarled close to my ear. As I tried to fight back he pulled all the rings off my trapped hand.

"Don't you dare hurt him," Jacob shouted through the dark. He called out an illumination spell, but it didn't penetrate the unnatural blackness surrounding us.

The man was already stripping me of the rest of my rings, taking away my ability to do magic. They clinked onto the wooden floor.

Jacob couldn't seem to figure out what spell would help me, but it sounded like he was trying, casting immobilizing spells and different kinds of illuminations, but the darkness seemed to have some kind of anti-magic property. None of the spells worked.

Once my rings were gone, and my shoulders both felt sprained from being yanked around, the man dragged me back toward the counter. He did something I couldn't see with his other hand and a light appeared between him and Jacob, who was still on the other side of the counter. "Now call Dean, or I'll break his arm."

I tried not to whimper as the man twisted my arm further behind my back, but I couldn't help it.

Jacob met my eyes. "Please Theo, believe me. I've had no part in any of this."

I nodded. "I know, it's okay."

I wasn't sure for any unimpeachable reason, only because Jacob sounded so genuinely sad. He was my friend and I didn't want him to have had anything to do with this. If he was in on it, surely he would have dealt with the man better, rather than acting like he had no idea what was happening. He would have shooed me away when I'd come in and spotted them together, and his attempt to help just now didn't feel like an act.

I knew Jacob better than that, and trusted that he hadn't been fake with me all these years. He hadn't been lying and sneering behind my back like Jason, or plotting to ruin and mess with me. Even as worried about secret judgments or motivations as I was, I knew I could spot the good people. I wouldn't doubt Jacob any more than I'd doubt Luca, or Marci for that matter.

The man shook me threateningly. "Make the call."

Jacob pulled out his phone, his hands shaking. He set it on the counter so we could see, then pulled up Dean's contact. He pressed call, and turned it to speaker.

"Hey, gorgeous," Dean answered in a shamelessly flirty tone.

Jacob closed his eyes. "Hey, I've got a friend of yours here looking for you."

"What?" Dean sounded surprised but still light and airy.

"At the bookshop. He's been saying some strange things. Um." Jacob's voice shook. "About dreams. And the apothecary next door. Your friend thinks you can help him with the dreams, but I have no idea what he's talking about."

The line was quiet. "Sorry, hun. Fuck. What the hell is Joe doing bothering you?"

"So you know what I'm talking about?" Jacob sounded dismayed, and looked hurt to hear Dean admit this didn't all sound unintelligible to him.

"Look, hun." Dean paused. "I know you can keep a secret for me, right?"

"Sure." Jacob sounded normal but narrowed his eyes, his mouth set into a hard line.

"Joe has been helping me with this little project. I'd hoped the dreams wouldn't affect him. The spell was meant to slowly dissipate from the crystal I'd placed it on, and it shouldn't have been with him long enough for the effects to stick."

"But you hired Joe to give bad dreams to my neighbor? Is that what you're saying? With a crystal?" An even deeper confusion seemed to overtake Jacob. His last question had sounded incredulous.

"Look, it's important the apothecary doesn't find out about this." Dean was very serious now. "He can't connect me with anything going wrong with his shop."

What, had this guy stolen my tea? I met Jacob's eyes in disbelief. He looked as shocked as I felt. There was no way Jacob had known Dean was doing this before now, Jacob wasn't that good of an actor. He wore all his emotions out in the open.

But what was Dean doing with the dreams and hiring some guy to hide a creepy coin in my shop? Was he causing me trouble to distract from the robbery? Setting up false leads with some mysterious crystal guy?

"Why can't Theo find out about this?" Jacob asked, sounding hollowed out.

Dean's answer came through in a knowing tone. "Let's just say I'm aware that the apothecary has had some things go missing from his shop."

"But I never told you about the robbery," Jacob blurted out.

"No, but you've been so good at telling me everything else."

I had no idea how well Jacob knew Dean, or if their relationship had gone beyond flirting, but it was looking like Dean had used him. Whoever robbed me would have had to know I wasn't home that night. Jacob might have told his crush I was out on a date, if they'd happened to be talking. Or if Dean had been fishing for information while putting on his charm for Jacob.

A similar realization must have been going through Jacob's head. He looked miserable, like he'd been betrayed, his grip on the counter strained. "You've been using me. Do you even—was none of it real?"

My heart ached for my friend.

"Okay, enough of this crap," the man—Joe—said gruffly. "Dean, get rid of these dreams or I'll be turning you in for robbing the apothecary, now I've heard what you've really been up to. Not to mention, it seems like you were setting me up to take the fall. Mystery game, my ass."

"What? Joe? You've been *listening in*?" Dean's voice was irate.

A loud boom came from somewhere behind us, and we all looked up. The ground shook and then the spell sealing us in unnatural darkness melted away.

The shop door burst open and Luca was there, his eyes burning with intensity. He didn't hesitate as he rushed up to Joe, an incantation already passing his lips. The tattoos on his hand flashed and Joe's body jolted against mine like he'd been shocked, then his muscles went limp and his hold on me loosened.

Sadie and Tobias rushed in after Luca and the two of them took hold of the dazed Joe as Luca reached for me.

"Ow, fuck." I straightened my arm. As Luca inspected me for injuries, my eyes fell on Jacob.

He looked like he might be about to cry. The phone screen had gone dark, the call disconnected. "We need to send someone to search Dean's place before he gets rid of the evidence he robbed you."

"Shit." I wasn't sure we'd get there fast enough. I had no idea where he lived. What Dean said to us over the phone might not be enough evidence for the Authority if he hid the teapot well enough.

"I've got back up coming," Luca said as he brushed my bangs back from my face. "Sorry we didn't come sooner. I was talking to your siblings a while before we realized how long you'd been gone. Then we saw the bookshop sealed off."

"You broke the spell?" I sounded slightly awed, maybe I was dazed.

"With Sadie's help." Luca shrugged. "My magic tattoos give me a boost but I wouldn't have been able to unravel it as fast without her."

I looked gratefully to my siblings who were frowning at the still dazed Joe. "Where's Stella?"

"Here!" She entered the bookshop, throwing the door wide. "With the back up!"

Edwin, Juliet, and a woman with blue hair followed her inside. The place was packed with people.

"Oh!" I reached exaltedly toward Edwin, then winced at the pain in my shoulder. "You can teleport us over to catch Dean!"

Edwin looked from me, to Luca, then at Jacob, who was wiping his eyes. "I have no idea what's going on, but sure. Tell me where you need to go."

29

THEO

After filling everyone in, I stayed behind with my siblings, Luca, Jacob, and Joe as Edwin and his two companions teleported off to Dean's house. Luckily Jacob knew where Dean lived, though I doubted Jacob was feeling lucky about anything right now.

Edwin's blue-haired friend, Mea, was associated with the Authority and apparently able to deal with Dean and any evidence he might be caught with. It seemed like Mea, Juliet and Edwin had it covered.

Hopefully my tea wasn't lost after all.

As the three of them disappeared, Luca called up the local Authority branch to report what happened. The officials promised to send someone to collect Joe as soon as possible.

Sadie, Tobias and Stella took up Joe-watch at the front of the shop, keeping an eye out for the Authority, while Luca and I held back with Jacob.

The bookseller had his head in his hands, elbows braced on the counter. "I'm such a fool. You even warned me."

I rested a hand on Jacob's shoulder. "Someone using you and taking advantage of your kind, open nature doesn't make you a fool. And I only warned you in the last twenty-four hours, when it seems it was already too late."

"I thought he liked me." Jacob looked up, his face red in what I suspected was anger. "Dean seemed so interested in my life and I thought—*this is someone who knows how to care.*"

I rubbed his shoulder. "Well, I like that you consider me an important enough part of your life to want the people you like to care about me too."

"Really?" Jacob raised his brows skeptically. "If I hadn't been so keen to talk about you none of this would have happened. I told Dean you were out for the night. He must have been planning this all along and I had no idea."

"How could you have? There's nothing wrong with you wanting to get to know someone." I could have held Jacob's gossipy nature against him, but none of it came from a bad place. The things that were important to me were important to him, he liked feeling included in what was going on with me, and had shared that with someone he thought would care just as much as he did. Jacob had had no reason to doubt Dean, and by the time Luca and I gave him one it wouldn't have stopped any of this from happening.

"Thanks, Theo." Jacob took a heaving breath. "But I don't think I'll be opening up so easily again."

I could understand that.

The same two women from the Authority who'd seen me after Graywoods was broken into arrived to deal with Joe. After they took statements and left, Tobias offered to get dinner for everyone and left with our sisters.

As the bookstore door swung shut, Jacob beckoned Luca and me behind the curtain. The bookseller took a bottle of gin out of the reading desk's drawer and slumped in an armchair. He poured a measure into three teacups.

I took the other armchair, exhaustion hitting me as soon as I sat down. One sip of my drink and the gin seemed to go straight to my head.

Luca hovered, taking small sips from his teacup, his eyes hardly straying from me. We were all quiet. There didn't seem to be much more we could say, but I knew Jacob needed the company.

We ended up having pizza. My siblings were uncharacteristically silent as we ate. Tobias took a moment to heal my sprained shoulders with a spell, leaving only a slight soreness for me to deal with, but he kept fussing, looking at me like he was trying to figure out if I needed anything else.

Jacob looked up from his second teacup of gin. "Someone's here."

Luca put his pizza plate down on the coffee table and made his way to the front. He returned with Edwin, Juliet and Mea.

"How'd it go?" I perked up, some of my energy returning.

"Well." Mea seemed pleased. "For us at least. We found Dean trying to escape with your teapot."

"Where is it now?" I looked between the three of them.

"With the San Francisco Authority." Juliet took a seat in the desk chair. "They'll be calling you, Theo, and hopefully returning the tea set to you tomorrow."

"Oh my god, thank you." I beamed at the three of them.

"Do you all want some pizza?" Tobias offered from where he sat on the floor. We were all gathered around the coffee table, not wanting to eat too near any of the grimoires or other books in this part of the shop.

Juliet, Mea and Edwin all accepted slices of pizza.

"Did Dean say anything?" Jacob asked from behind his teacup.

"He admitted you had nothing to do with this," Edwin assured Jacob. "He didn't stick to Joe's story that there was a joint plan."

"So he just used me for information." Jacob glared off into space. "I'm surprised he bothered to say I wasn't involved. What does he care?"

Edwin glanced from Jacob to Mea, and she explained. "Dean started to cooperate once he realized he'd be questioned by an Authority psychic, able to detect if he was lying. People tend to be forthcoming after that, not wanting to create more trouble for themselves by getting caught in more lies."

Jacob *humphed*, seeming distinctly unimpressed.

"Did he say why he took Graywoods tea?" Sadie asked from the floor beside Tobias.

"He probably wanted to sell it," Stella guessed. "A unique magical artifact like that would be worth a lot."

"Actually, Dean wasn't after selling the teapot itself." Mea frowned, finishing the last of her pizza. "He was trying to figure out how the enchantment worked. Since the tea spell was essentially reading people like a psychic, he thought he could study it, copy the spell with some alterations, and create something that could reveal things beyond a person's perfect herbal blend. The resulting creation was what he wanted to sell."

I made an angry, high-pitched sound. "That's horrible. Distorting the magic like that. The whole purpose of the tea is to read people in order to give them a better connection to themselves and their magic, not to expose them to others."

"It was a devious plan." Juliet wiped her hands on a napkin. "All the spells on the teapot seemed intact, but you'll have to check. It didn't look like Dean had much success in his analysis. He said he hadn't been able to create any spelled objects based off what he'd learned from the teapot, but the Authority will have to double check that."

"I doubt he could have." Tobias grabbed another slice of pizza. "The tea spell was created by our uncle, but he made it in conjunction with his partner, who was a psychic. I doubt Dean could have created the kind of warped copy he was after if he didn't already have psychic power himself."

It was a strange reason to steal Graywoods tea. I'd never have considered the magic used in creating perfect brews from this perspective, but I guess a lot of Witches coveted extra abilities. Being able to create an approximation of psychic magic to sell via charmed objects would probably be profitable, even if it was totally unethical.

"Did he say anything else?" Luca asked.

Mea grimaced. "As we dropped him off at the local Authority branch, he started raving about Marcella Mendez."

Luca's eyes narrowed. "She's a friend of Theo's and mine. He's been harassing her. But what does that have to do with this?"

"It sounded like he first heard about Theo's tea from Marci," Mea explained. "He was rambling something about how Marci was ruining his tech career, making it impossible for him to get a job."

"She was not," Luca interjected in Marci's defense.

"I'm sure she wasn't," Mea assured him. "But he said if Marci was going to keep him from getting another job, he was going to use the tea he'd heard her going on about to get himself a new income stream."

"So this is all because Marci didn't renew the guy's contract?" Luca shook his head. "She thought she'd seen the end of it when he stopped turning up looking for her."

I swiped a hand through my hair. "At least nothing worse happened. Not that any of this was good, but I'd rather I got robbed than some guy continuing to stalk Marci."

"I swear he didn't seem like the kind of person to do any of this." Jacob slumped further into his armchair. "I'm so sorry, Theo."

"You don't have to be," I insisted. "Of course Dean wouldn't want you to think he was capable of anything bad. Then he wouldn't have been able to use you."

"Still." Jacob set his teacup down with a sense of finality. "None of this should have happened to you."

"Or to you." I reached out and clasped his arm.

Jacob nodded. "No, it shouldn't have. But it did. I think I'm going to go upstairs to bed. Find a good book to read. Swear off men and save myself any more of whatever the hell this was."

I got up, put out a hand, and pulled Jacob up from his chair. "I'll see you tomorrow?"

"I'll look forward to it, Theo." Jacob embraced me in a quick hug, then patted me awkwardly on the shoulder before ushering everyone out of his shop.

The rest of us trooped back to Graywoods.

"I think we'll say goodnight too," Juliet said once we were all inside.

"But if you have any trouble with the Authority, give me a call." Mea handed me a business card and I thanked her.

With that, Edwin teleported them away, leaving Luca and me with my siblings. Luca put an arm around me and rubbed my back. There was a strained silence.

"Fuck, Theo." Tobias made a weird, twisted sort of face that looked painful, then he crushed me into a hug. Luca took half a step back, I guess not wanting to intrude.

I tensed in Tobias' arms. "I'm fine."

He loosened up and looked down at me. "You didn't seem fine last night."

I squirmed out of his embrace. Tobias, Sadie and Stella all looked at me.

"You're right." I ran a hand through my hair, catching a glimpse of Luca's steadfast presence out of the corner of my eye. "I meant I was fine after all tonight's drama. But if we're talking about other things, I haven't been fine for a while."

"We had no idea Jason was like that." Stella looked devastated. Probably because she knew him best out of my siblings.

I crossed my arms. "I'm not just talking about Jason."

They all shared a confused look.

"I don't like the way you treat me." I braced myself as Stella blinked in shock and Tobias opened his mouth, but I pushed on. "You're always harassing me, treating me like my life needs fixing. Like I need to change who I am. But I like my life the way it is. I don't need to change it to make it look more like yours."

"We didn't mean to hassle you, Theo. Not in a serious way." Tobias glanced at our sisters, who both nodded.

"Well you have been. Always telling me I need to do things that make me uncomfortable. Acting like you have to drag me along with you, like I don't do anything on my own. Which isn't true. I want to do stuff with you. But not when you're always judging my life. It makes me want to avoid you."

"We aren't judging you, Theo." Sadie stepped forward and took my hand. "We thought we were being encouraging."

"You're not." I looked down at our hands. "I know you all want to look out for me, but the way you're going about it comes off as condescending and negative."

"I'm sorry, Theo." Tobias pulled Sadie and me into one big hug. "Hassling you was supposed to be friendly teasing. We don't think you have to be just like us, or want you to change who you are."

"We didn't realize it didn't feel friendly to you," Stella added from behind our brother.

"But now we do and things will change." Tobias squeezed me. "We'll do better."

"We promise," Stella added as she joined in the hug.

"Thank you." My eyes were damp. All of this felt uncomfortable, but I knew it would be worth it.

My siblings loved me and I trusted they'd put in the effort to fix what had gone wrong between us. I would too. I needed to communicate better with them. Tell them when their comments or behavior bothered me, and not be worried that doing so would prompt them to judge me more.

"I'm so proud of you, Theo," Tobias said in my ear. "You're talented, passionate and caring. You're such an amazing man, and I'll do better at expressing that."

I nodded into his shoulder, lost for words.

"Come here, Luca," Stella said after a moment. "I see you all shiny eyed over there."

They made room and Luca joined the hug, his arms around me. Stella was right. He looked like he was welling up. "My chat with my father didn't go anywhere near this well today."

I pulled him close. "You'll just have to join our family then."

Luca smiled. "I'd love that more than anything, Theo."

So would I.

30

LUCA

I entered Graywoods two weeks later to find Theo counting jars of moss near the back of the shop. The teapot gleamed on its pedestal, looking every bit as magical as an enchanted item should.

"Luca." Theo beamed at me as he closed his notebook.

It was Friday and I'd come over for a date night of movies and takeout. I gave Theo a hug before leaning against the counter, glancing at the teapot. "I was thinking, maybe you could make me a cup of tea before we head upstairs."

Theo's whole face lit up. "I'd love to."

I hadn't yet tried Graywoods tea. Things had been bumpy the last couple weeks. The teapot hadn't suffered any damage, and had been returned to the shop not long after it had been recovered, but there hadn't seemed like a good time to ask for a cup before now.

I wanted this to be something Theo and I could share as a special moment. I knew making me my first cup of perfect tea would mean a lot to him, and I didn't want other distractions getting in the way.

I'd be resigning from my job on Monday. Now that I'd

committed to this change in my life, I felt good, but that didn't mean the last weeks had been easy, or that getting to this point hadn't been stressful in its own way. Still, I was glad I'd forced myself to really sit and think about what I needed, and finally come to terms with everything. That was worth celebrating. I was excited for my future in a way I hadn't been in a long time. What better way to commemorate that than with Theo's unique kind of magic?

Theo pulled me behind the counter. He rolled up the sleeves of his forest-green sweater, crystal rings catching the light. "I've been wanting to share this with you for so long."

I tugged Theo into a quick kiss. "I wish I'd asked that first day I came to your shop."

"No." Theo smiled. "This is perfect. Though, if the teapot had been lost and I'd never gotten to make you a cup, I'd have been devastated."

There was a tracking spell on the teapot now, just in case. Not that anyone would be able to break into the shop again, with the extra protections from Edwin in place.

Theo seemed to shake off any negative thoughts of what might have been. His eyes were bright with anticipation. He was practically brimming with excitement. "Are you ready, Luca?"

"Yes." I took a relaxing breath as we gazed at each other. I took his hand and he sighed dreamily. Stars, I like him so much.

After a quick kiss we both looked over at the teapot.

"Hold the cup in both hands." Theo passed it to me.

The ceramic was cool but quickly warmed as the glazed pattern swirled in response to my touch. Theo turned his attention back to the teapot, heating it with two hands on the metal. His rings flashed and magic hummed in the air.

Theo picked up the teapot and faced me. He held my stare as he poured the hot water and spoke the incantation, his green eyes full of tenderness. Once he set the teapot down, we both looked at the cup. The water swirled and glittered as it slowly turned red. Sweet aromas wafted through the air.

"Oh, a hibiscus tea," Theo whispered in an awed tone.

The rich smell of the tea inspired a sense of calm in me. It was familiar and soothing even though I couldn't remember having hibiscus tea before. I brought the cup to my lips and blew on it gently before taking a deep breath in. Spicier notes cut through the hibiscus scent, ginger and something else.

I took a sip. The warmth of the tea spread out through my whole body. It was like being wrapped up in a blanket in front of a fire. I felt safe and whole, connected to my inner self as my magic thrummed, resonating with the sensation the tea was giving me.

It was like my own magic was revealing layers that I'd never realized existed. I was very familiar with my power and how strong my magic was, but this was something else. It felt like my essence. Somehow I'd never noticed my own magical intricacies with this kind of clarity.

I took another sip, getting a hint of cinnamon and allspice. I took a shaky breath, almost overwhelmed with the new magical connection I was experiencing. It was strong. Even my link to celestial magic didn't feel like this.

My eyes found Theo's. He was watching me closely, a tiny joyful smile on his lips. As I drank the rest of my tea, I let the new feelings inside me grow and meld with my feelings for the man in front of me. As much as this tea grounded and comforted me, I felt those things with Theo too.

Us together was like its own magic.

When I was finished, I set the cup down and pulled Theo close. His arms wrapped around me and I leaned in to kiss him. It was deep and soul exposing. Theo met me with joy and tenderness, and I never wanted to let him go.

"I don't know how to describe that tea in any way that would do it justice," I murmured against his lips. "Thank you."

"You're welcome, Luca. I want to share all my favorite magic with you." Theo squeezed me tight. "That's the first time I've ever tasted someone else's tea. On your lips, it was almost better than my own perfect cup."

My smile felt like it was going to split my face in two. "What's your tea like?"

"I'll show you." Theo cleaned the cup with a puff of smoke then repeated the spell, holding the cup in one hand and the teapot in the other.

As the liquid swirled, the scent of lavender and vanilla filled the air.

Theo gazed adoringly at the cup. "It's been a while since I've had any myself. Mine's a chamomile based tea, but it's nothing like the teabags I have upstairs."

Theo brought the cup to his nose and inhaled, his eyes closed. He was so beautiful, and looked completely and uncomplicatedly happy as he slowly sipped his tea. When Theo opened his eyes, his gaze met mine, turning tender.

After his last sip, Theo set the cup aside and pulled me in to kiss him. Warmth spread through my body as pleasurable chills ran down my spine. His tongue swept over mine and I tasted hits of vanilla and lavender alongside the lingering taste of my own tea. I felt so close to him, like we were creating something special.

"I could get used to this," Theo whispered.

I ran a hand through his hair. "Me too."

THEO

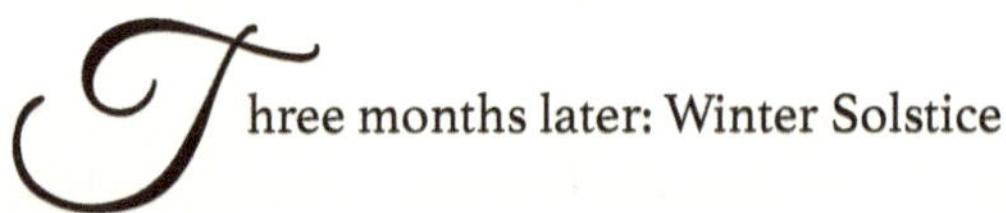

Three months later: Winter Solstice

I LED Luca deeper into the snowy forest.

It was dusk, the last of the light fading from the sky. The trees glittered around us, their bark shimmering, evergreen leaves glowing. The surrounding snow reflected the light, making the whole world dazzle.

"Wow," Luca breathed.

I squeezed his hand. We were almost to the clearing.

As we got closer, we could feel the magic in the air. Both summer and winter solstices were important days as far as earth magic went. Witches like my family celebrated them reverently. They were the days when earth magic was the most tangible. Even people without an earth affinity like me could feel a heightened connection to the world around them today, if they took the time to look.

I loved it.

This year I loved being here with Luca. He'd told me he'd

never experienced anything like my family's solstice celebrations. His family hadn't practiced any rituals on the holiday, only marking it with a dinner or a party.

I found solstice magic soothing and couldn't wait to share it with Luca.

We entered the clearing to find a spectacular display of glittering magical lights. The bark of the surrounding trees had been enchanted to shimmer, lanterns floated in the air, and candles were set in swirling patterns on the snowy ground.

A path led to the middle where my family was waiting. We were greeted with hugs and kisses, Tobias not letting Luca and me escape after greeting us. Apparently he needed extra hugs.

Things had been better with my siblings. I'd been more open with them, and they'd reined in all their teasing remarks. It allowed us to actually talk about things. I felt like I was sharing more with them than I had in a long time.

"So glad you could make it," Tobias said to Luca.

Luca took hold of my hand. "I wouldn't miss this for anything."

Luca seemed happy. Our relationship was going really well. I loved being his boyfriend and was sure he felt just as intensely for me. But beyond that, in the last month and a half I'd sensed a change in him. Like he'd finally settled into the new life he'd chosen.

Luca had been doing some legal work for Marci's tech company. It was worlds away from what he'd been doing at his old firm, with much shorter work hours. He'd said it was fun, and there was no question Luca had made the right call.

Unfortunately his parents didn't seem to agree. Luca had barely talked to them, but I hoped they'd come around eventually and accept the changes he'd made. For the most part Luca acted fine with how things with his family had ended up. He'd said he wasn't surprised.

We'd be seeing his sister in a few days. Aria and the rest of the gang down south were awesome, and Luca seemed just as keen to spend more time with them as he did to spend time with my family. He couldn't get enough of the teddy bear pancakes, even after several trips to Tahoe. It was so sweet I just wanted to wrap him up and keep him forever.

Which was basically my plan for us.

I leaned in close to Luca. "It's almost time to start the ritual."

We both looked up at the night sky. It was clear and full of stars. The moon had risen high. It was gorgeous.

As a group we were going to do an incantation to connect with our earth magic. It was a more spiritual type of spell than one that 'did anything' as some Witches might say. I loved it. It was like Graywoods tea but on a different level.

Luca squeezed my hand. "Being here with you is like a fairy tale."

My smile echoed his, and it didn't feel like we'd ever stop grinning.

THANK YOU FOR READING
WITCH BOYFRIEND WANTED

Please consider leaving a review on your favorite site to help others find magical books they love. 

Would you like a free **bonus scene**? Head over to my website coletterivera.com and subscribe to my author newsletter. I'll send you a short story about Luca & Theo's Southern California Christmas with the rest of the Love & Magic gang, full of sugar and spice, and keep you updated on my future book releases!

ACKNOWLEDGMENTS

Once again I would like to thank my editor May Peterson. It has been so great working with her on this series. I would also like to thank D and M for their help pinpointing the location of Theo's apothecary shop, as it's been a long time since I've lived in the San Francisco area myself.

As always, I would like to thank TK for his support of me and for his continued love of my Witchy worlds.

And finally, thank you to Sam Palencia for her beautiful cover art, exquisite color palettes, and bringing these characters to life.

ABOUT THE AUTHOR

Colette is an author of queer paranormal romance novels. She loves to write couples who take care of each other and show their soft sides when in love. Sugar and spice are key ingredients in all her books. She's an avid PNR reader and loves all things magic. Colette once lived in the US but now calls New Zealand home. As a bisexual she has to resist making all her characters bi. When she succeeds you'll find a variety of representation in her books.

Colette can be found on Instagram @colette_rivera or on Facebook under Colette Rivera Author and at her website coletterivera.com.

ALSO BY COLETTE RIVERA

Love & Magic

Keep Your Witches Close

One Wicked Night

Witch Boyfriend Wanted

Moonlight Falls

The Fall of Elijah Gray

The Seduction of James Gray

The Cursed Sebastian Storm

The Heart of Moonlight Falls

Lovers of the Damned

Demon's Mate

Demon's Heart

Demon's Desire

Devil's Mate

Shearwater Landing Shorts

I Think I Found a Vampire

Lockwood Coven

Her Ghostly Embrace

Bound In Blood

His Eternal Temptation